About the Author

My name's Janie. I'm in my mid-twenties and am not a hundred percent sure who I am. I write because it helps me navigate out my jumbled head. I love mermaids, space pirates, romance and a million other crazy things.

These are my experiences with gender issues and sexuality. I do not expect our experiences to be the same, and I'm sorry if they offend you or make you angry in any way. I was just trying to explore different sides of myself through varied characters. This book has a long, underrun story of me looking into my own gender and trying to figure it out.

WHEN THE NAME FADES

J May

WHEN THE NAME FADES

Vanguard Press

VANGUARD PAPERBACK

© Copyright 2023
J May

A CIP catalogue record for this title is
available from the British Library.

ISBN 978 1 80016 710 0

Vanguard Press is an imprint of
Pegasus Elliot Mackenzie Publishers Ltd.
www.pegasuspublishers.com

First Published in **2023**

Vanguard Press
Sheraton House Castle Park
Cambridge England

Printed & Bound in Great Britain

Dedication

To Ellie, Ry and Cleo

Acknowledgements

I have no idea where to begin in thanking people here. I'm lucky enough to have tonnes of inspiring, wonderful people in my life who not only encourage me on the average day but push me when I'm being an idiot and doubting myself.

Firstly, to my partner. My favourite human. I've never known a person who can take me out of the world the way you do. We've been through a lot while I've been writing. Weird jobs and moving, lockdown after lockdown after lockdown, long distance. But through all the stress and all the self-discovery and just, everything... You always find ways to make me smile. I'll never fully be able to articulate how much you mean to me, because I don't think the words exist, but thank you for holding me when I'm scared and for telling me to go for things when I'm overthinking. You're amazing in ways that you don't see, and I love you more than you could possibly imagine.

Secondly, to my mother. My mother: the gay fiction enthusiast who got me addicted to Roswell: New Mexico because of freakin Malex. Your enthusiasm and encouragement is overwhelming sometimes, you push me in weird ways and a lot of my ideas come off us bouncing stories off each other and you're just...nodding along and telling me my ideas are great. It comes from us talking about TV shows and ships and just, everything. I'll always be grateful for our stupid conversations, the ones that only make sense to us, and a lot of them are how I come up with the things I do. You've always been an inspiration to me with your kind, selfless heart, and I love you to pieces, even when you're driving me mental.

To my sister, Amy. My partner in crime, my best friend. I honestly don't know what I'd do without you. You're selfless, amazing, hilarious and little Cleo is the luckiest girl on earth to have you as a mother. When the world is swirling out of control, when it feels like I have a hold of nothing and I'm completely stuck, you're always there, and I always know you're on my side. I'm always on yours too. I love you so much, it's ridiculous.

To my dad and his crazy crime novel ideas that keep me up at night sometimes. You've inspired me in ways that I probably won't be able to tell you. Thank you for always being steady; for teaching me to be good with money; maybe making me a little paranoid about certain things. (Like pick pockets in London) You do drive me crazy a lot of the time, but I know it comes from a place of love. I love you too Dad, so much.

To my nanna, thank you for calling me and singing Cliff Richard through the phone with me on varied days. Some days sucked, and I needed that. Thank you for always being a person I can vent to and for always being there. You're wonderful, and I couldn't be more thankful to have you in my life.

To the rest of my crazy family... To Terri, Alycia, Jimmy, Gill, Sam, Cleo, Willow, Bailey, Buddy, Diesel ... To everybody I haven't seen in the longest time, and I hate the fact that I haven't. To my grandma and grandad, my uncle's, aunt's, cousins. I love you all so much and if you are reading this, grandma...sorry about chapter 5...it probably wasn't your favourite?

This book was a lot of self-analysis for me. I figured out things through writing about characters being trans and gender fluid... I still haven't fully figured it out, in all honesty. I wake up a lot of days uncomfortable in my body. The idea of this story came from my obsession with varied animated shows and ships, my number one being Klance from Voltron. I've written bits of Fanfic for it but have mostly been obsessively reading it for over a year, and I wanted to give a mention to all the fanfic writers out there who've written wonderful stories about wonderful characters and created their own worlds through them. I'll never get tired of them.

I want to thank my editor, Faye. I hired her through Fiverr and was terrified because I'd never done that before. She was amazing, encouraging and very good at her job; spotted a lot of weird, grammatical errors that I wasn't aware of. Would highly recommend her services.

I also want to thank my dissertation Supervisor, Kate. This project started out as the basis for my creative writing MA dissertation which I turned in in April 2022. You were always supportive, patient and encouraging, even when I was a little flaky, because I was, and I'm sorry. Thank you for loving my story even in moments where I didn't and laughing about stupid things on video call with me. Thank you for adding so much to Enzo's character and making me fall in love with him too.

To my ex-English professor and current pen pal, Pete. I couldn't really do acknowledgments without mentioning how much your encouragement and faith have pushed me over the years; how I love our emails. I wouldn't be writing at all if it wasn't for your class in college, so thank you Pete, and I look forward to seeing you again soon.

And finally, to my friends. To Alice, Hayleigh, Luke, Dave, Amelia, Nicole, Sheila, Nic, Charlie, Molly and there's a fair few more, but I'm scared that I'm gonna miss someone and make them feel bad. Just know that I love you and love that you're a part of my life. Thank you for letting me vent to you about random crap and for always smiling when I talk about things that mean a lot to me and probably mean nothing to you. I wouldn't be who I am without you guys, so thank you for everything, you're all the best.

Special thank you to Amelia for designing the beautiful cover to this book. It's genuinely one of my favourite things ever.

Chapter 1
DANNY

He still heard her voice. He heard her voice every time he spoke, everywhere he walked, every time he thought. His heart would rattle to the tune of it, his eardrums would thrash to the tones of it. The world around him felt smaller and hollower, as her voice skittered around him in a painful whirlpool of torment.

She was his. He was hers. They were happy, weren't they? They laughed and they joked. They ate every meal together, spent every night in the same bed, woke up to the same alarm and the same morning breath. Their house was always a mess, but neither cared when they were wrapped in each other's arms. It felt right. It was supposed to. They were soulmates, after all. They'd heard each other's voices months before they met, but when they did meet, it was like they'd always known each other. It was like their lives followed the same pattern; like their hearts already beat in sync. They were bound to each other; souls intertwined like they were woven together. It was weird. No one ever knew how to describe it.

When he heard her voice for the first time, he was eighteen. Most people were. He fell asleep a single person and woke up bound to another; a person that he never expected to meet; a person that could be in the North pole or America or Jupiter. She could've been anywhere, but one day, he was walking down the street, and her sweet, melodious voice hit him like a cold bucket of water. Her name warped through his mind then danced on his tongue. He said it before he could think better of it. 'Allison.' And she stopped. She stood in the middle of the street, frozen. Her blue eyes pierced him when she turned around. Her expression stuck somewhere between shock, confusion and awe, while her short, blonde hair blew back in the breeze. His name left her lips a few moments later, and the entire world stopped. 'Danny.'

It'd been two years since then. Two years, and they'd gotten a house together, bought a mattress and a washing machine, been to Disneyland, discussed kids and marriage and planned an entire future that never happened.

Now, he was three beers down at their local bar – the place where he'd kissed her for the first time. So many memories stood within the weak, burgundy walls. Painted golden, hollow flowers gleamed on the wallpaper in the low, lamp light. A couple of candles flickered from the far corner tables, highlighting the newly varnished, dark wooden tables. Chairs scraped the ground in repetitive, painful patterns as Danny clenched his teeth and pressed his palm into his beer bottle, the condensation aching over his fingertips and causing them to wrinkle. His old, blue tartan shirt was tied around his hips, covering the top half of his grey, ripped jeans. A black T shirt covered his upper half, little rips on his shoulders and under his armpits. His black Doc Martens remained untied and muddied on his restless feet. They swung and swayed, a couple inches from the floor on the old bar stool. The door to the bathroom stood directly beside him, while ten small, round tables sat around in a random pattern on the old, grey carpet. A TV stood behind him, currently playing something that no one was paying attention to. The bar was practically empty, and Danny wasn't turning around to see who was there with him. He was alone, anyway. No matter how many people were here, he was alone.

"Well, this is a classic scene," a deep, smooth voice stated from Danny's left.

"I half expected there to be a guy in a fedora playing jazz in the corner," Danny smiled, despite himself. Admittedly, this bar did have 'Casablanca' vibes.

"So, what's got ya down, buddy?" the voice asked, and Danny blinked in surprise. The words flowed over him, twisted his gut and flooded anxious smoke through his nostrils. The bar suddenly felt crowded as screeching voices collided in his brain, and Danny's blue eyes turned to the stranger.

The voices silenced. The bar fell black and warm lights appeared around the perfect stranger in a flame-like pattern. It beamed into his sharp cheekbones and slightly upturned nose. His eyes were an intense lightened brown that glittered light-gold in the orange light. His long, black hair was tied back loosely in a little ponytail, and a rush of cool electricity flitted through Danny's bones. Light pieces of fringe fell into the guy's pale face, drawing attention to his strong, pointed chin. He wore a pair of blue jeans, a light-brown jumper and blue, relatively destroyed trainers.

A steamed breeze filled Danny's brain, stilling his body completely, as the label from his beer bottle slipped and finally fell to the bar. A warm tingle darted from the back of his skull to the base of his spine, and Danny's eyes slammed closed for a moment, the warmth overwhelming him in a strange flood of cell-bursting comfort.

The calm steam continued to rise through his head like water swirling through a kettle. It filled his heart, nestled into his muscles and caused all of limbs to fall to relaxed heaps. The silence was serene, like the silence you'd find on a beach in the very early morning, full of warmth and anticipation as the tide flowed in, and colour slowly bled through the indigo sky.

It took several moments for the world to fade back into normal rhythm. The dull sounds of the news penetrated his ears lightly, the warm light glowed back over the bar and the darkness faded away. The stranger was still there. His eyes still gleamed, his smile still gentle, and the warmth flooding Danny only got hotter as he opened his light-pink lips.

"Hey, buddy, you all right?" he asked.

Danny shivered and turned away from him. "Y ... uh... yeah," he muttered, picking at the now non-existent label on his bottle. "Uh... uh... you?"

The guy smiled and gently pulled himself onto the stool next to him, causing another warm shiver to quake through him. Their eyes caught again, and every thought in Danny's brain disappeared except one. One word. One voice. 'Enzo,' the deep, smooth, horrifically familiar voice stated.

Danny froze. The grip on his bottle disappeared, as the glass slipped through his fingers and rolled down the wooden bar, falling to the floor with a light *crash!*

Glass and pale-brown liquid erupted below. A tug gnawed at Danny's heart as he watched the liquid fade into the wood and the burgundy carpet. Glass covered everything in a spiky circle. Crap, he had to clean that up. He had to clean that up before someone got hurt or someone slipped or something. The stranger, 'Enzo,' followed Danny's gaze and scoffed with a little eyeroll, before a bar man appeared with a little brush.

Danny's mouth opened shakily, his heart started thundering, blood pumped through his ears, and a dull ring stabbed through his brain. How... was this... possible? This wasn't... how was...A person only gets...

"Okay, Danny, calm down," 'Enzo' stated, placing his hands up in a placating gesture.

This did almost nothing to quell Danny's shock, because he knew his name. Fuck, he knew his name. He heard his voice too. How was this possible? Wait, Danny liked guys? He guessed that was true, but his soulmate was a woman! So... just, what? This was too much. It was all too much for him. Plus, he was three beers down. This was just... was this even real? Was this a beer-induced hallucination? How long had it been since he drank? Had he passed out? Was this a dream?

"That's not calming down, Danny. I can explain, but you need to breathe. You're okay, everything's okay."

"How... is... how is..." Danny gasped shakily. His tongue grasped at words like hands trying to get a solid hold of water.

Enzo smiled gently, placed his hands at his sides and fully turned to face him. The warmth between them grew to an impenetrable bubble. Their cheeks heated in unison, unconscious smiles hitting their faces as each of their hearts stumbled to a stop, and it suddenly felt to Danny that he was talking to an old friend –an old friend that he hadn't seen in decades; an old friend that he knew before he was sure of himself; a friend who he'd had a crush on but had never had the courage to admit to. A big crush – a first crush.

He still remembered his first crush. He was fifteen. Her name was Kathy, and she had freckles on her cheeks and eyes that beamed light green in the sunlight. He remembered her bright-orange, curly hair that fell to her shoulders and tickled her nose when it got windy. He remembered the way that she'd chew the rubbers off her pencils when she was thinking too hard, and the way her nose scrunched and drew her freckles into a new pattern when she laughed. He never talked to her or did anything about this crush because he was waiting, but a part of his heart hoped she was his soulmate. He was saving himself for his soulmate; wanted to be able to say that he'd only ever kissed his soulmate, but there was a time when all he could think about was kissing Kathy and dating Kathy, holding her hand and just getting lost together.

"I'm not sure, but it is," Enzo stated gently, his voice falling to small warble that shuddered through Danny's heart like a warm breeze. He gasped it in and held it in his throat while staring into the guy's sparkling eyes. "I'm sorry, it always freaks people out." Enzo rubbed a hand on the back of his neck nervously.

"What... uh... what does?" Danny stammered with wide, terrified eyes.

"This," Enzo stated firmly. He lifted his hands then gestured to Danny, then himself, then back to Danny. "I feel it too, just so you know."

"Feel what?" Danny asked.

Enzo cocked an eyebrow at the guy. "This weird sense that I know you when I don't?" he stated in confusion. "This nervous flutter. My heart is beating so

21

fast right now and my hands are… I'm sweating…" He sighed then stared down at the bar. "This always happens with cute boys," he stated then shook his head as Danny blinked back in surprise.

"Cute, uh… cute boys?" he asked, pushing a lock of his mousy hair behind his small, rounded ear.

Enzo cocked a brow with a little smile. "Yeah, you're cute, Danny," he stated in his low, smooth tone and Danny's heart shoved back into his own chest like a shot.

"I'm uh… I'm uh n…" He began but Enzo grinned and stole all of Danny's words.

The smile lit up the dull bar. It was bright, breath-taking and utterly earth-shattering.

"Ah, modesty," Enzo stated and his grin fell to a warm smile. "That just makes you cuter," he added with a shrug, widening his smile and tilting his head down.

Danny's face grew hot enough to evaporate sweat.

"Sorry, not used to the flirting – noted."

"Fl… fl… uh… flirting?" Danny stammered and Enzo scoffed, rolling his eyes playfully.

"How old are you?" he asked. "And how drunk?"

Danny bit his lip. "Twenty and uh…" He stared over the bar with awkward eyes. "That was my third."

Enzo nodded with a polite, little smile. "And… excuse me for asking, but…" Enzo placed his hands into a placating gesture once more. "You don't have to tell me, but…" He gulped. "What happened to your other soulmate?"

The atmosphere in the bar suddenly got heavy. The air tasted like rotten egg-y smoke that injected its way into every vein in Danny's body. He stared at Enzo, the word 'other' swaying through his brain in a cursed whisper. So, Enzo was... this was... how could this be real? How was this possible? A person only gets one. It's soul*mate*, not soul*mates*. Your soul can't be connected to multiple people. It's just not possible.

"O... uh... other?" Danny asked meekly.

Enzo nodded, his golden gaze, calm and sweet. It flew through Danny's heart like warm honey.

"Yes," he stated slowly. "I swear, I'll explain, but I need to know first, so I know how to help you." Enzo's eyes appeared with a kind sheen, as a little smile glowed over his face. More pieces of fringe fell over his eyes and his nose, highlighting freckles and little crinkles under his eyes. Danny's knees stuttered against the bar stool as he tore his eyes away from Enzo, choosing instead to stare at a half-empty bottle of old scotch behind the bar.

"She left," he admitted slowly, his body falling in on itself.

"So... you've met her?" Enzo asked, his eyebrows rising through his hairline.

"Yeah," Danny whispered, turning his gaze to a full bottle of Smirnoff vodka. He suddenly craved another drink, his throat falling dry and scratchy. "About two years ago."

"And what happened?" Enzo asked gently.

Danny's gaze turned to him, and those placating hands came back for a moment. It looked like he was trying to save himself from falling off his stool. Danny didn't want to, but a little laugh escaped his trembling lips, as Enzo smiled warmly.

"I swear, you don't have to tell me. I can help either way, but I, um..." Enzo's golden eyes turned and looked around the bar before turning back to Danny. "You don't seem okay, and you ever heard the expression 'a problem shared is a problem halved'?" he asked rhetorically, but Danny nodded anyway, and Enzo tapped his shoulder with his hand.

Danny's eyes snapped wide open and stared down at Enzo's pale, long fingers, as they pressed into his shoulder. It caused a quake of inexplicable warmth to flood through the muscles, trailing through his entire body, as a terrified shiver almost knocked him off his stool. "I... don't seem okay?" he asked with a little, dry gulp.

Enzo cocked his eyebrow in a way that screamed 'seriously?' then nodded politely over to Danny.

"Danny, you're alone at a bar on a Friday night – peeling labels and ripping up napkins," Enzo stated. "There's nobody coming. No dates, and you're not going anywhere – this isn't exactly the picture of 'okay'." He sighed then pulled his hand away.

Danny lowered his eyebrows with a little, shocked scoff. Where did this guy get off? He didn't know him. They were apparently 'soulmates' but still, they were strangers. You don't say that kind of thing to strangers. You can't just imply that a person is a pathetic loner. Danny scrutinised Enzo. He glanced over his little ponytail, specifically focused on how scuffed it was. It was loose and falling out with little pieces of hair floating all over the place. He looked windswept. There was a black stain on his jeans. And the scuffs on his trainers were strange. It was like the soles had been rounded. Did he ride a bike? He must do. Holy crap, this guy drove a motorcycle. He also smelt the tiniest bit like petrol. What, did he live on his motorcycle? His knuckles did look a little scuffed, his eyes were the tiniest bit sunken, and his shoulders were tight and straight, like he didn't exactly feel comfortable here. Where was he from? He didn't sound like he was from Yarmouth. What the heck was he doing here?

"How do you know there's nobody coming?" Danny asked, eyebrows lowering as a defensive wave crashed through his mind. Enzo sighed, his shoulders fell and a little scoff escaped his lips.

"Danny, you've been here for hours; you've drank three beers. You haven't turned around once, and you haven't checked your phone."

Danny jolted, then stared with wide eyes and a little headshake. How long had this guy been watching him? That had to be a red flag, right? Right? Although he was his... they were... crap, what were the lines here?

"If you were waiting for someone? Well, after drinking one beer alone, you'd probably know that they

25

weren't coming, so either you're here alone, or you've gotten stood up. And just judging by... well, your reaction to me flirting?" he questioned, pressing his lips up in slight accusation. "Well, I don't think you were prepared for a date, so—"

"I'm here alone," Danny concluded with a sigh, while turning back to the bar anxiously. "Can I at least get another beer if you're gonna be explaining how pathetic I am all night?"

Enzo smiled, put up his hand and pointed to the beer in the fridge, putting two fingers in the air. The bartender dropped the beers, popped the caps and slid them over to Enzo without a word. He disappeared to the other side of the bar, as Enzo slid one over to Danny.

Danny cocked an eyebrow in surprise, sipping at the beer with a wavering smile. "Thanks."

Enzo nodded in acknowledgment, sipping his beer in unison.

"You're not pathetic, Danny," he said after a moment.

"It's been two months, Enzo," he replied, and Enzo fell back in surprise, forgetting that Danny had already heard his name through his head.

"Two months since what?" he asked kindly, and Danny sighed heavily, eyes falling to the bar, as he gulped down a chunk of unspoken words.

"Since Allison left," he said. "We were together almost two years, and she just... we were soulmates." He muttered these words, processing them through his mind as he spoke. "Or, well…" His eyes tilted to Enzo. "I thought we were."

Enzo rolled his eyes in a light-hearted fashion.

"You were, are. Don't worry about that, just keep going," he stated gently with an encouraging nod.

Danny blinked in surprise then lowered his eyebrows at Enzo. Were? Are? Enzo suddenly felt like a gatekeeper holding his answers hostage. His heart squished in his chest, as if a metallic device had locked it down. Who was this guy? What did he know, and why did he know it? Was he tricking him? Was this false? How could someone fake being someone's soulmate? You couldn't, right? This feeling had to be real. It felt real but just… how? And could he trust him? Danny's drunken mind was having trouble not trusting him in that moment. Everything felt too real, every pound of his heart and every dart through his mind. Everything felt fantastical and shocking, but still – he was a stranger, wasn't he?

"I don't know," Danny admitted uncomfortably, turning back to the vodka bottle with a sigh. "We broke up and she left." He shrugged. "Typical story, except, oh… I could still hear her voice in my head and feel her pull on my heart, and she was just… gone."

"That's not abnormal," Enzo stated evenly, and Danny's gaze snapped to him.

"I know it's not abnormal, but she was my *soul*mate. *Soul*mate. The person who was literally made for me – we all know the stories. We all know what it

27

means when you hear that stupid voice in your head. This wasn't meant to happen. She wasn't meant to leave. We're together. We're together forever. That's the deal, otherwise it wouldn't be called 'soulmates.' It'd be called something impermanent; something less…" Danny rambled off then gulped, turning back to the bar. "Important."

Enzo gulped then placed his hand back on Danny's shoulder, hoping to quell the anger.

"I know, I know," he whispered. "And I'm sorry, Danny." Enzo gently rubbed Danny's back, smoothing over the muscles, as he sighed and slumped down. Danny's eyes closed as he leaned into the action. "It's okay, you're gonna be okay." Enzo's voice was a wave that crested through Danny's heart. "This soulmates thing is weird, okay?" Enzo gulped, and Danny turned to him with a lowered eyebrow.

"What do you mean? And aren't… we… uh…" Danny asked, swaying a hand between the two of them.

Enzo nodded, retracting his hand. "Yeah, yeah, we are."

"H… h… how?" Danny asked.

Enzo smiled warmly. "I don't exactly know how it works," he admitted with a shrug. "I just know who… and where."

Danny's eyebrows lowered further, his brain tangled in harsh confusion, his heart twanged into his ribs like a baton into a gong, as Enzo's golden gaze softened.

"Everybody feels different but no less wonderful, and I just... find them," he stated wistfully, eyes drifting, as a smile crept up Danny's face.

"What does that mean?" he asked. "And... them?"

"Man, you have a lot of questions." Enzo chuckled with a bright smile.

"Wouldn't you?"

"I suppose," he admitted with a shrug. "But sadly, I don't have all the answers." He sighed, bright smile falling to something gentler, as his own heart wavered. "I'm just here to help."

"Help with what?"

"With you, silly," Enzo stated, a grin appearing on his face once more, as he playfully nudged the blue-eyed boy's shoulder.

Danny gulped and desperately tried not to fall off his stool. "With me, how?" he asked.

Enzo sighed deeply, taking a sip of beer. "Well, first, I think we should get out of this bar and head somewhere that feels less... Shaun of the dead-esque," he stated, glancing around the dully lit, abandoned bar. "Why are you here, anyway?" The warm, comforting flame glowing through Danny's heart disappeared, leaving a rush of cold smoke. "This was our place," he admitted plainly, swallowing a million stories.

Enzo sighed sharply, shoved his stool back and stood up. "Okay, then we're definitely getting out of here," he stated, holding a hand out to Danny.

Danny blinked at it then stared into Enzo's brown eyes in serious confusion.

"Come on, man. Let's go somewhere fun, and let's just… let me take your mind off her, okay?"

Danny stared at Enzo, glaring into his eyes sharply like he was analysing a painting. Could he trust him? He felt so familiar and was just… Fuck, he was easy to talk to and cute and just, funny. He felt like an old friend, but he wasn't. He smelt like cinnamon and caused warm tremors to quake through his body, but what was he? What were they to each other? Who was he? Where was he from? Could Danny trust going with him?

His eyebrows squeezed into his eyes, and his eyes squished into his nose and caused little wrinkles to appear, while Enzo just smiled. He just smiled a clean, straight smile. No hint of sarcasm, frustration or pushiness. He appeared perfectly content with his straight lips and kind eyes. The warm light from the bar gleamed and glowed over him in waves. He almost looked angelic with his smooth skin and glittering, golden irises. Little pieces of hair continually fell into his face, the light gleaming through them and highlighting his defined cheekbones. Danny suppressed a gasp, as his heart leapt into his throat.

Moments passed like days, as Danny stared into Enzo's eyes, then at his outstretched hand, then back and forth, his internal debate clear in his wide eyes and slightly parted lips. What was doing here? Why was he debating this? He should just go home. You shouldn't go places with cute, mysterious strangers. It's not okay. That's how you get murdered, but Enzo didn't feel like a stranger. He felt like a friend, plus, he made Danny curious. This town wasn't that big. Enzo was new, or Danny just hadn't been out in a long, long time. Enzo didn't feel or look local. There was... something – something about this guy that he couldn't just leave here. Could he? There was more to it. There had to be.

Enzo never wavered. He never moved his hand and his smile never dropped. He just looked at Danny with genuine kindness and understanding. It'd been a while since anyone had looked at him like that.

A warmth grew on his cheeks, a gentle smile grew on his lips and his chest fell forward as his heart shoved into his ribs happily. Maybe he didn't have a clue who this guy was, or what they were to each other, or what was going on but... well, he wanted to find out and before he knew it, his hand was in Enzo's grasp –pale, soft fingers weaving between his own and causing his heart to lose control.

Danny stood, then gulped while staring down at his hand. "Okay," he muttered, leaning his chin into his chest, as Enzo's smile grew to a wide grin.

"Love the enthusiasm."

Chapter 2

"Why are you looking at me like that?" Enzo asked with a cocked eyebrow and a weirdly knowing smirk that made Danny roll his eyes in exasperation.

"Bowling?" he asked. "Seriously, let's get you out of your head, Danny. Let's get you to stop thinking about the fact that the person the universe paired you with forever decided to up and move away. Bowling? Bowling was the big plan?"

Enzo smirked as the pair slowly walked down the centre of the alleys.

Claw games, little sweet machines, those shelves with the big balls and standing bars full of beers and cheap burgers passed by them. Danny's feet were already uncomfortable in these shoes. All of him was uncomfortable. All of this was uncomfortable. It was weird seeing the young girl put his shoes in that little cubby, it felt like he was trapped. He felt like he had an out until that point, but now? He was wearing red and blue trainers that were currently scraping the sides of his feet. A part of him innately trusted Enzo and that freaked him out. A huge part of his heart, mind, soul, everything was drawn to him and wanted to be around him, but the other side of him wanted to walk out of here. But there was another side that wanted answers, and he didn't want to leave, but he did, but he didn't. He was in a never-ending internal conflict, as the pair hit the final alley.

The place was empty. There was a couple on the opposite side of the room and a little birthday party going on behind them, but nothing and no one else. It was eerily quiet, even with the soft pop music playing from the TVs above them.

"Yes, bowling," Enzo eventually responded, standing up with a little smirk and heading to type in their names.

Danny slumped into the bench and folded his arms while looking over the new guy curiously.

"Bowling is physical; it's competitive; there's not much time to think on anything, and just F.Y.I..." He listed off while tapping in letters. "I'm gonna kick your ass, Dann-O."

Danny blinked in surprise then lowered his eyebrows. "Dann-O?" he repeated. Enzo chuckled.

"Seriously, I'm a kick-ass bowler – used to play with my siblings all the time. They never beat me," he stated, pride flashing through his golden irises, as he stared down the aisle determinedly.

Danny couldn't explain the little fire that erupted in his gut, as he caught the cockiness in Enzo's glare. He wanted to snuff that out – he wanted to win. Heck, he was a good bowler, too. Allison never beat him, and his friends never beat him. He was stumbling down drunk on sambuca shots once, and he still got a turkey, but he wasn't competitive. He'd never been competitive. He was one of those kids who collected participation ribbons, just had fun and didn't care if he won. He didn't even care if he looked stupid, he just played the game. He smiled, laughed, joked and probably got his ass beat, but he didn't care. What was Enzo drawing out in him?

"Sure," Danny uttered sarcastically, with a challenging glint in his eye.

Enzo caught the glint, golden irises lining with blue, as the pair had a small stare-down. The weird, competitive tension drowning out the pop music.

"Think you got what it takes, blue eyes?" Enzo asked, folding his arms and cocking his brows.

Danny smirked in response, teeth glinting slightly in the fluorescent lights, as he stared up and caught sight of the currently empty scoreboard.

"You first—" His brain scrambled for a nickname, glancing over Enzo's features and scrutinising each one – the dark hair, golden eyes – until he found something and grinned. "Freckles," he stated, referring to the light dusting of freckles over Enzo's nose.

Enzo jolted back in surprise, fingers smoothly gliding over the top of his nose. They were cute, simple and sweet; they reminded Danny of something. But it also seemed to ground Enzo a bit. He'd been looking at Enzo as this big pile of questions hidden by a pretty face, but he was just… a dorky, freckly person.

"Oh… uh, okay," he stated, his smooth and confident demeanour crumbling for a moment.

Enzo picked up the ball –orange, but golden in the white lights. He strolled past Danny, turning to him slightly and hiking up an eyebrow before he reached the foul line and stopped.

He swung his arm back casually, bending down and leaning over the aisle. Danny followed the ball but found his eyes drifting elsewhere, his cheeks reddening whenever he caught sight of Enzo's ass. He was having small doubts about being into guys, having been with a girl forever and never really having a lot of chance to think on it. His soulmate was a girl. Well, his other soulmate? He didn't understand that, but Enzo was hot –the freckles, the golden eyes and the dark hair. His cheeky smirk made his heart flutter, and the deep tones of his voice seemed to go straight to his… well, the less said on that, the better.

Danny wasn't sure he was into guys, but he was into Enzo. There was something about him that drew him in. Hence, why he was currently turned around on the bench, elbows leaned on his knees and eyes awkwardly falling to his ass every few seconds before he caught himself and watched his bowling arm instead.

Danny's eyes drifted up slightly, as Enzo's jumper rode up his back. He almost gasped, as a little colourful thing appeared on his left hip. Danny squinted and stared through it, hoping to make out the vague shape. It seemed to be a line. It was pointy. Lightning? Enzo had a little lightning tattoo on his left hip! It was tiny – probably about the size of a 50p coin – coloured purple and blue, with stars over it like a galaxy. It was pretty and practically glowed off Enzo's pale, perfect skin. When did he get that? Why?

Enzo drew the ball back, turned and smirked at Danny for a second before raising his eyebrows and gliding the ball down the aisle smoothly. Danny watched as Enzo stood up straight and folded his arms. It hit the end dead centre and every single pin clattered to the floor. Danny's jaw dropped.

Enzo turned his golden gaze on Danny then strolled back towards the bench, jumping down from the aisle with a wide, proud grin. "And that, blue eyes," he began, turned and smirked in Danny's shocked face, "is how it's done."

A little scoff escaped Danny's throat, as his eyes rolled. "Beginner's luck, freckles," he stated, then folded his arms and let out a little challenging eye-squint.

Enzo was not perturbed. He just gestured to the aisle then slumped onto the bench, crossed his legs and folded his arms. "Your turn, hotshot."

Danny scoffed, air escaping his nose in a hot rush, as he shook his head and picked up a light-green ball.

His fingers went into the holes, as he turned to the aisle and began marching forward. The metal barriers dropped the pins, and Danny didn't hesitate. He chucked his ball down with a gentle amount of force that shot it dead centre.

Enzo's eyes widened in Danny's peripheral, as the ball trampled all ten pins. "Whoa," he gasped. "Not bad, blue-eyes."

Danny just rolled his eyes, scoffing out his nose.

"Tell you what. Let's make this interesting, I'll cover the first round, but loser buys the next," Enzo challenged, and stretched a hand out,

Danny squinted with a proud smirk. "You're gonna be buying a lot of drinks," he replied, then took his hand and shook it harshly.

"Love the confidence," Enzo muttered, then cocked his eyebrow before wondering to the bar.

Danny really didn't know where this competitive streak came from but he was completely lost in the challenge and so determined to win that he completely neglected his drink, wanting to keep his mind in check, so that Enzo would have to buy the next round.

Both guys got a turkey in the first three turns, but then Danny missed a pin and got a spare, while Enzo got another strike. Enzo then missed two pins and got a spare. The game went by fast and ended with Danny getting three strikes in his last turn. Enzo wandered off to the bar once more to get their ciders.

Danny was just smirking, watching him leave. A weird buzz then quaked through the bench and Danny jolted as Enzo's phone appeared beside him, beaming and jumping off the bench.

He shouldn't look, right? That's an invasion of privacy. It was wrong and just... Whatever else he was thinking fell out his brain, as his eyes read over the screen.

'Enzo, where are you?' was the first message he saw. Several other messages appeared from this person, and each one built a certain level of anxiety through Danny's throat. 'You're late. I thought you could work tonight?' 'Enzo, we need you on the phones. We are understaffed.'

Danny lowered his eyebrows at that one. On the phones? What did Enzo do?

A message from a new person appeared. 'Enzo, can I stay at your place tonight? He's drinking again. Xxx'

A gulp rang through Danny's throat at that message. An even stronger one went through him when he read the contact as 'Mum.' The screen then went black, and Danny decided not to read more. This wasn't fair. He didn't know Enzo – looking through his messages was wrong. He just blinked, shook his head then shoved those messages to the furthest corners of his mind, deciding not to ask about them.

He just grabbed his cider and began chugging it before the golden-eyed guy got back and slumped into the bench beside him, pressing another cider into his hand. Their sides tapped, and their arms pressed into each other. A rush of warmth flooded through Danny's entire body.

He didn't think he'd feel that feeling again. Much less about a near-stranger and… a guy. Allison was his soulmate. His only soulmate. That's how these things worked. Everybody got one and that's it. That was the person you were supposed to be with, but explain this? Explain the voice and the weird familiarity. Explain Danny's need to be near Enzo and him wanting to learn more. This was weird for him. Explain the fact that he wanted to be closer to him, and why this game had gotten so competitive, and why they just got on like old friends. Danny wasn't a socially capable person but with Enzo, it was easy. He was being competitive, weird and sassy, and it didn't feel awkward. Heck, he barely acknowledged it, and he wasn't drunk. It was weird, to say the least.

Danny side-eyed Enzo and found himself getting lost in his golden irises, as they reflected the dull lights of the bowling alley. His dark, tied-back hair was falling over his face, as he smirked and sipped on his cider. The bobble was slowly slipping and causing more and more hair to cascade over his shoulders. Shadows glided over his sharp features and highlighted the little freckles over his nose, and he was just… beautiful.

Danny almost gasped when Enzo's golden gaze fully turned to him, and a little grin lit up his features. "I see I've finally met my match," he muttered deeply, causing Danny's heart to warble. Enzo's shoulder-bopped him, grinning wider when a smile unconsciously appeared on Danny's boiling face.

"So um... you're my... you're my soulmate?" he asked nervously, and Enzo's grin dropped to a gentle smile as he nodded. "How? Why? I don't..."

"The universe tends to decide these things," he replied.

Danny rolled his eyes in exasperation. "But people only get one,"

Enzo rolled his eyes. "See, that's what people think, but it's not true,"

Danny blinked in surprise. "How many have you had?"

"About twenty? Twenty-five?"

Danny's eyes widened. "But... how? How do you... how does this..." he began, then gestured between the two of them.

Enzo shrugged. "I've never known how it works."

"How long does this last for you? And do you just... run off? Like, what happens? Do you stop hearing my voice? Am I like a... temporary soulmate?" Danny asked, with lowered eyebrows and shaking fingers, his heart beating harshly as he gulped in horridly solid breaths.

"I'm not leaving until you're ready for me to. It lasts a different amount of time for everybody, and nobody's voice completely fades. You're important, Danny. Don't doubt that," Enzo stated simply, while staring into his blue eyes. "I know this is a lot to take in, but you must trust me. We're soulmates. It's that simple. The same way you and Allison were."

"So, she's not my soulmate anymore?" Danny gulped.

"Did she feel like your soulmate when she left?" Enzo asked.

Danny's breath caught. Did she? Did she feel like his soulmate in the end? Danny's soul tremored, his flat didn't feel like home anymore. They were soulmates. Together forever – that was the deal – so how could she leave? He wasn't ready to let her go. How could he let her go?

"Did it matter if she did? We were soulmates," Danny argued in a slow whisper, his gaze falling to the floor.

"So, you just assumed that meant you'd be okay forever? Not having to work on anything or try?" Enzo asked, and Danny's gaze snapped to him.

Enzo backed up slightly, his hands up in surrender. "I'm just saying, Danny. Regardless of what the universe had planned, relationships take work. They always do. You can't just assume you'll work because you're supposed to."

"What's the point of soulmates then?" Danny asked.

Enzo shrugged, turning back to look over the alley. "Personally, I'm not the biggest fan of this whole 'settling down' thing," he stated. "There's so much to experience in the world, so much to do and so many people to meet, plus, everything's always changing, and nothing is just set in stone. What's the point of pretending it is?"

Danny blinked in surprise as a strange silence flooded the pair.

They each turned back to their drinks, taking long sips through the confused, quiet bubble. Danny's brain swam; so many things tangled his mind and made him dizzy. Was he naïve to just believe that him and Allison were set in stone? His parents were. His grandparents, too. His friends. They were happy. Him and Allison were meant to be that. They were set in stone.

Or were they? What did any of this mean? What was Enzo to him? Just… temporary? A soulmate for *now*? That's it – would Allison's voice come back? He hadn't heard it since Enzo showed up. His brain felt oddly hollow in places. It felt like he'd forgotten something fundamental to his being, something important, but he couldn't dig it out from the depths of his own head. It felt wrong, but Enzo's voice filled those gaps and flooded his mind with warmth and familiarity.

The boys played the next game, but Danny's head wasn't in it. Enzo smiled at him and nodded between turns, but Danny couldn't concentrate. The words 'nothing is just set it stone' kept spinning through his mind and falling to his heart in a cold, dizzying heap. Enzo had just come in and completely muddled how Danny felt about everything and it felt… good? His world felt murkier, and there were things that made no sense, but there was this flood of calm that came with Enzo.

It wasn't anything like Allison. It felt nice and familiar with Allison. They felt like soulmates, but maybe he was fooling himself in believing that their relationship was ever perfect and easy like everyone else's? Maybe everyone else's weren't as perfect as they seemed? Something in him shattered with that realisation. Soulmates were soulmates. They were pre-destined and meant to be, was that not it? Was that not enough?

"Hey Dann-O. You all right?" Enzo asked, and slowly appeared on the bench beside him, hand on his shoulder, golden gaze flickering into blue.

"Yeah." He gulped and Enzo cocked a brow.

"You sure? You haven't scored above a nine on the past three turns," he said. "And just based on your cockiness in the first game, I'm gonna say that's unusual."

Danny rolled his eyes. "Guess I'm buying the next round?"

"Not until you tell me what's wrong," Enzo responded instantly, with an encouraging shoulder squeeze.

Danny's eyes trailed the loose, dark hair that swirled around his face, pieces got caught behind his ears and above his eyebrows. His freckles gleamed like stars in the dull light. His cheekbones were sculpted out perfectly, and it only just occurred to Danny that Enzo smelt good. He smelt like apples and cinnamon; warm, wonderful things that made Danny feel cosy. It was all so friggin weird. Danny didn't know what to think, and he didn't like it.

"It's Allison, isn't it?" Enzo asked, with an exasperated frown.

Danny's shoulders slumped, and a little sigh escaped him.

"Look, Danny, okay," Enzo said, then placed his other hand on Danny's other shoulder. "I can only help you with this crap if you start believing me and stop freaking out."

"What exactly are you helping me with?" Danny asked and leaned his gaze back up.

"Whatever you need – getting over the girl who left you, maybe getting rid of your idealistic view of soulmates? Because they're not idealistic. Relationships take work, regardless of whether you're soulmates or not – and sometimes things just don't work out, and that's okay. The world keeps spinning. You don't need to be with somebody to be yourself and be happy, Danny," he stated simply, eyes swimming back and forth between Danny's.

Danny stayed frozen, mouth collapsing open and closed every few seconds while he stared at Enzo. The hands on his shoulders made his body swoon slightly, the look in Enzo's eyes made him feel weird, and what Enzo said made this weird flash of guilt jab him.

"But what if she comes back? What if her voice is still in there when you're gone?" Enzo shrugged.

"Regardless of anyone, Danny, you need to be happy in you," he said seriously. "What happened with you and Allison?" His eyebrows raised and Danny gulped, gaze falling to the floor.

"She moved to America," he stated. "We were going to move together but, uh, one day, I got home, and she'd packed her clothes and left. Her key was on the counter, and that was it. She left a note but, uh, yeah…"

"You still have the note, don't you?" Enzo asked, with cocked eyebrows.

Danny just numbly nodded, and a deep sigh escaped Enzo's throat. "Okay, we're going to your place."

Danny looked up to Enzo in shock. "We're uh… we're what?" he asked.

"We're going to your place. I'll book a taxi," Enzo stated.

"Why are we… uh…" Danny began.

"Just trust me," Enzo interrupted.

Chapter 3

Danny's flat was small. It was a one-bed with a tiny living room and kitchen. The bathroom had a shower that teetered off the wall and splattered water over tiles at ridiculous hours in the night. The carpet was grey, hard, and rough due to ware. A two-seater couch sat in the centre, with a small TV in front. One cushion sat in the centre of the cream couch – a little, rounded, pink cushion with a small red stain on its left side. Several unopened letters sat on the rickety dining table behind the couch. Danny's old, clunky laptop sat in the centre with a pile of papers next to it. There were two chairs at the table, both old and used. The one behind Danny's laptop had an uneven leg and a missing screw.

The kitchen was beside that. It was a basic, squared-off room with an oven, microwave, fridge, bin and kettle. One person could comfortably stand in it and cook, but two people? One would be crushed into the gleaming white cabinets. A note sat on the fridge – a little, pink post-it note that was hung by a circular magnet. The writing was rushed and scribbled, and the paper was thin and weak, but it seemed to weigh down the magnet, dragging it towards the floor awkwardly. The white, spotted, laminate flooring was polished and clean, as were the hobs and the sides. The room looked untouched, besides the note on the fridge, the takeaway containers on the side and the little, chipped mug by the sink that seemed to have pink lipstick on the rim.

The bedroom was dark, the windows covered with purple blackout curtains. The bed was a small double. It was brand new, made of shiny, smooth oak with a drawer on either side. They mainly stored old clothes and books. Danny didn't know what was in them anymore. He hadn't looked since she left. He especially hadn't looked in the one on the right side.

The red tartan quilt was clean and smelt like wildflowers and washing-up liquid, as it surrounded the small, memory foam mattress. Danny remembered the day that they'd gotten it. It was backordered, and they'd waited two months, while sleeping on their crappy, old couch bed. They were so relieved when it arrived, they fell asleep at two thirty in the afternoon – no quilt or sheet or pillows, just a bare mattress on their living room floor. It was the best they'd both slept in months.

The bed was perfectly made, with the red pillows sat up against the headboard and two little, black cushions sat in front, with a fluffy, grey throw on the foot of the bed. A dressing table sat across from it and was currently covered in little bottles of perfumes, deodorants and lip balms that appeared half-used, old and in disarray. A mirror stood behind it, covered in powdered foundation and lip gloss that glittered when light shone through gaps in the curtains. Danny's clothes were organised and piled up on shelves, typically arranged by season, but he tended to move them around when he procrastinated marking. They were currently arranged by colour and piled on the three small shelves by the window –trousers in the middle, T shirts at the top and a single, unused suit at the bottom.

Danny unlocked his door shakily, then pressed it open and walked through to the living room. Enzo followed slowly behind him, as the warm air and familiar smell of wildflower and Christmas cookie candle thwacked their nostrils.

The cab ride had been silent. Danny gave the guy his address, and they disappeared down the road to the tiny apartment building in the middle of nowhere.

Enzo stayed silent as the door closed and Danny gently hit the light switch.

The living room lit up, and the weirdness of this scenario hit Danny like a shot, as he wrapped his arms around himself and stared down at the grey floor, his head swimming in a bath of warm beer.

Enzo wasn't looking at him. His golden eyes trailed around the room when they walked through the door. His gaze specifically fell to the letters on the table, the stained cushion and the magazines hidden under the couch. "Nice place," he muttered, after a moment of deathly silence.

Danny jolted at the words, feeling them pelt him from the side as he stared at his couch, anxiety eating through his stomach lining as he gulped and tried not to think about what was potentially about to happen.

"Uh... I, uh... thanks," Danny stammered, then ran a hand down the back of his neck. His gaze landed on the magazines and the cushion, the stain specifically, as he had this sudden desire to run over and flip it. He gulped then gestured to the couch with one arm, while his gaze slipped to the kitchen door. "Uh... you, uh... want a drink?"

Enzo lowered his eyebrows as Danny turned to him. Blue eyes linked with gold and a sharp squeeze quaked through Danny's heart.

"Oh, I see," Enzo stated then bit his lip while looking into Danny's nervous eyes. "Danny, this isn't what you think it is so don't worry."

Danny shook his head and a small smile formed on Enzo's face as the man reached forward and placed his hands on Danny's shoulders. Danny jolted then stared at Enzo with un-endingly wide eyes, his mouth going dry like someone had aimed a leaf blower at it.

"Nothing is going to happen. I swear, this is just so I can help you... you know... move on and..." His eyes glanced the magazines. "Be happy? I don't know. I don't really practice these speeches before I do them. This isn't the first time I've gone to another soulmate's place on the first date, so, yeah, I can see why your mind went there. I'm sorry."

Danny blinked several times then shook his head, while Enzo's face gained a bright-red, glowing sheen that brought dramatic attention to his freckles. The pair gulped in several shaky breaths while looking at each other, both of their faces getting redder and redder, as the air between them started steaming.

Enzo cleared his throat suddenly turning his gaze to the ground. "Yeah... I'll, uh... take that drink," he stammered, placing a hand on the back of his own neck and looking everywhere but Danny's eyes, while Danny nervously shuffled over to the kitchen.

The heated tension made Danny's guts tighten and twist before he came back into the room with two open bottles of cider. Enzo hadn't moved. His eyes darted about the room like a pinball, while his hands clenched and unclenched. He rocked back and forth on his heels and lapped in breaths like a paddling dog. Danny nudged him with the cider, and Enzo snapped his gaze to him.

"Do you uh... do you wanna sit?" Danny asked, while Enzo took the cider from Danny's hand.

Enzo just smiled lightly, nodded, and the pair wondered over to the couch. They were about a foot apart, each perched on the edge of their cushions. Danny took a slow sip of his cider, while Enzo put his on the ground and stood up, grabbing the magazines in one fluid motion. Danny stared at him with wide eyes, while Enzo began flipping through an old Cosmo. He could still see her handwriting on a couple of the quizzes.

"Guessing these aren't yours?" he asked, while tilting a suspicious eyebrow down at Danny.

"Allison's," he confessed.

"And you keep them there because?" Enzo asked, eyebrows rising.

Silence ached around them, crickets chirped, and tumbleweeds rolled along the floor. Danny didn't need to answer that question, did he?

"Because I… uh… they're hers?" he muttered, tilting his gaze to Enzo for a moment, then turning back to look at his cider.

"And she's not here, Danny," Enzo said gently, then placed the magazines on the ground before turning to the candles by the TV.

His words punctured Danny's heart, letting the air out of it. Enzo placed the candles on top of the magazines then grabbed the letters off the table, glancing through them quickly to the check the name on the top. He was unsurprised when they all read 'Allison Docker.' He placed them on the pile, too.

"What are you doing?" Danny asked.

"The cushion was hers too, right?" Enzo asked and gestured to the little pink cushion on the couch.

Danny lowered his eyebrows and turned to it before Enzo snatched it away and chucked it on the pile.

"What are you doing?" Danny repeated, then stood and grabbed the pillow.

"Danny, she left. You can't just keep a shrine to her in your own home. Does having her stuff around really make you feel good?" Enzo asked and grabbed the cushion once more.

Danny opened his mouth to retort but couldn't find the words. He couldn't find it in himself to say 'yes', when looking at those magazines, and smelling those candles made his heart feel like it was getting juiced.

But what else was he supposed to freakin do? He heard her voice in his head and smelled her perfume on his coat and his quilt. He could still feel her around the flat on most days. She was coming back – she had to.

That's what happened to his parents. They were soulmates when they were eighteen. They met at college, but his mum was forced to move away when her dad joined the RAF. They were apart for months, but his dad cycled down to see her at the base every few weeks before they decided to go to Uni together.

His grandparents met on holiday. It took one look for them to see that they were soulmates, but they lived miles apart on the other side of the country, before his grandfather hopped on a train and bought them a house. He came back, and they were together because they were soulmates.

That's how soulmates worked. Not one soulmate then you hop to another like you're playing leapfrog. Everyone gets one. You meet them and then you're together. That's it. Your souls are interlinked, your lives are interlinked. You're meant to be together, so you're together; it's that simple. It's been that simple for hundreds of years now, hundreds of years of people hearing the other's voice then finding them when destiny chooses you to find them, then you're together. Simple.

Allison was coming back. Their story wasn't over. It couldn't be because Danny and her were soulmates. They got each other and loved each other and that's just how these things worked! Soulmates weren't temporary. It wasn't crazy to wait for each other. It's what his parents would do. It's what everyone did. There was a reason he hadn't told anyone yet or posted about it. Everyone knew that soulmates were forever. It's how they worked, how the world's worked forever. He couldn't be the only guy on the planet who completely lost his soulmate. He just couldn't be. What would people think of him? What would his family think? Everyone expected him and Allison to get married. He expected it. He expected them to have kids and get a house with a white picket fence. He wanted a life with her. He couldn't be the only guy in the world who fully lost his soulmate. He just couldn't be.

He could hear her voice still. He *always* heard her voice —her light, lifting tone and the way she always sounded like she was smiling. He heard it every day, every time he woke up and every time he felt sad. He'd heard it in his head more often than he'd heard his own voice. She was his soulmate. There was just no getting around that.

"I can't just get rid of it," Danny answered eventually, while staring down at his cider.

"And why not?" Enzo asked with a cocked eyebrow.

"Coz she's my soulmate, Enzo," he argued, and Enzo groaned.

"And she left, Danny," he stated.

"I know that," Danny muttered, while collapsing further into himself, his thumb nail unconsciously scratching at the label on his bottle. "But she's coming back."

"And how do you know that? And even if she did, is it worth putting your life on hold until then? Just having all this crap reminding you that she's not here? Is it worth it?" Enzo asked and placed the cushion back on the pile.

Danny stared at his cider, thumbing the label and biting his lip as the vessels in his heart started to twist, and his brain started to fog to the point where it felt like his eyes were floating in warm whipped cream.

"It doesn't matter," he ground out, then sighed. "It doesn't matter if it's worth it or not. She's my soulmate, and she's coming back. Soulmates aren't a temporary thing. It doesn't matter how I feel or whether she's gone for long or not. We're meant to be and that's it."

"Then explain this," Enzo said then pointed back and forth between the two of them, as Danny's gaze jumped to him then drunkenly followed his finger.

"I, uh… it… uh…" Danny stammered then turned his gaze back to his cider.

"Look, Danny. I'm not trying to freak you out here," he stated. "You're a good person. I can feel that, and you deserve better. I can't make you freakin see it – you have to work it out for yourself – but I can give you a start. And to start, you have to get rid of her stuff and admit that your feelings fucking matter, regardless of whether Allison was your soulmate or not," Enzo finished, slowly and calmly, while looking over Danny's sunken form.

The silence that followed felt like they'd been dropped in the middle of the Baltic Sea. Their ears popped and the world froze, as Danny stared at anything but Enzo, and Enzo refused to look anywhere but Danny.

Enzo's golden eyes were squinted and serious as Danny tilted his gaze back and ran slowly through what was said. "How can you say that?"

"Which bit?" Enzo grumbled, as Danny got to his feet and grabbed the cushion once more.

"Just… she's my… we were…" Danny began, then groaned as his mind desperately reached for the right words. "Are. She's my soulmate, Enzo. Whether she hurt me or not, or whether she's here or not, she's my soulmate. My feelings aren't important because we're just… it's just it. We're soulmates. That's it. It doesn't matter how I feel, because she's coming back, and we'll be together coz that's just how these things work."

"So, okay," Enzo began, then stared lightly at Danny as the blue-eyed man blinked up at him, feeling an odd surge of anger and righteous indignation flood his sinuses. "Just, okay. Put this soulmate thing aside for one moment. Forget the fact that Allison was anything more than just your girlfriend. Just for one second." He leaned forward and pressed his hands back into Danny's shoulders, bringing attention to the fact that Enzo was an inch or two shorter than him. "She left," Enzo continued seriously. "How did it feel?" His voice fell to a slow, calm whisper.

Danny's mind fumbled for an answer. Words swirled around in a deafening tornado of heavy smoke and sticky mist. It felt... wrong. Forget about her being his soulmate? How? He tried to press through his mind and reach out to grab any words or anything that made sense in the spiral, but nothing came up; nothing at all, until Enzo squeezed his shoulder and squinted his golden eyes with a tired smile.

A rush flew through Danny's mind. It felt sunshine-y and hot. It alleviated parts of the mist and caused a gulp to rifle through his throat. He remembered when he read that note. He remembered coming home and seeing half of the drawers empty. The flat still smelt like her. It smelt like sugared strawberries and piles of fresh roses. Her toothbrush was gone, as well as her shoes and her coat. The key on the side was the last straw, until he found the note. The words 'I'm sorry but I have to do this for me' were scrawled on a little post-it, like those words explained everything –like it justified anything.

He'd called her, but it went straight to voicemail. He'd texted her, but there was no reply.

He didn't understand it. He thought it was some awful prank and that she was going to jump out from behind the door with two plane tickets and a camera. His whole body fell numb as he slumped into the couch and read and re-read the words, hoping that something would occur to him, that something would make him understand, but he didn't. They were moving to New York together. That was the plan. She got a writing fellowship, they had boxes and suitcases ready, Danny was handing in his notice. That was the plan, and he was ready. Scared, but ready. But no, she just decided to go. Their souls were interlinked; their lives were planned out. They were meant to be everything to each other, the universe had decided that, but no. She walked away. She walked away as if that meant nothing, as if Danny meant nothing to her.

Danny's heart collapsed in on itself, as cold, ink-black sludge stabbed through the ventricles.

Enzo just squeezed his shoulder tighter and grounded the man.

"It hurt," Danny muttered, his gaze falling to the ground and his vision blurring, as light bits of moisture fell from his eyes.

"I know," Enzo gulped, then ran a finger under Danny's eye, removing a tear before placing his hand back on the man's shoulder. "But you're going to be okay," he whispered, then pressed Danny's shoulders back.

Blue eyes linked to gold again, and Danny was surprised by the kind, genuine smile on the man's face.

"Trust me."

Danny looked back and forth between Enzo's eyes, spotting small strands of green and blue in his light-brown irises. They sparkled like sequins. Shaky heat rushed through and inflated Danny's chest as he gulped.

Enzo's arms slacked slightly, but the grip on Danny's shoulders remained as the two boys stared at each other, and a strange rush of warmth flitted around them. Danny's heart quaked through several stunted beats as he pressed out slow breaths. Enzo felt his arms slack further and his feet drift slightly over the rough carpet. Their eyes drifted from one to the other, until Danny's eyes fell to Enzo's lips and the world stopped.

Danny looked at Enzo's soft lips, gulped and slipped forward. Enzo followed, and their eyes closed, lips falling into each other.

Enzo's lips were softer than they looked. They were warm and gentle while being firm and unyielding, his arms wrapped around Danny's back as Danny's hands wrapped Enzo's waist. Their hearts fell into succinct rhythm. Their heads tilted to the sides as the kiss deepened slightly, and the world got warmer and kinder as the air in the flat swirled through Danny's hair. Danny's mind fell blank and blurry in wistful, drunken happiness that felt like a warm blanket wrapping his heart.

They didn't pull away until Danny's knees felt like jelly and Enzo wound up being the only thing holding him up. The pair blinked open their eyes and stared at each other. Each wore shock on their faces, lips falling to 'o' shapes and eyes staring ridiculously wide. They were an inch or two apart, maybe more? Maybe less? They didn't feel the distance in that moment. Neither could feel much more than stunned, and neither spoke for several long moments, while they just breathed and willed their hearts to slow.

Enzo didn't make a habit of kissing all his soulmates. He'd only kissed his first –the first voice he heard when he was eighteen; the voice that he thought he'd end up with forever. His name was Tim. They went to college together, studied English in the same class and were just friends, until they both woke up one day and heard the other's voice through their minds. Neither knew how to react and neither knew how to speak to the other about it, until Tim kissed him, and Enzo was stunned further. He hadn't kissed anyone before then, so wasn't sure how it was meant to feel, but it felt like magic –something that Enzo could do forever.

They dated for three months and planned on going to Uni together until Tim left. They got into the same Uni, but Tim decided to take another offer. He apologized and said that they could do long-distance but Enzo knew he didn't mean it and the pair broke up a week later. A week after that, he heard a new voice in his head, then another, then another. He didn't know what it was or what to make of it, a part of him was thankful for the distraction. He never really believed in this soulmate stuff, anyway. His parents were never happy, despite being soulmates. He didn't want that. He wanted the ability to relax in relationships. He didn't want to be shackled to another person forever because the universe decided it. He wanted to be in control of his own happiness. He moved about and helped people where he could. He met some great people, took them on adventures and got them out of their shells. He loved it and he wouldn't want anything else, but he never stuck around, so he never kissed them. They were people who needed comfort and support, they didn't need some guy showing up, kissing them and then leaving.

Why'd he kiss Danny? Did Danny kiss him? It was hard to tell in that moment, but both wanted it –that much was obvious. And that kiss? Holy crap. Did Danny feel that too? It felt like his heart stopped then was shocked back to life. The soft, warm fingers pressing into his back both grounded him and sent him flying. It felt ridiculous and magical in so many ways. It'd been five years since he'd been kissed but kissing Tim hadn't felt like that. Would kissing all of them have felt like that? Did Danny feel like that when he kissed Allison? That thought caused a weird stab of black sludge to jolt through his still-calming heart.

"Whoa… um… I'm sorry… I… uh…" Danny rambled, then pulled back slightly as Enzo snapped back to reality and shook his head.

"It's okay, Danny. You're okay," he said quickly, while gently nudging him back onto the couch.

"I'm sorry, I shouldn't have done that. I don't know why I did that. I just… you were just… I… crap," Danny continued to mutter, then aggressively shoved his head into his hands. Enzo slumped onto the couch beside him, his red face steaming slightly.

"Has anyone ever told you that you're kinda high strung?" Enzo asked with a little smile.

Danny scoffed. "My mother."

A sharp laugh escaped Enzo's lips.

"Seriously, I'm sorry. I don't know what that was. You said nothing was going to happen, and I just… I don't normally do that. I'm sorry."

Enzo rolled his eyes. "I invited myself over to your flat, and uh… well, it takes two to tango, Dann-O," he replied, then nudged Danny's shoulder while cocking his eyebrows. Danny blinked as a deep blush flooded his entire face. Enzo's eyes then fell back onto the pile of stuff on the living room floor, as a weirdly comfortable silence flooded the flat.

Danny was freaking out. Every part of his brain was on red alert and blearing alarms through his temples. Why did he kiss Enzo? And why did it feel like that? It felt so… it was… there was so much to it. It felt shocking. It felt ridiculous and wonderful and lit up

61

every part of his heart in a warm glow. Kissing Allison had not felt like that. He didn't know how kissing Allison felt now, but it didn't feel like that. Holy crap, it didn't feel like that, and, he just kissed a guy! And he liked it. If there were any doubts about him being bi, well, they were gone. Holy shit, there was so much to unpack here. His head was beating painfully as he ran his fingers through his hair.

"Where was this note?" Enzo asked, then jumped up. Danny jolted, his gaze falling to the kitchen door. Enzo smirked, then walked through it, wandering back into the room immediately with a post-it in his hand. "She broke up with you with a post-it note?" Enzo asked with a cocked eyebrow.

Danny just sighed and nodded.

"That's brutal." He placed it on the pile before turning to look back at Danny. "You're getting rid of this crap, and from today onwards, you're letting Allison go and focusing on you, okay?"

Danny gulped and his eyes caught the corner of her things, as he gulped and bit his lip. This room already felt empty. Every corner and every crevice felt lonely and cold – it hadn't felt like home since she left. Every now and again, he'd look in the dressing table mirror. His eyes would trail to the lip balm and a lump would form in his throat. He'd stare at his reflection through the lip gloss stains; he'd go into the bathroom and see only one toothbrush, and his heart would ache; he'd struggle to breathe until he turned away. The curtains in the bedroom hadn't been open in months now because Allison chose them, and Danny couldn't bring himself to drag them apart.

He couldn't bring himself to do anything. He only headed out tonight because his room felt too quiet. It was Friday and work was manic, as usual. He still had a million papers to mark and a few lessons to plan. He hadn't been a trainee teacher for long, but he was drowning in work, which he was grateful for. You can't really overthink when you're drowning in work.

He glanced up at Enzo and watched his golden eyes trail him as a little smile appeared on his face. Weird thing was that this place didn't feel as empty with Enzo here. A part of Danny's soul was breaking at the idea that someone who wasn't Allison was standing on his carpet. Someone who wasn't Allison was in his head. Someone who wasn't Allison had kissed him. Someone who wasn't Allison was his soulmate. It was a lot to digest and process, but maybe it would be less if this place stopped feeling like it was half-empty.

His eyes glanced at the stuff again, as a strange longing tugged at his heart, dragging it into his ribs as Danny gulped down a shuddering breath. He really did feel empty. He hadn't noticed it or acknowledged it before, but he'd spend hours sat on his couch, looking through those magazines and lighting those candles. He'd dread waking up in the mornings to an empty bed; he'd actively avoid looking in that mirror. Nothing had felt right in months, and that was okay because she was coming back. They were soulmates and things were going to make sense again, at some point. At some point in the future, she'd come back.

That's what Danny was leaning on, but what if Enzo was right? What if she wasn't coming back? And even if she was, he couldn't keep living like this. He was just numb and waiting, driving himself slowly mad, falling into a corner. It'd been two months, but it felt like decades had gone by. He felt like he'd aged ten years in the past sixty days.

He couldn't keep living like this. He couldn't keep looking at that pillow or smelling those stupid candles. He needed to get rid of that mirror and those curtains. He needed to remind himself that he was still here and the world was still spinning. He needed to stop drowning. He needed to stop falling, before he fell too far and couldn't pull himself back up, but how was he supposed to do that?

Danny gulped and looked over the little pile once more, the note screaming through the back of his mind as his heart inflated like a water balloon. 'I'm sorry, but I have to do this for me.' The paper still smelt like her; everything still did. It wasn't right. It wasn't right that she was gone but she was still here. There was something so detached and unnatural about it, something uneasy and cold. It made Danny feel like he wasn't existing in the world unless she was sleeping beside him. The last two months felt like he was just watching life roll past him.

Until now.

Danny reached a trembling hand forward and tugged the note free from the pile. He stared at the writing, his eyes trailing the lettering, his fingers falling numb as he let out a breath and grabbed the cushion off the floor. He scooped it up in his arm, then grabbed the magazines and the candles, cupping everything in an awkward cradle. Enzo just watched him silently with wide, gold eyes.

Danny walked to the door and reached a weak finger out from under the pile.

Enzo's resolve dropped with a little scoff. "Need some help there, Dann-O?"

"Please," Danny replied, and Enzo appeared at his side, tugging the door open. Danny walked through and disappeared to the lobby, Enzo hot on his heels as they appeared in the street.

"So, what's the plan? Bury this stuff in the forest? Burn it? Chuck it in a river?" Enzo asked, and Danny cocked an eyebrow at him before walking to the side of the building and chucking the pile in the bin.

"Ah." Danny scoffed at him with a little side smirk, as he sighed and stared over the crap at the bottom of the dumpster.

He felt guilty about it. But there was something else. Something freeing. It felt like the synapses in his head had pulsed through refreshed shocks, like he was blinking back to life. His shoulders slumped as he sucked in a breath of cool, Autumn air. His feet turned and wandered back to the front of the building, and he slumped onto the small patch of grass outside. Enzo followed and leaned against the small oak tree with a smile on his face, as the moon gleamed over them in calming, wistful silence.

Danny let out a deep sigh and leaned on his hands, fingers trailing the grass as he looked up at the oak tree. He smiled beneath it, tether on his heart pulling away. His mind fell blank as time started to pass, and the moon simply trailed over them. Stars glittered and glowed. His eyes wandered the sky as he laid down and closed his eyes, the world engulfing him in a warm, comforting embrace that flooded his very being to the core, reminding him that he wasn't alone and that he was going to be okay.

Chapter 4
ENZO

Enzo had been planning on working that day. He'd told Gemma that he was available but he was sat in his flat on the couch, staring blindly at the TV. He wasn't sure what he was watching, at this point. Some kind of gameshow, possibly? His flat was a tip. He'd just made chilli and was slowly spooning through it, paprika aching through his nose and causing it to twinge before he gave up and put it down. His eyes turned to his headset and his laptop, as a deep sigh escaped through his lips.

He worked as a customer service operator, and he didn't hate it. He just handled incoming calls for an energy company. He'd been doing it since college and was just used to it, he guessed. It wasn't exciting or especially fun, but it was easy and he could do it anywhere. He just needed his laptop, headset and Wi-Fi. His manager was nice and the hours were flexible – perfect for his crazy-ass jumping from place-to-place life.

He slowly slumped off his couch, not bothering to turn the TV off. His headset just hit his palm when feedback squeaked through his temples and a grunt quaked through his heart. The headset rolled on the dining table, and Enzo shook his head to alleviate the growing migraine, a weird combination of anxiety and frustration pressing hot air through his chest.

A small voice whispered through him. The word 'Danny' flooded all four corners of his brain as Enzo smirked and grabbed his bike keys off the side, completely forgetting about work, while turning off his TV and marching out his front door.

He never knew how he knew where. He knew that that was probably the weirdest part of all this, and he rarely had a day or more between getting a new person in his head. He'd just gotten back last night after helping a girl named 'Katie', who had moved across the country for her soulmate, only for them to fall for another person and leave. It'd happened a week ago, and she wasn't sad, shockingly. She was pissed and Enzo spent the whole time smashing all his belongings. He'd be remised to say that he didn't enjoy it. Katie didn't really need his help to move on or let go. It was more about relieving her frustration, and Enzo was more than willing to do that when this guy was a prick to Katie.

Katie was a sweetheart. She had a kind smile, bright-blue eyes, a positive outlook. She was one of those sunshine-y people and they had a lot of fun together. They never kissed, never even hugged. They had a handshake at the end but that was it, and Enzo knew she'd be fine. It was probably the shortest time he'd spent with a person in a long while. He was there for two weeks. He was used to spending months with people.

The longest he'd spent with another person was four months. But they were grieving, and Enzo became a bit of a lifeline for Charlie. He didn't feel right leaving him, so he stayed until the voice fully and completely faded. He even moved into his flat for a little while, did a bit of couch-surfing.

His mum was very worried. Enzo lived in Wickhampton, Charlie lived in Swansea. The commute was crazy so Charlie just gave him the couch. He was a kind-hearted person and Enzo had felt his whole heart break for him when he heard his story.

Charlie's soulmate was diagnosed with inoperable liver cancer when they were sixteen. They were in remission when they met and they dated for a year or so. He'd proposed and they were getting married, but then it came back. Charlie was unable to speak when Enzo showed up. He felt like the universe was betraying him. It took a long while to talk him off the ledge. It wasn't an easy one, but Charlie was better by the time Enzo left. He was smiling again. He was ready to let go and find a way to move forward.

He kept in touch with everyone. It was a weird deal he had. They added each other on Facebook and messaged back and forth. He'd been drunkenly messaged by a few of them. A couple asked for booty-calls, but they lived across the country, and it was no-go, anyways. He didn't sleep with any of his soulmates.

Him and Tim got close, but then he moved away, and Enzo couldn't picture himself trusting another person like that. He didn't know how long he had with these people, he didn't want to just bed them and run off –not only for their sake, but for his, too. So, he was twenty-three and a virgin. He hadn't kissed anyone in five years, but he was okay.

He met a lot of great people with his weird, self-proclaimed 'curse.' There had been a time where he hated it and just wanted the voices to stop so he could relax and do nothing, but he knew where they were and he knew they probably needed help, and Enzo was not a person who could just leave well enough alone.

He never really fell for his soulmates. Hell, he wasn't sure he'd been in love since he was eighteen. He wasn't even sure back then, but the more time passed and the older he got, the more people he met, the better he got at disassociating. He loved spending time with all these people and going on adventures and learning about them. He loved making friends and going to different places. He loved riding his bike all over and just spouting nonsense that he assumed was 'wise.' He wanted more than anything to be a good influence on people.

His mum didn't understand what he was doing, and he wouldn't dare talk to his dad about it. Heck, his dad didn't even know he was bi, and with all the references his dad made to gay people in TV shows and movies being 'fruity' and how much he just couldn't stand watching them kiss, he never wanted to have that discussion with him. Ever. His mum had implied something about him liking guys in front of his dad once, he glared like someone had slapped him. Enzo had paranoid moments where he thought that was why he drank. All his siblings were straight and happily married. They found their soulmates and stuck with them. Most of them seemed happy. His parents weren't but he couldn't see them breaking up anytime soon. They'd fight about stupid things like the remote and phones. God knows why but their biggest issue was Enzo. That's what he felt, anyway. His mum worried about him but he couldn't stop what he was doing.

He heard the voices. He knew where they were, and he didn't want to settle down. He couldn't imagine a day where he would. The worst nights of his life were him sat alone in his flat. He didn't want that. Who would want that forever? Just to be with another person, slowly decaying; finding new things to fight about and haemorrhaging money on bills and rent and stupid things, while fighting about bills and rent and stupid things. Then you have a kid and life becomes even more of a headache, and you can't even get away from it. Enzo didn't want that. He dreaded the day that he would. Though some days, he did just want someone to vent to –when people at work were annoying or when he was tired. Some days, he just wanted to talk to someone about something he was excited about. He had moments of being jealous of his siblings when their photos popped up on Facebook but he wasn't built for those things. The universe decided he wasn't, so he had to keep going, and he was happy with it. His life was full of great people and good stories. What more could he want?

'Danny' rang through his head sweetly, and Enzo hopped on his bright red bike, shoved his helmet on and tore down the street, speeding and spinning round corners, as the sun slowly faded around him. His phone vibrated through his pocket, but he didn't dare look at it. The wind swept through his lightly tied back hair. The bobble was slipping but he didn't care, he had plenty anyway. The sun set and night slowly crested through the sky, stars twinkled between the pale-grey clouds. The moon rose behind, and everything appeared in a glowing, nature-themed shadow show. White light glistened and glowed in lines that beamed up and around the slowly fading blue.

Enzo's motorcycle was old, but safe. He had it looked at every month and was trained in how to fix little, stupid things on it. It was always gassed up and ready to go, always had a second helmet locked to the handlebars, and a pile of clothes plus bathroom stuff (soap, razor, toothpaste, toothbrush) in the little box on the back. He'd learned early on to be prepared for anything when he just rode off to meet a new person. He drove across the country once and wound up staying in

Wales overnight, with no supplies or anything. He had to buy all new clothes and a new toothbrush. It was annoying, so now he had everything in that little box. If he ended up staying in a little hostel somewhere, he had clothes. If he wound up in a crappy hotel, he had a toothbrush. He had pyjamas and soap. If he ended up on a soulmate's couch, he was prepared.

He didn't know how he knew where to go. It was a beacon, like something from over a long distance dragged him forwards, and it wouldn't stop until he got there. It was an unspecific Satnav that dragged his heart through his chest, causing his lungs to turn gooey and his breathing to feel off, then it was fine. Then Enzo got there and warmth erupted through him in a firework of relief and familiarity. Every time. Always the same. It always felt weird, cold, uncomfortable and uncontrollable until he got there, and he saw them. Even from behind, he always knew.

'Danny' didn't live too far. It was twenty minutes from Wickhampton to Great Yarmouth. Enzo was thrown when the tether on his heart retracted. It whiplashed him as he appeared in the car park of a small bar named 'The Monarch.' A giant, red butterfly sat on the front of the run-down, redbrick building. Six cars sat out front and no lights shone through the window. The place was dead. It was a post-apocalyptic bar, a place for sad, lonely people to drink their troubles away.

Enzo chained his bike up, combed his hair and adjusted his bobble again, before making sure that his jumper covered that stupid tattoo. Why he ever got that thing, he'd never know. He forgot about it on most days, then would look at his back in a mirror and be like, 'When did I bang my b… oh.'

He appeared through the glass bar doors with a nervous smile. One shaky breath, and his eyes zero-ed in on the guy at the bar. Warmth flooded his sinuses and overwhelmed his cells in a flurry of soul-quaking heat. A black, blue and white tartan shirt dangled over the bar stool and hid half of the man's slim calves. It seemed to be a shirt tied around his hips, covering a pair of distressed, faded, grey jeans. A black top with short sleeves covered his chest, with little rips over the shoulders. His hair was short, curly and mousy. It fell just below his ears with little wisps flanking off in odd directions. His neck was pale, his arms were slim and slightly toned, and it took a couple of nervous breaths for Enzo to get up the courage to speak.

He could hear his voice in his head. He already felt this weird air of familiarity about him, the sense of kindness and warmth, heartbreak and nerves. 'Danny' gave off so much without even looking at him.

The bar was empty. The news blared from somewhere. There were maybe three other people here, but Enzo could barely see or hear them. His eyes were stuck on the back of Danny's head, on the bar around him, on the bottle in his hands, on the label he was scraping with his nails, and on the sigh that escaped him. His back was hunched, his eyes were glaring down at the bar while his body shook and sighed on the awkwardly tall stool.

He never thought much when talking to his soulmates. He was a thoroughly nervous person but he pressed his shakes and awkwardness to the side when he talked. He wanted to be confident and fun, so 'fake it till you make it' was his motto.

And on that note, he wandered to the bar and started the strangest night he'd had since this weird, little curse started five years ago. Danny was nervous and sad, like he expected. He was cute –bright, blue eyes and charming smile. He was a teacher, judging by the papers on the table and the stern but calm, gentle vibes he gave of.

His soulmates always felt familiar. They always felt like old friends. They were always cute and wonderful, sweet and kind. They all had similar ways of speaking and similar ways of seeing the world while having different passions, different looks in their eyes and different hopes, but they all typically had one thing in common.

None of them knew it was possible to have more than one. They thought soulmates were forever and were deeply, deeply cut when their soulmate left, or when things didn't turn out as 'they were supposed to'. Enzo had understanding for those who had never met their soulmates – the frustration within them was palpable. He had more understanding for those who had lost their soulmates in unforeseen circumstances. He'd met a few and his heart always broke for them. A few were relieved at the idea that they didn't just get one. Enzo renewed their faith in life and reminded them that the world kept turning, things kept changing and things would get better. His time spent with them was always a wake-up call. It was always a reminder that what he was doing was important, that these people were important and deserved better.

For people whose soulmates had just up and left, he understood a little less. Tim left and it hurt, but Enzo saw it coming and he understood. A part of him was relieved that Tim left, that it wasn't his own choice to leave. They were young and stupid, life would've torn them apart. And if it hadn't torn them apart, they'd be trapped together.

Danny was different. Blue emotion filtered through Enzo when he spoke of Allison. Tim was naïve and lovesick like Danny, but Tim was more impulsive. Then again, Danny did kiss him. His heart overflowed and drained when the blue-eyed man smiled, and his heart roared in anger when he thought of how much Allison had hurt him. There was so much going through his head and so much beating through his body and his heart. He wanted to make Danny feel better. He wanted Danny to see that he deserved better. He felt his kindness and his generosity. He found his competitive nature intoxicating and his smile entrancing, but there was more to it.

The pair stared up at the moonlight. Danny was lying on the grass with his arms behind his head, eyes gently closed, as Enzo smiled and slowly lowered himself onto the ground beside him. Danny didn't shuffle or twitch. He just sagged into the ground with a wistful smile on his lips. Enzo watched as his mousy hair floated into the grass, revealing his gentle features. A million emotions flitted off him in spinning wisps. He was beautiful. Everything that Enzo felt from Danny was beautiful, kind, simple and sweet. He deserved better than Allison. Had he realised that now? Or was this just a…

A vibrating chuckle warbled through Danny's throat and shook through the earth, as Enzo blinked in surprise and turned his head to the blue-eyed man. "What's funny, blue-eyes?" Enzo asked, and Danny scoffed, turning his head to face Enzo.

"Nothing," he muttered, then shook his head and turned back to look at the sky. "It's just been a weird night." He sighed. "Guess this is par for the course for you, though."

"I'm not some kind of nomadic whore, you know, just travelling from town to town and kissing cute teachers with crappy apartments," he said.

Danny's eyes jolted up and stared down at Enzo, a guilty gulp ringing through his throat. "I didn't mean to uh…" he rambled, and a hearty chuckle warbled through Enzo, as he grinned and sat up.

"Relax. I'm not offended," he stated. "But for the record? This night wasn't exactly typical for me, either."

Danny blinked then lowered his eyebrows.

"None of them are. None of them are the same."

Danny just rolled his eyes and fell back to the ground. "How does this work again, and what do we do here?"

"Still with the questions," Enzo chuckled, and Danny scoffed. "You still hear my voice?"

"Loud and clear," Danny muttered, and Enzo grinned lightly, a little warmth flushing his heart as he gulped. "You still hear mine?"

"Can't see it going anywhere for a while, Dann-O," he stated.

Neither had any clue what was going to happen. Enzo had done this a million times, but it was always different. Some wanted him to stick around for a while, and some wanted distance to adjust. Some were in denial, some were drunk off their face and needed Enzo to babysit them. A guy clung to him once and wouldn't let go. He was nineteen and it was... awkward. Finding your soulmate at a university when you're not a student at said university, is just awkward. Everyone was playing this weird card game. Enzo joined in and everyone got drunk. He fell asleep on the kitchen floor of his soulmate's dorm.

He had no idea what Danny would want. He didn't strike him as the 'cling and never let go' type or the 'I need distance to process' type. What type did he strike him as? Nervous and cute? Sure. Awkward, but oddly competitive? Definitely. Kind of naïve, but in a sort of endearing way? Sure, but none of these seemed to hint at what tonight's activities would be.

"So, you're uh... you're uh... you're sticking around until the voice fades, right? You're not just gonna, like, run off when I turn my back, are you?" Danny asked, his calm demeanour fading, as his blue eyes caught Enzo's gold.

Enzo's heart clenched as Danny's nose twitched awkwardly.

"I'm around as long as you need me and as much as you want me," he said, softly. This part made him feel like a fairy godmother. He didn't know how to explain it. It felt like he was being used, but he wasn't really. He was doing this to himself – it was self-inflicted. Maybe he was more like the genie from Aladdin, minus the being free part at the end. No, that's not fair. He didn't feel trapped in this life. Well, okay, it was all complicated. He was free, and he didn't want to settle down, but it didn't change the fact that the universe had kind of decided that he was an unattached person flitting about the world forever. He was the person who helped the other misfit people. He was the guide for the leftovers –the people who were lost and needed someone to remind them that they were going to be okay. He was that person. The universe decided it when he was eighteen. He probably wasn't the only person out there like this but it sure did feel like that sometimes.

Danny blinked at Enzo then tilted his head to the side, like a confused puppy. His blue eyes gleamed. "So, you're like Nanny McPhee?"

Enzo blinked then lowered his eyebrows.

"Or Mary Poppins?"

"Here till the wind changes, Dann-O." Enzo grinned. "Got any plans till then?"

"You don't have a clue how long this uh… this…" Danny began, then gestured between them. "Lasts, right? Could be a day, or a week, or a month, years?"

"I haven't had one that's lasted years, yet," Enzo conceded, and Danny's eyes got wide. "But, yeah, there's no real way to determine so…" He jumped to his feet and offered his hand to Danny. "Might as well enjoy the time we have." He gave Danny a hopefully encouraging smile.

Danny took the hand slowly and was dragged up beside Enzo, stormy eyes lining gold as nerves flooded the night air. Their hands slipped apart speedily, Danny placing a hand on the back of his neck and nervously gulping. "So, it's uh… it's still early. Do you uh… do you maybe wanna go somewhere? Have you eaten yet?"

"I mean, not really. What'd you have in mind?"

"I mean… uh…" Danny began, then glanced the building. "I could cook?" he offered, and Enzo blinked in surprise. Had anyone offered to cook for him before?

"How good a cook are you?"

"I mean, I'm not Top Chef material, but I make a pretty good spag bol?" he answered. "I think I have garlic bread, too?"

"And I'm sold."

Chapter 5
DANNY

Well, this was shaping up to be the weirdest night of Danny's young life. Enzo held his hand as they headed back to the apartment. He made a beeline for the kitchen, while Enzo settled in on the couch and their hands disconnected. He shoved some spaghetti in a tiny pan with boiling water and wandered back into the living room, leaving the kitchen door open.

Enzo was settled on the couch., His curly hair flowed around his pale face, the moonlight bled through the curtains, highlighting the little freckles on his nose, and Danny was mesmerized by the golden gleam in his eyes.

This was so weird. Weird to new extents of weird. There were so many warning lights going through Danny's head. He felt guilty that someone other than Allison was in their apartment. No, wait. His apartment. It was just his now. It felt more like his, but just. Yeah, it was going to take some adjusting.

Enzo leaned against the back of the couch with his legs crossed, a little playful smile on his lips.

"What?" Danny asked before he could stop himself.

"Nothing," Enzo replied. "Just been a strange night."

"What are your nights usually like with your… uh…" he fumbled. "The… uh… others?" He was going to say 'conquests', but his brain pinged so hard that his cheeks burnt.

"Not this," Enzo admitted with a gentle smile. "I mean, it's been a long time since a night has just been… well, actually, no one but my mum has ever cooked for me." He shrugged.

"Hope you're not expecting much," Danny replied.

Enzo grinned as Danny blushed and sped back into the kitchen. He really didn't know what was going to happen tonight. Did he want anything to happen? He hadn't slept with anyone in over a year. Him and Allison had been drifting for a long while. They had been overworked and stressed. Time got away from them and it'd been a while for Danny. And he'd never been with a guy. This was all *a lot*. He was trying to keep his head straight but he didn't know what he wanted. His mind was a tumbled jumble of desperation, confused attraction and trying to let go of the person he thought he'd be with forever. God, his pasta was going to burn.

"Nothing has to happen tonight, you know." Enzo's voice slipped through the kitchen door, and Danny's heart tumbled to a stop. "Look, I don't know what you're thinking, but I know what I'd be thinking, so, yeah…" The door creaked and Enzo wandered through with a tentative smile. "I don't sleep with all my soulmates, okay? I don't, or well, uh…"

Danny lowered his eyebrows as Enzo's face lit on fire.

"Enzo," he said, and Enzo jolted. "Are you a… you have… you have before, right?"

"Would it change anything if I hadn't?" Enzo asked and Danny's eyes widened.

"Whoa, okay. No, no. It doesn't change anything. This night is just… it's just a lot. I just… there's just so much, and I just… I'm not very good at processing things quickly. I don't know. I don't know, Enzo! You appeared like, what, a couple of hours ago? And everything's changed. I didn't even know I liked guys! Like, just… God, I don't know." Danny rambled off then pressed a hand into his beating head.

"Look, it's okay," Enzo began quietly, then placed a gentle hand on Danny's shoulder. "I know it's a lot, and no one's expecting you to get a hold of yourself quickly. Take all the time you need to process, Danny, and if you need me to go, then that's okay too. I'm just here to help you."

"Help me with what, exactly?"

Enzo shrugged. "It's different with everyone," he admitted. "With you? I think it's about moving on and letting you know that there's more to life than being with another person."

"That's what you think?"

"It's just the impression I got. Sometimes, it's about helping people let out their anger and frustration. Sometimes, people just need a shoulder to cry on, but all of you seem to have this fantastical view of soulmates, and when your soulmates turn out to just be human and normal, and when your relationships turn out to be difficult, and you just keep this whole 'Well, they're my soulmate, things have to work out' viewpoint in your brain, then they don't. You're alone, and you just think that the only thing that can make you happy is that person coming back. That they're half of who you are, and that the universe just decided you were perfect. So, you just kind of guessed it would be easy. Then, when it's not, well, you know what happened with Allison better than I do," Enzo rattled off quickly, eyes fixed on the pasta pot.

Danny's eye twitched as he folded his arms over himself. "I'm not helpless, Enzo."

"I'm not saying you are," Enzo replied, then put his hands up in a placating manor. "I'm saying that it's not hard to deal with the idea that soulmates aren't this fated, easy thing. It's hard to move on from a person who you believe is yours forever – the person who is, like, made for you. It's different than just getting over a boyfriend or a girlfriend. There's more to it, especially if you're the one that was left behind."

Danny gulped, and his gaze fell to the floor.

"I'm not saying you're helpless, or that it is an easy thing to deal with. This is a lot, and I know it is. It was

85

when I got my second soulmate, too. You're allowed to be a little lost and confused, and you're allowed to think about her. Everything is down to you, Danny. I'm just here to… I don't know…" He shrugged with a little smirk, as Danny turned to him. "Show you that there's more to life than soulmates."

"But you *are* my soulmate," Danny argued in confusion.

"For now," he stated, and Danny jolted. "Neither of us know how long it'll last, and that's okay. Nothing is set in stone, Danny."

Enzo moved closer. The slightly shorter man slipped his hands into Danny's, entwining their fingers as their eyes linked, and every breath in Danny's throat got lodged.

"I'm here for as long as you need me, and I think we're pretty good. I can just be someone to talk to, someone who exists to watch movies with you, someone you can make food for. I don't know. It's different… it's always different, and I do care about you," he said seriously. "And we are soulmates, but there is so much more to life than being with another person. You have to take care of you, work out who you are and what you want. You're not going to be ready to be with someone if you don't *know* who you are and what you want."

"So, you know what you want?" Danny asked quickly, eyes squinting down at Enzo as he jumped back in slight surprise.

"What?" Enzo asked, then shook his head. "Doesn't matter what I want, Danny. We're talking about *you*."

Danny's features collapsed into a disbelieving frown.

Doesn't matter what I want. Enzo's voice rattled through his head, making Danny's heart twinge.

"How could you not think it matters?" he whispered, blue eyes staring into gold.

"It just…" Enzo shrugged, then tugged a hand free and ran it through his long, wavy hair. "It doesn't matter, Danny. I'm okay, I'm happy. What I want is to make sure that everyone else is okay before I just move on and your name fades."

"How many names have faded through your head, Enzo?" Danny asked. "How long have you been doing this?"

Enzo gulped and pulled his other hand away, gaze turning to the floor as he nibbled his bottom lip.

"Are you actually happy?" Danny had no clue where this was coming from, no clue what possessed him to ask. He didn't like being told what he needed. He didn't like the idea of needing someone to dig him out of the Allison hole. He didn't like being told what to believe, or that he was wrong about soulmates. Everything was changing tonight, but he didn't like the idea that everything he believed was wrong.

There was nothing wrong with having someone to sleep next to, nothing wrong with having someone to confide in. He knew who he was, didn't he? He wanted to be a teacher. He loved working with kids. The paperwork and the lesson planning were a lot but he enjoyed it. He always knew that's what he wanted to do. He loved dogs and puzzles and stupid comedy shows. He was shy and awkward, made weird comments at the wrong times, and got drunk off a cider or two on a good night. He loved reading cheesy novels. He loved his parents and his aunt, he loved rainy days and crappy, superhero movies. He was stubborn and smart, lazy but dependable. Danny wasn't a puzzle that he had yet to figure out. Danny was a whole picture.

"Uh... about twenty-three? Twenty-five? You want a list?" he asked with a little smirk, eyes tilting back to Danny's as the man turned back to face him. "I've been doing this since I was eighteen, Danny. I'm twenty-three now, so five years. I've met a lot of great people in that time, and their names always fade, but they're always better off by the time it does." His golden eyes were gentle and calm, a small frown tugged at his lips. "I know it's a lot, Danny, and I didn't mean to insult you or make you get defensive. I'm not the best judge of what you want or need. I only do my best with this crap, and I'm just going off what I know."

"And what you know is that relationships are meaningless and that people don't need people?" Danny asked, while turning around and folding his arms.

Enzo clenched his teeth. "That's uh... not..."

"Then what did you mean?" Danny asked, eyes squinting intensely, as their gaze fell back to each other.

"Okay, I don't know," he admitted. The atmosphere was harsh and horrible. The air in the room disappeared, all the oxygen had been sucked out and both boys were just struggling to breath. Danny's blue eyes were flaming and intense, a sharp frown laced his lips, and his posture was stilted and straight while staring down at the shorter man. Enzo hadn't experienced this before. It was another new thing, he supposed. Most of his soulmates just accepted what was being said and moved on, but Danny? He seemed to take what Enzo was saying in a different way. A way that was making Enzo's heart harden through his chest.

"What's the longest relationship you've been in?" Danny asked.

"Uh... four months? Three months?" Enzo answered, then scratched the back of his neck.

Danny's eyes widened. "Then how can you say all this? You don't know..."

"It's not like I have a choice, Danny. The voices fade, and I move on. It's just the way it is. I know what I know about relationships, and I've just..." He shrugged. "I've made it so I didn't need anyone. I don't know. I just think there is more to life than dating someone."

"No. No. I get that." Danny sighed then glanced out the window. "And you're right. It's just..." He gulped and turned his gaze to the floor. "Why are you like this?"

"I uh... I don't know," Enzo answered awkwardly. "I thought my first soulmate was it because it made sense. Yeah, but then he left, and another voice came, and another, and another. It's been going on for five years now. I'm used to it and I like it."

Danny blinked in surprise then lowered a sceptical eyebrow.

"Really. I don't want to settle down or wake up to the same person every day. It's just... it sounds too stuck. And I don't wanna lose myself in another person. I've seen it happen."

"But you don't *know* that'll happen to you."

"It happened to you, didn't it?"

A harsh stab pressed through Danny's heart and the man fell back.

"See? It happens in relationships, Danny. I don't want to sacrifice myself and what I want for another person."

"Even if they're your soulmate?" Danny asked sadly.

Enzo gulped and ran a hand up the back of his neck. "I've had plenty of soulmates, Danny," he explained, while looking deeply in his stormy eyes. "It's not that simple. Relationships are hard. Not everyone ends up happy, whether they're destined for each other or not, and most of the time someone just ends up getting hurt. It's better this way."

Both boys sighed in the heavy, cooling atmosphere. The kitchen was quiet; silent almost. They breathed and stared through the floor, each twiddling their fingers and nibbling at their lips. Neither bothered to look the other in the eye. Neither knew what to say. Danny wanted to keep talking about this, but Enzo was getting sadder and sadder, and it didn't seem worth it.

"You can head back into the living room. I'll just finish up dinner, okay? The remote's by the TV." His voice was weak and gentle, it barely penetrated Enzo's ears, but the man still turned and headed out the kitchen, closing the door behind him as Danny sighed. He didn't know what possessed him to say that. Heck, he wanted to say more, but why? Why did he want to defend relationships when his girlfriend left him?

Danny shook off his thoughts, then put the spaghetti Bolognese together before grabbing the garlic bread and chucking it in the microwave. A few minutes later he plated the food up, then awkwardly wandered through to the living room, opening the kitchen door with his elbow. Enzo looked up and grabbed a plate off him, before the pair wandered over and sat on the couch, the stony silence stretching once more as they started slurping at their spaghetti and munching at their garlic bread.

"You know, I get it," Danny muttered, slicing the cold atmosphere slightly, as Enzo jolted. "Relationships are hard, and having a soulmate is much harder than I thought it'd be. I uh…" Danny gulped, then placed his fork down on the plate before staring at the blank TV screen. "My parents were soulmates, and I just... I always thought they had it easy, you know. They seem happy and I just... that's what I thought it'd be like. Like you meet them, then you fall in love, and that's it." Danny clapped to exaggerate his point and Enzo scoffed.

"No, that's what most people think."

"I know relationships are harder than that, and I uh... I think I know myself, but maybe you're right that I um..." Danny sighed, and Enzo looked at him with kind curiosity, his lips pressed into a small smile and his golden irises swirling in the moonlight. "It's easy to lose parts of yourself in anything, and being with another person, well, when you love them and want to be with them, you want to be the best you can be *for* them, but also for you. It's hard to explain."

"No, I get it."

"I'm not sure you do, Enzo," Danny argued gently, blue eyes staring into gold, as the man blinked and leaned back in surprise, his small smile falling to a confused frown. "I'm sorry. I didn't mean to um... okay." Danny sighed and snapped his gaze to his plate. "I get not wanting to lose yourself, and I get thinking that relationships are restricting, because they are, but when it's the right person, it's all worth it somehow. It doesn't feel like you're losing or like you're trapped. If anything, it's like being free." Danny stared across the room, and a warm breeze filled his heart. "I get um... I get feeling like they're standing in your way, because I felt that when Allison wanted to move us across the world. I felt trapped and obligated, and I hated it. Plus, I didn't know what to do because she was my soulmate and I just… There didn't feel like a way out, and I didn't really want to be thinking about a way out because soulmates are kind of an eternal thing. It's just… yeah, it was hard, and I hated it."

Enzo sighed gently, a sad smile tugging at his lips.

"But it doesn't make it not worth it," Danny muttered, then turned to Enzo with kind eyes. "I don't regret being with Allison. I mean, I don't uh… think her leaving… it um… it well…" Danny gulped, phantom pains pressing through his heart. "It hurt, but I don't know, what we had. Maybe it wasn't even about her. I just…" Danny sighed, then looked up to Enzo, a shadow passing between them as the blue-eyed man steeled his expression. "I imagined meeting my soulmate for years before it happened, and I don't think I'm wrong in um… having a soulmate is amazing. It's terrifying, but I didn't have to try, you know. That's what I thought, anyway. We were just good together. We talked and laughed like old friends and the parts that were good were really good, and, well…" Danny gulped, then stared back at his feet. "She left and that hurt, but there was a time where we were meant to be, and a time where we were good together and in love, and I… that feeling when we hugged, or when she smiled, and I just…" Danny's eyes tilted back up to Enzo, as a jolt stabbed through his heart and a warm, familiar breeze flittered through his brain. "I never thought I'd feel that about another person," he added with a smile, as Enzo smiled and tilted his gaze away. "I'm not saying that relationships are easy or that everyone is the same, and I uh… well, I can't imagine this from your perspective, or, maybe I can a little, now? Coz you're my soulmate, and we're uh… yeah…" He gestured awkwardly between the two of them, as Enzo lightly chuckled.

"Yeah."

"I think what you do for your um… for uh… I don't understand why you're like this, and I'm hoping that I'm not now?"

"You're not," Enzo denied instantly. "It's not like an infection, Danny."

"All right," he stated. "Yeah, I don't understand why you're like this, and I think it's pretty awesome that you go around and use this to try and help people, and like… but, okay…"

Blue eyes searched gold, as the pair stopped and stared at each other.

"You never get to experience what it's like to be with your soulmate. To be with someone and like, want them and lean on them. You don't know what it's like from like… the other side… I just…"

"I'm okay, you know," Enzo argued quietly, folding himself over slightly. "I don't *need* to be with someone to be okay, you know."

"I know, and I'm not saying you're not okay," Danny argued, then shrugged his plate off his lap and slid over to Enzo, tugging his plate off him and placing it to the side. He grabbed Enzo's hand, entwining their fingers, as his heart stilled and his head spun. "You don't have to *need* someone to be with them, Enzo." Danny let out several, strong, nervous breaths, while gently staring into Enzo's eyes and taking his other hand, entwining those fingers too. "It's not about needing another person. It's about..." He gulped, his voice falling to a gentle, warm whisper. "Wanting them."

"I... uh... I..." Enzo stammered nervously. His heart quickened, and his breath stuttered through his throat. His cheeks warmed as Danny's hands squeezed his. "I uh..."

Danny pulled a hand free and ran it over Enzo's right cheekbone, pressing a piece of hair behind his ear as the room got smaller.

"What are you doing?" Enzo whispered, and Danny pressed their lips together. Neither knew where the world went when their eyes closed and the warmth blew around them in a kind embrace. Everything felt charged in that moment. Nothing felt complicated or confusing. Soulmates didn't matter and relationships didn't matter – Allison didn't matter. Everything and nothing made sense as Enzo got lost in Danny, and Danny got lost in Enzo. Their hearts pounded in a hard heat, heads swooning. Neither made any move to pull away or stop, even when breathing became a challenge.

Enzo gasped as Danny's chest pressed into his, hands properly tangling through his hair. He had no clue what was going on. He had no idea what he was doing and no idea what he wanted, but there were sparks flying all over the place. It didn't feel real. Danny didn't feel real. How was this the nervous, twitchy guy who Enzo found at the bar? He was confident and sexy and just... whoa. What was this? Why was he doing this? And why did it feel so... it didn't feel real. He couldn't find the words in his head. It was just unfathomable.

Danny wrapped around him, and drew him closer, the warmth drilling through him, his fingers trailing the man's back. It felt like Enzo was watching from above them, air tunnelling through his chest warmly and holding him straight, while his fingers nervously trembled and fell to the man's lower back.

Danny pulled away first, slowly letting out deep, desperate breaths, as his blue eyes blinked open. Enzo followed and blinked up at Danny with a shocked look, arms still wrapped around him.

"What was that for?" Enzo whispered, and Danny grinned wickedly, causing Enzo's heart to fall through his chest.

Danny then shrugged, his grin falling to a warm smile as Enzo's cheeks flushed a light pink.

"Have you never just kissed someone coz you wanted to?"

Enzo blinked and lowered his eyebrows, trying to drag a memory to the front of his brain. "Yeah, but uh…" He bit his lip. A long time ago. It was a long time ago.

"But what?" Danny asked, then leaned forward, pressing their noses together as Enzo's eyes widened. "I just…" Enzo sighed, then scoffed out a strong breath. "What the heck are you doing, Danny?"

The blue-eyed man leaned forward and kissed his cheek slowly, pressing his hand into the other one, as Enzo fell back in surprise.

"Danny," he whispered, gold eyes staring into blue, as more raspy breaths escaped him.

"What?" Danny asked, leaning their foreheads together once more, revealing his own light-pink cheeks and ruffled hair.

Enzo gulped and his heart pooled. "Nothing." Danny wasn't thinking, and if he was watching himself back right now, he would've been screaming at himself to stop. He wanted this, and he didn't care what happened after or what happened next. He was lost and that was unlike him. It was an outer body experience, and it caused every part of him to go on high alert. His heart thrust horrifically through his chest, and his face was on fire as he pulled Enzo closer, and the man leaned his lips back into Danny's.

They got lost once more and the warmth enveloped them again before Danny leaned up and kneeled on the couch, moving until the men were standing opposite each other, Enzo's arms wrapped around Danny's back. Danny's fingers traced Enzo's cheekbones before falling back into his curly, ruffled hair.

Danny pulled them apart after a moment and let out a gentle breath while looking at Enzo's flushed face, resting his arms on the guy's shoulders. "I know you don't normally do this," he whispered slowly, looking back and forth between Enzo's eyes. "And well, I uh... yeah, I don't either, and I've actually never been with a guy in that uh... but..." He gulped, his confident demeanour falling slightly. "Do you trust me?"

"Yes," Enzo croaked, and Danny smiled, pulling away slightly as both men dropped their hands to their sides. Danny reached forward and took Enzo's warm hand in his own, entwining their fingers then pulling him towards the bedroom. Enzo gulped down a wave of nerves as his heart rattled, and the boys disappeared behind the door.

Danny kissed Enzo softly, running his hands up his torso while leading him blindly to his bed. Enzo's knees bent backwards at the edge, and Danny pressed the man back into his mattress. Enzo gasped, but Danny kept their lips pressed together, then slowly crawled on top of him, knees landing on either side of Enzo's hips as the man slid up and pressed his head into the pillows. Their lips pulled apart momentarily while Enzo leaned up and pulled Danny closer, tangling his hands through the man's mousy hair as Danny's hands wondered to the bottom of Enzo's jumper, fiddling with the soft wool as his heart stilled.

"Danny," Enzo gasped, then leaned back to look into Danny's blue eyes. "Are you sure about this?"

"Why? Want me to stop?"

"God, no, but just... you're getting over some... I don't wanna just..." Enzo gulped down the rest of his thought.

"Trust me, Enzo," Danny whispered. "This isn't about her. It's about us. Just trust me." He leaned over Enzo's ear, brushing their cheeks together. He placed a kiss on Enzo's forehead softly and leaned up to look in his face. "You need to know that you're important too," he whispered, and every muscle in Enzo's body stiffened. A look of awe and slow shock flooded his sharp features, as his cheeks lit up a warm, deep pink.

Danny leaned back and kissed him once more, gently fingering the ends of Enzo's jumper as the man leaned up slightly, and Danny wasted no time in tugging the woollen top over the man's head, scruffing his hair up in the process, before Enzo leaned up and kissed Danny once more. He fiddled with the ends of Danny's T shirt, then tugged it quickly over his head, tossing it to the side.

Both men stopped still for a moment, eyes fixating on each other's faces as they each caught a breath. Enzo leaned back into the pillows, eyes falling to Danny's chest, as all the breath fell from his throat in stilted shock.

Danny's eyes wandered down Enzo's chest, settling on his stomach as a nervous croak quaked through him, and his heart started trying to escape once more. He'd never been with a guy. He never thought that he wanted to be, but Enzo was beautiful with his curly hair, his cheeky smile and those glinting eyes. Danny couldn't stop himself getting lost, and he couldn't stop the blush deeply engulfing his entire face, leading down through his neck.

He leaned down slowly, taking in the man below him, claiming his lips once more and allowing himself to get lost when Enzo's hands reached up into his hair and pulled him closer.

Danny's fingers pressed into Enzo's stomach, then ran up his warm, smooth torso as all the breath in his throat got tangled and trapped. Enzo's hands trailed down him slowly and gently, trembling slightly as he gasped out a small breath. He tilted his head, and their positions changed. A warm, comforting glow floated through them, and the corners of their mouths tilted happily as the kiss deepened once more.

Danny's hands wandered and wandered before landing on the waistband of his jeans. A gasp fell through Enzo's throat and Danny pulled back, looking into the man's golden eyes, with nothing but care and patience floating in his blue irises. "Are you okay? We can stop if you…" he asked, but Enzo's warm, pink lips pressed back into his.

Danny's heart stopped as Enzo wrapped himself around him, fingers gently gliding down his smooth, warm chest before landing on the waistband of his jeans. Danny's eyes opened widely with a little gasp as the boys pulled apart and looked at each other, their hearts falling back through their ribs.

Moments passed, and Enzo nervously bit his lip, fingers still awkwardly jostling Danny's jeans as the man gulped and shook his head, looking over Enzo with kindness and understanding in his blue eyes. They nodded to each other, gulps collapsing through their throats, as the air in the room got warmer. Anticipation ran through every air particle, like static through carpet fibres.

Danny shakily undid Enzo's jeans while Enzo nervously undid Danny's, and the pair shuffled out of them moments later, throwing them on the floor and remaining in their boxers. The world froze when Danny looked over Enzo, stopping on his eyes, his flushed cheeks and the rounded shock on his swollen lips.

"What?" Enzo asked, eyes darting back and forth from one stormy blue eye to the other and back again.

"You're just..." Danny began, then leaned forward, gulping as his heart pounded out a particularly harsh beat. His lips found Enzo's ear lobe, and dark hair tickled his nose as a small smile appeared on his face. "Beautiful," he whispered, then kissed Enzo's warm cheek before pulling back and looking over the man. Enzo's shocked expression got significantly more shocked, as his cheeks puffed up a brighter red. "Is that um… is that okay?"

"Yeah," Enzo breathed out, then moved a shaky hand up, smoothing his fingers over Danny's cheek, reaching around the back of his head and pressing him forward. Their lips crashed together as the pair fully fell into each other, quickly spinning onto their sides as they let out little chuckles.

Beaming smiles crossed their faces as they leaned back, their cheeks red and breaths rattling as a comfortable bubble formed around them. Enzo's arms fell to Danny's shoulders while Danny's wrapped around Enzo's back, and the pair sunk slowly into the quilt.

They smiled and chuckled lightly, faces getting hotter and hotter as Danny ran the pads of his fingers up and down Enzo's spine. Neither knew how much time passed as they murmured happily and dissolved into the warmth, smiling and chuckling like idiots.

"So…" Danny began, clearing his throat. He glanced back and forth between Enzo's golden eyes. "What now?" he asked, and a deep chuckle escaped Enzo, as a dark blush flooded Danny's face. "What?" he questioned, as Enzo grinned and shrugged.

"I don't know, Dann-O. You're the one with experience here," he quipped, and cocked an eyebrow, as Danny's face hit a thousand degrees.

"Uh not uh… not with…"

"You wouldn't think I was the virgin here, would ya?" he muttered sarcastically, grin widening as Danny's face burned and a little, very unheated glare appeared on his face.

"You're destroying the ambience, you know," he stated, and Enzo tilted his head back with a laugh before looking back in Danny's eyes, a relaxed smile on his blushing face. Danny blinked in surprise, his heart rattling through his chest. "Okay, never mind," he stated, then leaned forward and kissed Enzo once more.

Enzo squeaked but dissolved into the kiss, hands tussling through mousy hair, as Danny's hands glided down his back.

They landed on the waistband of his boxer shorts and both men froze, pulling back and staring at each other with wide eyes.

Danny shook his head and smiled sheepishly. "I uh… I don't really know what I'm doing. But do you… um… Are you ready for this? Coz if not, I am just perfectly happy making out with you until the seasons change outside."

Enzo blinked in shock while staring into Danny's eyes. He was so weird; so cute, sweet and awkward, but it was like he had this switch in his head. He could go from nervous and cute to sexy and confident with no delay. 'Perfectly happy making out with you until the seasons change outside.' Who just says that to a person? More importantly, why did those words cause an anxious pool to form in Enzo's stomach? What was going on? Every vein in Enzo's body was buzzing and quaking. His heart had not stopped pounding since Danny landed on top of him. A cooling fire danced over his skin with Danny's fingers tracing the top of his boxers. A shaky pit formed in the base of his stomach, and a dizzying heat wafted through his heart. It was elating but terrifying. He didn't know what to do or what he wanted.

He liked having lines. He liked having rules when it came to his soulmates, and he'd gotten used to it, so there was never any temptation there. He befriended his soulmates and helped them; that was all. He never thought about kissing them. He never thought about crossing that line, but Danny had crossed it for him. And that kiss? That kiss caused a swirl through his soul, made his heart float through his chest and his head spin. Would kissing all of them have felt like that? He couldn't imagine feeling that way about anyone but Danny. He wouldn't have gotten this far with any of the others. Would he have wanted to?

Danny's fingers toyed with his waistband and all the breath in Enzo's throat tightened and constricted, until a shaky gasp escaped him and Danny pulled away.

"You okay?" he asked.

Enzo gulped and nodded, though his heart was causing seismic tremors up and down his muscles.

Danny pulled back a little further, retracting his hand from Enzo's hip and holding it up in the air. "If you're not ready, it's okay," he stated calmly, holding Enzo's gaze with gentle, blue eyes.

"It's not that," Enzo gulped out, closing his eyes and forcing out a calm breath before blinking back up to Danny. "I'm just…nervous," he stated, wincing at his own words, as Danny smiled.

"Me too," he admitted and a warm, charged flurry swam through the air around them. Danny's hand fell and began tracing Enzo's cheek. The man's golden eyes closed as he let out a calm breath. Danny's wistful warmth rang through his face, echoing through his entire body as he slumped, breaths falling to a slower rhythm and heart stuttering through beats. Danny's hand fell to Enzo's shoulder as the golden-eyed man smiled and leaned forward, pressing his lips slowly into Danny's while running his hands through his hair.

Danny ran his hand over Enzo's cheek and drew him closer. Sparks flooded and flittered through the air between them. Every touch, every heartbeat, every breath came in shocking waves of comfort and closeness, rattling through their bones in anticipatory waves. Enzo's hands slipped first, falling from Danny's hair to his chest, as Enzo's heart tunnelled through him.

Danny's hand slipped to Enzo's hip, as the man pulled Enzo closer and pressed his lips in harder. Enzo's hand fell opposite Danny's and began to trace Danny's waistband, as he gasped into Enzo's parted lips. Enzo's hand tugged at the tight material, jostling it down as his heart began to dance through his ribs like a mallet playing a xylophone. Danny followed his gesture, and Enzo felt all the blood in his heart freeze as the pair discarded their underwear on the floor.

Danny was on him in a flash, rolling on top of him, pressing his knees into the mattress and kneeling over the man's hips. He leaned down and pressed gentle, slow kisses onto his lips, hands wondering down his chest smoothly, while Enzo's hands fell back to the pillow in shock. Danny trailed featherlight kisses from Enzo's lips to his cheek to his neck. The man released a gasp and tilted his head back. A gust of cell-quaking pleasure flew through him, while Danny continued to press kisses down his bare chest. Enzo watched and shook in nervous anticipation, as mousy hair peppered his abs.

"You are so insanely attractive, you know," Danny whispered gently, appearing over Enzo's face with a gentle smile on his blushing face.

Enzo blinked at him, face burning. His freckles glimmered through the blush, as a shaky smile appeared on his face. His long, dark hair splayed against the pillow. His eyes stared unendingly up at Danny as the man leaned over him, mousy hair falling around his blushing face, while his bright blue eyes gleamed.

Enzo's heart began to stammer once more, as a shaky gulp fell through him. "Back at ya," he breathed weakly, and Danny grinned.

"No, seriously. I uh… I thought it at the bar, too. You're just… I've never seen… just your eyes and your hair. You're just…" Danny explained, hand slipping to Enzo's cheek as he placed their faces a couple of inches apart. "Perfect." he finished, warm breath trailing Enzo's face as the pair silently stared at each other, smiles falling in heart-wrenching shock.

A moment passed and neither made a move, until the anticipation drilled through Enzo's veins in a cold flood. He reached a hand up and gently ran it down Danny's back, breath getting stuck in his throat as the man gasped, a cool, burning sensation appearing over his fingertips. Danny leaned down further, lips pressing warmly into Enzo's as the pair breathed each other in, hearts falling in sync as their hands trailed down each other. Shivers quaked through their skin as they kissed, warmth gathering until they could feel nothing more than each other.

It was weird how natural this felt. Danny had never been with a guy, but kissing Enzo caused that thought to fall from his brain. He was nervous, but all of that was numbed by how kissing Enzo felt like nothing he'd ever felt before. If seeing Enzo was like a warm breeze, then kissing him was like a windstorm. It was overwhelming in a million ways. Danny could barely breathe. He barely had time to process what he was saying. It was okay to call a guy beautiful, right? It didn't matter. He'd said it now and causing Enzo to turn that colour was worth it. All blushing did was make his freckles twinkle, and Danny's gut twisted happily at the sight. He felt every ventricle in his heart collapse as

Enzo gasped and smiled. His gold eyes staring up at Danny caused every sensor in his body to crumble and stutter. It felt like the realest thing he'd felt and the most unreal thing in the world. He didn't know how to process anything, and it was terrifying. It was like jumping off a tightrope in the middle of a mountain range. The view was beautiful, the sky was warm and alight in golds and oranges as stars fell through the clouds, but you were still falling. His throat closed when Enzo's hands fell on his chest. His heart stammered through breaths whenever he tugged at his hair and fell in and out of rhythm whenever they just stopped and stared at each other.

His hands wandered lower, little bits of hair tickling his fingertips as Enzo gasped and leaned out of the kiss. Danny's hand froze, and his eyes tilted open to look over Enzo. His golden eyes were wide and unblinking; his lips were bright pink, warm and swollen; his hair was a curled, tangled mess and Danny had never seen anything as entrancing before. "You okay?" he whispered.

"Yeah. Just keep going," he breathed, heart pounding around his words in a shaky, awkward rhythm.

Danny blinked in surprise as Enzo let out a slow breath and closed his wide eyes for a moment, blinking up and giving him a kind smile, cheeks rounding and freckles glowing, as all the breath in Danny's throat bawled up and froze.

Danny's hand shuffled down, Enzo's hand mirrored and Danny rasped out a slow breath.

Something clicked through the room. The air turned heated, their eyes closed and tension started to spark through their fingers. The moonlight beamed over and through them like they were moving with waves in the ocean. Enzo kept gasping in air, Danny kept tilting his head back and moaning deep enough to vibrate the bed.

He didn't know what to think, well he wasn't thinking. Neither were, neither had the mental capacity to focus on anything but each other. It was like the world faded away, like shadows smothered everything except themselves. It was a whole new kind of wonderful. It was messy and scary, Danny felt like a teenager again; like he was losing his virginity for a second time. He was almost giddy with anticipation, totally lost in awe and completely overwhelmed by the fact that he got to feel this again, that he got to know what it meant to have a person completely see you in this state and know that they care, know that they want you.

Danny always worried a lot with sex, he was terrified when him and Allison first did it. He was shaking and nervous, overthought it for months before it happened and it was perfect. Exactly as Danny wanted it to be. They were clumsy, they laughed but Allison was beautiful and it was everything Danny wanted.

He hadn't thought about not feeling that with another person before now. The idea of not feeling like this again, not knowing what it meant to be close enough to someone, to trust them and care about them this much, to want them to be comfortable and pleasured. It was scary.

Enzo was a whirlwind in so many ways but Danny never would've seen this coming.

He was beautiful like this, perfect and unravelled. He kept running his hands through his hair, gasping in little breaths and pressing his hands onto Danny's chest, he kept pulling them closer, breathing over his ear and making Danny shudder happily.

It felt like years passed as they got lost in this new reality, as they got closer and closer, as they moaned and breathed, as they trusted each other and left all their thoughts and fears behind.

Enzo forgot all of his lines, forgot all of his stupid principles when it came to soulmates. He let himself embrace this, let everything go and didn't think. He was terrified, a part of his mind was screaming but every other part was lit up excitedly and vibrating in pleasure. It was weird, weird enough to cause anxiety to pool through his stomach when Danny pulled back gently.

"You okay?" He asked. Enzo blinked blearily, wolfing down air as his heart pounded through his throat.

"Yeah." He whispered slowly and they breathed in sync, blinking into each other's eyes and slowly smiling before Danny slumped down and appeared beside Enzo.

The silence that followed was odd. Neither looked at the other, they breathed together and stared at the ceiling as moonlight quaked through the curtains. They laid bare on the mattress, clothes scattered on the floor and eyes tiredly closing as warm air trickled over them.

"So, this is what it feels like to not be a virgin." Enzo realised aloud and Danny choked out a laugh, tilting his head to him.

"How does it feel?" He asked and Enzo smirked, turning to Danny.

"Weird." He admitted and Danny rolled his eyes lightly. "But good. It's a good weird."

"You sure this... you know, counted?" Danny asked and Enzo cocked a brow.

"It's my virginity, Danny. I choose what counts."

"Fair enough."

"Why? Do you wanna do more?" Enzo asked cockily and Danny's eyes went wide.

"Uh... yeah uh... right, uh..." He gulped, confident demeanour completely fading through the air.

"I'm kidding, Dann-O." Enzo stated and Danny sighed lightly.

"I mean it's not that I... don't want to... I uh... well, I..."

"Danny." Enzo stated seriously, pressing a hand into his shoulder and shaking him slightly. "We've got time, relax."

"Right, uh... right, yeah."

A part of Danny thought of Allison for a moment. He thought of this bed as a home they'd shared, they bought it together and lived on it together. A part of him thought having someone else here would feel like he was betraying her but... it didn't. Danny didn't know how to feel.

His head was a tangled mess, blood was barely pounding to it now as he came down slowly, hand on his chest and eyes on the man beside him.

Golden eyes glittered through the moonlight, freckles beaming like constellations as he gently smiled and tiredly blinked. His hair was mussed, the air around him was a whisper of kindness and fading ecstasy. It was perfect. He was perfect and everything else faded away when Danny leaned forward and kissed him once more, grabbing his arm gently when he pulled back.

"What was that for?"

"Just making sure you were real."

"That prove it?"

"Not really." Danny admitted and Enzo smiled lightly, blush flooding his face as both their hearts fell to a slow rhythm.

The ceiling stared down at them, moonlight beamed over them and stars swirled through the air. It felt like magic as they smiled and breathed, Enzo yawning and slowly snuggling into Danny's chest as Danny pulled up the quilt and wrapped his arm around him. It was weird how natural it felt, like they'd been doing this for years, like it was a rehearsed dance, like they were just two puzzle pieces fitting back together after a long moment. Danny was warm, his heart was alight, this room felt like home when he fell asleep and the world fell away once more.

It'd been a long time since Danny slept that well. It'd been a long time since he'd woken up not feeling empty and sad; not having a moment of 'Hey, Allison's not here', and feeling that moment stab his heart like a lance. It'd been a long time since this bed hadn't felt big and empty. It was weird and completely terrifying. Feeling a body wrapped around him, when the sunlight bled through his eyelids, was so weird and new that he had a moment of thinking he was still dreaming.

Then Enzo yawned, snuggled deeper and Danny's heart tunnelled into his chest, as a shock of elation flooded every vein in his body. This was real. He was here. Last night happened.

Holy crap – last night had happened. He'd slept with Enzo. He'd slept with a guy he'd just met. He got a new soulmate. Enzo was his soulmate, and he was sleeping right there, but for how long? And were they dating now? What were they? What was last night? Oh, crap, what had Danny done? This was so not like him. And what should he do now? Does he make breakfast? Does he ask Enzo out? It seemed a little late for that.

Danny shook his head and closed his eyes tight, as a small headache rocked his eyebrows. He sucked in a breath, his eyes finding Enzo once more as the man snoozed on his chest, causing warm palpitations to float through Danny's heart. Maybe it didn't matter if Enzo was here. Neither knew how long their voices were going to…

Danny's heart plummeted and his eyes widened, as he pushed himself to sit up, Enzo squirming and tiredly following, while Danny let out long, shaking breaths.

"Danny?" Enzo asked tiredly, hands rubbing his eyes when Danny turned to him. "What is it? What's wrong?"

Danny gulped, heart darting into his throat, as the reality of what happened last night, and this entire situation, stabbed through his chest like a trident.

"Danny?" Enzo whispered gently, then pressed a hand into his shoulder.

Danny looked back to him then shook his head. "Enzo, your um…" He gulped, then shook his head once more, forcing out another strong breath. "Your voice… your name. I… I can't hear it anymore."

Chapter 6
MARLOW

It came in waves. Marlow would have days where he didn't think about Charlie; days where he couldn't picture his smile, couldn't smell his cologne or see his toothbrush sat by his in the bathroom. There were entire days where Marlow blanked it out, where he forced himself not to think about him, but they didn't exactly make him happy, either. No, every time he didn't think on Charlie, he felt empty. Every time he did, he felt empty. He was always lonely, sad and cornered. There was no escape to feeling this way. There was no escape to feeling worthless and tired. Every bone and every muscle within him kept collapsing in heated heaps of sticky mess, while his brain reminded him just how pointless his existence was.

Marlow hated existing on most days. He wished he didn't. He wished he could hide in a corner and disappear, had days where it felt like he had. He couldn't remember a time where he'd felt like himself. Maybe he never had? Maybe life was that cruel. He didn't know who he was or what he wanted. His family never loved him, his friends hated him and he was just going through life like a leaf floating in the breeze. There were millions of people like him, billions of people in the world. What difference did it make if he was happy or not? What difference could his existence possibly make? He was pointless. His existence was pointless. His life was pointless. What was the use in pretending otherwise?

Well maybe, there was use in pretending otherwise. People would worry, and people shouldn't worry about Marlow. He wasn't worth worrying about. He was going to be fine. He was just having a bad time. Things would pick up soon.

He hadn't left bed all day. A dark cloud hovered overhead, flooding his cells like dust flooded a hoover. Nothing hurt – he wasn't ill. He just couldn't move. Work called once or twice. Marlow turned his phone over and laid on his front. His eyes were closed but daylight peaked through the slightly open curtains. Marlow found no motivation to close them. He found no motivation to do anything, until he started to think about his friends; until he started to think about his mum and about how selfish he was being; about how much he hated hiding away and making everyone wonder where he was. Just how selfish could you get?

It caused more dust to flood him, his drowning muscles clenching and straightening, before he dug his phone out. His eyes squinted at the bright screen while he sat up, his gaze tilting to the left side of the bed as his heart tumbled.

Right, Charlie was gone. He had left him. His soulmate had left him and he couldn't hear his voice anymore. The name was gone. It'd faded a month ago and was just a long-running, unfunny reminder of how Marlow was alone and how he had lost the one person who was meant to stay by his side forever. Of course, he had. It was only a matter of time before Charlie realised how worthless Marlow was; how stupid he was; how ugly; how un-talented; how much he didn't matter.

Marlow shook his head speedily, forcing his focus onto his phone as he slowly sat up, his long, curly, brown hair flopping into his eyes in a greasy heap. His small, rounded stomach folded slightly, and his thighs squished together as he folded his legs. He was currently in his underwear, wrapped in a double quilt with a floral quilt cover that Charlie had bought to 'brighten up the place'. It was bright yellow and orange with sunflowers all over it. Marlow thought it was garish but wouldn't dare tell Charlie. Charlie was too happy about it, and it wasn't like his opinion would've mattered. Charlie would've gotten it to mess with him, in that case. He was funny like that.

Marlow smirked at the ghost of a memory, then remembered that it was over, and a blank, sober wave of grey flooded him. No tears fell, no anger clenched his gut. He just felt resigned. Charlie was gone. It wasn't a shocker. Marlow was never good enough for him. It was only a matter of time.

He texted his boss speedily, saying he had the flu but should be okay for Monday. Aiden just said to let him know and a twang of guilt struck him while reading the words 'I hope you feel better soon'. Marlow knew Aiden meant it, and that killed him. He was a manipulative, lying jerk. Aiden shouldn't care.

Marlow slumped out of bed with a sigh, grey overloading his brain as he sent a text in the group chat. 'Hey guys, anyone up for drinks tonight?' A million replies flooded his phone, as the ghost of a smirk appeared on his lips. He wasn't up for it but going out and pretending to be, was the only way that he didn't feel alone. He needed to pretend and keep pretending until he felt good again; until the world made sense again; until the grey stopped flooding him, and he could smile without feeling like he should prop up the sides of his mouth with his fingers.

Marlow trudged to the bathroom, recoiling as the light switched on and stabbed through his eyeballs. "Urgh," he grunted, then squinted his eyes until they adjusted. He turned to his mirror and sighed at himself.

He looked pale. His eyes were sunken. His shoulder-length, curly brown hair was a mop atop of his head. He had spots over his eyebrows and his chin. He had bits of random, uneven ginger stubble on the sides of his face that needed to be taken care of. His light-green eyes looked grey in the dull light, or were they just grey nowadays? He couldn't remember.

His face looked rounder than usual, his arms and his chest, too. He hadn't been exercising as much, so little pieces of flab had formed over his thin frame. Marlow hated it but getting up the motivation to go back to the gym or cook was asking a little much right now. He'd been living on ready meals and takeaways, gorging on chocolate and crisps to try and make himself feel whole again. He felt like he'd crumbled to pieces, and nothing was making him feel right. Charlie used to make him feel right.

Marlow tore his gaze away from the mirror, turning to his shower and turning it on. It took twenty minutes for him to be dressed and ready – a white T shirt with the Jack Daniels logo, and a pair of ripped jeans that Charlie had given him when they were too big for him. He threw on some old, battered socks with holes dotted around the pinkie toes, then wandered to his kitchen and turned on the kettle, checking the time on his oven before sighing. It was four p.m. already. The whole day was gone, and he was meeting up with his friends in a couple of hours. His eyes glanced up and out the window to see sunlight slowly fading through the clouds. It was November, after all. Everything was cooler outside. Christmas was coming soon.

Christmas was Charlie's favourite time of year. They always spent it with his family and watched movies and ate Charlie's mum's cooking. They'd done that for four years. Marlow didn't have a clue what he was going to do now. He didn't want to think on it, but he always had this thought in the back of his head, this deep, shaking fear in knowing that he'd be spending Christmas alone in his crappy, little apartment that he had rented when Charlie had dumped him out of the blue and taken the house.

That was a month ago. A month ago, he had come home and Charlie had told him to sit down. Marlow shook his head. He never wanted to relive that day. He never wanted to relive the day that his reality crumbled. He didn't even want to think on it. It felt like his heart turned to stone, then fell to sand. It felt like his veins and muscle fibres had bunched up and solidified. He never wanted to go through that again. Heck, he couldn't. Charlie was his soulmate; his only soulmate, and he'd shattered his heart after four years.

He was twenty-four and alone, with no hopes of meeting anyone else. There were no names in his head. Maybe this was just how it was meant to be? He never felt like he was worthy of Charlie, anyway. Charlie was happy with his new guy and their old house, and life went on. Well, yeah. It didn't feel like it, but things had to keep moving. Marlow had to keep moving.

His phone buzzed to life on the kitchen side, and Marlow jumped before grabbing the device in cold, shivering fingers.

"Hello?"

"Marty! Dude, where are you?" Dennis yelled, and Marlow's eyes grew wide. "We've been waiting twenty minutes – you coming or what?"

Marlow blinked and lowered his eyebrows before turning back to the clock. "It's four seventeen," he argued, and a deep sigh retched through his phone.

"So? It's Saturday!" Dennis yelled.

Marlow scoffed lightly. "Fine, you at the botanist?"

"Yep."

"Get me a beer; I'll be there in a minute," he stated, then hung up while the guys cheered through the phone. He rolled his eyes, grabbed his jacket and shoved on his shoes.

He appeared at his door; opening it, slamming it, and locking it in a few, rapid actions, before racing down the stairs and out of his apartment block.

The canal appeared on his left, the sunlight fading and trickling through the water, as the night sky appeared in a swirl of deep blues, blacks and indigos. Stars beamed in the darkness and hovered over Marty expectantly through the clouds. It wasn't too cold a night, but fog hung in the air like an eerie, grey shadow, distorting everyone's feet through the dull street lamps.

Marlow lived in a small apartment block at the edge of Chester town centre. Him and Charlie had studied at Chester Uni, loving the city so much that they stayed after graduating. It was a pretty place, and Marlow was still unsure how he felt about living there without Charlie. It'd only been a month, but this place started to feel much smaller and tighter without him. Marlow started to be convinced that it was more about him than Charlie; that this place was home, but he was being too fussy and scared. The idea of running into the tall, toned man anywhere was enough to make him want to flee the country. He wasn't worried about a fight or about it being awkward. He was worried about seeing Charlie happy and realising that he was never enough for him. He was worried that it'd make their time together seem pointless, and that his heart would shatter all over again. Could Chester feel like home when Charlie was here? Had it ever been home, or was all of it a lie? He didn't know anything anymore. It just felt like he was trailing along, time fading through the air around him.

He arrived at the botanist and wandered through half-crowded tables full of half-drunk university students who were blowing off steam with weird, garden-themed cocktails. Fairy lights shone dully through trellis-style holes in the ceiling. The bar shelves displayed colourful bottles of sparkling nonsense that glittered and gleamed in the warm, yellow light. Marlow moved slowly forward, his friends appearing loudly and speedily in the background as he slumped onto the old picnic table. A beer was slid over to him as he swung his legs around and slipped off his jacket, the warm, yellow lights enveloping him as he sighed and stared up at his friends.

Dennis, Ashley, and Lexi. Dennis was a thick, tall man with ebony skin. He always wore tank tops that dropped under his armpits and revealed all his ripped chest – even in the winter, and even when he was shivering. He always chucked a leather jacket on top and just shrugged like, 'I'm not cold, leave me alone.' Marlow could always tell he was cold when he started ordering bourbon instead of beer. Currently, he was sipping on a small glass of bourbon, and Marlow had an urge to hand over his jacket.

Ashley sat next to him, arm around his hips and a light grin on her blushing face. She was paler than pale; her skin was as white as a sheet on most days. She had freckles all over her face and long, curly, ginger hair that tickled her nose and got behind the lenses of her black, square-rimmed glasses. She was short, quite curvy and lived in long, floral dresses and boots. Her hair was typically half up in scrunchies and headbands, but it did nothing to prevent it falling into her face.

Dennis was twenty-six, and Ashley was twenty-three. She was studying a master's in geography at Chester, while Dennis studied a PhD in microbiology. They were soulmates. They had been together since randomly meeting at roleplay society three years ago. Dennis was the club organiser, and Ashley was a new member. She recognised his voice immediately, and the pair moved in together about six months later. Dennis had been planning on proposing for the past year but kept chickening out because he didn't know how to make it 'special enough'. Marlow knew that he was scared she'd say 'no'. He kept telling him that she wouldn't, but Dennis was stubborn and terrified.

Lexi was the last member of their group. She was twenty-one and currently finishing off her undergraduate degree in economics. She was the only one in the group who still went to roleplay society. Dennis dropped out when he started his PhD. Marlow finished his mathematics degree and left to join an accounting firm, and Ashley left when Dennis did. They met her on a night out with the society, and she just got dragged into the crew. She was the baby of the group, but you wouldn't think it. She had long, brunette hair and a permanent intense look on her face. She made it her mission to figure people out; believed everyone was a math problem that she had yet to solve. She always wore overshirts and old, movie T shirts, with jeans and Doc Martens. She never wore make up, never wore a jacket, and her hair was always up in a tight ponytail. Malow was deeply afraid of her sometimes. He always felt like her deep, green eyes were glaring through his soul.

They were the only friends that him and Charlie didn't have in common. Charlie didn't want to join roleplay; he was always off with the rugby society. Marlow got dragged there by Dennis when they met at the student bar on campus, and he loved it, shockingly. He wasn't exactly an outgoing person, but he loved making up characters and putting on stupid voices. It was the one place where he felt completely free to let go and be himself. There was no pressure and no expectations – everyone just joked and had fun. It was refreshing, and the four of them managed to keep in touch, even when most of them finished their degrees.

Heck, Dennis, and Ashley weren't even a part of the society when Lexi joined. She just became their friends out of 'convenience', as she always said.

"So, how you doing?" Lexi asked, then tilted her deep, green eyes to Marlow, as the group fell silent and stared at him. He almost choked on his beer when she reached a hand forward and pressed it into his shoulder.

A squelchy, uncomfortable feeling pressed into his lungs, as he gulped down a million answers to that question. "I'm good," he managed to say, with a little, shaky smile. He then raised his beer and chugged half of it, as his friends smirked at each other.

"Ooh, we're doing shots tonight," Dennis said cheekily, while Marlow smirked, and a strange weight lifted off his shoulders.

"Rosie's?" Lexi asked, eyebrows tilting to Marlow as his smirk widened.

"I'm down," he agreed, and Dennis grinned wickedly, eyes glinting in the dull light, as Ashley looked over him curiously.

"I'm getting the shots; anyone need a top up?" Dennis asked, tilting his gaze to Marlow and raising his eyebrow.

Marlow just shrugged and finished the rest of his beer, a wave of cold dizziness stabbing through his brain and jittering into his muscles, as a little smile hit his face.

He didn't tend to drink a lot. His friends took him out on occasion, but it was maybe once or twice a month, and he never drunk at home. He didn't like it. He didn't like losing control, and most alcohol tasted gross anyway, but he indulged his friends when they took him out. He didn't want to let them down and be the boring, frustrating friend who wasn't any fun. He always worried that they would just stop inviting him to places, so when they went drinking, Marlow was *all* in. He chugged his drinks, did shots, went to the club and danced until his calves lit on fire. He hadn't done it in a long while, but he was good at pretending. He was good at having fun and being socially capable, when he felt like hiding away and pretending that he didn't exist. He was an expert at that now.

The rest of the night devolved into drinking games. Marlow was five beers, four vodka shots and a burger down, when the foursome decided it was time to go clubbing. The world was blurry, and the air tasted like barley, as the gang wandered out onto Chester high street and walked speedily over to 'Rosie's'. Dennis got everyone a beer, but Marlow was already out on the floor.

There was no theme tonight, just a DJ playing some weird, base-filled music that vibrated through the floor and messed with Marlow's eardrums. Rainbow lights beamed and glowed around the dark, square room lighting up the squished pile of humans who were grinding and jumping. Everyone was grinning and holding drinks. It was a nice place, but it always, always smelt like beer and sweat. Even when drunk, it smelt like beer and sweat. It would've made Marlow feel nauseous if he wasn't completely smashed. The world was a rainbow-lit blur, and everything felt light and airy as he danced, arms rising and falling, chest convulsing and legs moving on their own. It wasn't graceful, by any means. Marlow wasn't even sure what song was playing at this point, but he was smiling, and he wasn't thinking about Charlie or how lonely he felt. The world was wonderful, full of light and smiles, and Marlow needed this. His jacket was long since forgotten and his body was dripping sweat, but he couldn't feel it. His face was on fire and his hair was a mess, but he was grinning.

Dennis, Ashley and Lexi appeared and danced beside him, laughing and joking, grabbing his arms and leading him through a few moves, until Ashley and Dennis wrapped around each other and got lost in a slow song, and Lexi got bored and disappeared.

Marlow was left breathless on the floor, wolfing down air like a lion wolfing down a steak. His arms numbly fell to his sides, as he awkwardly shuffled through the crowd and into the bathroom. Dennis and Ashley appeared in the corner of his eye, and his heart clenched. Dennis was wrapped around Ashley, his arms around her waist, while hers rested around his back. They leaned into each other and grinned, while loud music bounced around them. Neither seemed to know or care where they were or what was going on, as they swayed and spun slowly to a pop song. Marlow felt a twinge of green through his vision, as the grey cloud started to infest his mind once more, but he shook it off and pressed his way into the bathroom.

Silence hit his eardrums and caused a strange ringing before he turned to the mirror and fell back in surprise at his dripping, red face. He smirked, then chucked a pile of cool water at himself, ducking his head over the sink and allowing it to dribble through his hair and down his shirt. A wash of cold, calm relief flittered over him as he smiled and closed his eyes.

Dennis and Ashley flitted through his mind's eye, and Charlie appeared speedily behind them as a sharp, hideous tug dragged his heart down. The grey started to infect his muscles and his bones, weighing them down as he began to collapse like a masterless marionette puppet. His hand pressed into the cool ceramic of the sink, as he forced out a strong breath and desperately tried to focus on something.

"Hey, hey," a voice suddenly muttered, and a sharp, heavy screech began inflating his brain as Marlow's heart squelched. He slowly crumbled to sit on the floor, pressing his hands into his ears and biting his lip, while tilting his gaze around to look at the other presence in the room. His eyes widened in surprise as a pale, freckly man with brown eyes and long, dark, wavy hair appeared with his hands out in a placating manor. He wore a pair of loose, blue jeans and a navy jumper, with some lace-up boots and a shoulder bag. He was smiling nervously, before he kneeled in front of Marlow and stared directly into his eyes. They were a few inches

128

apart, but Marlow actively felt all the saliva in his mouth evaporate, and his heart crumpled to a scraping stop as he stared into this man's bright, beaming eyes, the light of the bathroom making the brown light up a subtle gold.

The screeching stopped and a silence hit the room, flooding Marlow's brain as his shoulders slumped and he blinked and blinked and blinked, before one word puffed into his head.

"Enzo," he whispered, as the two syllables took over his brain, the grey fading to the back of his mind, his eyes staring at the stranger and his heart palpitating painfully, as he shakily and forcefully got to his feet.

Enzo followed and blinked nervously. "Yeah," he whispered. "Marlow?"

Marlow jolted at his own name, falling backwards into the sink and gripping it with his hands.

"How is... what is... you uh..." he began, then pointed to his own head, as a familiar warmth spun through his heart. His head collapsed forward in happy, drunken, dizzy relief. His lidded eyes stared at Enzo, his heart skipping beats, and his breath getting stuck while words desperately tried to get out.

"It's okay. It's okay. I know this is... it's uh..." Enzo began, then bit his lip while looking through his nervous, jittering fingers. "Yeah, it's a... uh... a lot, and yeah, but you're fine. You're not crazy; everything is okay," Enzo said softly, moving forward, placing his hands on Marlow's shoulders and forcing him to look into his eyes.

Everything inside Marlow lurched forward as he let out a deep, shaking breath. Vodka and burger rushed up and into his throat, but he gulped it down and stood up straight, focusing on the cool ceramic beneath his fingertips. He was really trying to keep himself grounded, but the alcohol, loud music and cute stranger were not helping. Everything was a sickly-sweet, drunken blur, and he was starting to feel sick –sicker than he'd felt in a long, long while. He could taste everything that he'd eaten and drank tonight, at the back of his throat. He felt it rising, but he was not throwing up in front of Enzo.

"Are you uh… are you my…" he began, and Enzo nodded with a little gulp.

"Yeah. Sorry, I know this is a lot, and you do not look good. Do you wanna head out? I could take you home. I bought my bike, and I haven't been drinking," Enzo explained quickly and awkwardly, while gently looking into Marlow's green-grey eyes.

Marlow shook his head quickly, thinking of his friends, and turning to the door. "I uh… I have friends here," he stated, and Enzo nodded in understanding. "Uh… you wanna join us? We were gonna go to um… to the the…um…" Marlow squinted and desperately fumbled through his mind for their next plan. "The place with the science-y cocktails – the alc…"

"Alchemist?" Enzo asked, with a little smirk.

"That's it!" Marlow responded loudly, with a grin.

Enzo rolled his eyes slightly, smirk falling to a little smile. "Sure," he replied. "If your friends won't mind."

"Pfft." Marlow instantly denied, shoving his hair back as a weird rush of dizziness flittered through his body. He stumbled slightly but Enzo caught his shoulder, and a jolt of static darted through them.

"You uh... you really are my soulmate, aren't you?"

Enzo nodded awkwardly, biting his lip as he did. "Yeah," he grunted out. "And before you say it, it is possible for a person to have more than one, and I do hear your voice in my head, also. This isn't just a one-way street."

Marlow blinked, his mind slowly wrapping around those words, before locking his eyes onto Enzo's face. He spotted the creased, nervous eyebrows, the strange glint in his eye and the analytic look on his face, before looking at his shoulders and his arms, spotting the awkward slump and the weirdly strong stature. He looked kind of sad, maybe a little awkward. There was something familiar about Enzo that he couldn't quite put his finger on; something they had in common that was tugging at Marlow's heart strings so hard, the organ fell to his ribs.

"So..." Marlow began, shaking off the weird familiarity with a little, awkward smile. "Can I get you a drink?"

Enzo smirked, and the pair wandered out of the bathroom.

Chapter 7
ENZO

It had been a few months since he had heard a name, and he could honestly say that he had hated every second of it.

The universe must really freakin hate him, or he just screwed up and indulged where he shouldn't have indulged. He *knew* it was a bad idea to get intimate with his soulmates. He knew it, but he let Danny kiss him, he'd let himself get drawn in. He let that night happen, and honestly, it was freakin great. Danny was hot and sweet and gentle, and he wasn't a virgin anymore. Being a virgin was getting a little old but hey, he wasn't sleeping with someone who's name was going to disappear in a week, or a month – or a day, as it turned out.

He sat in his apartment. He'd been working a lot recently. He did take Danny's number, and he'd been texting him on and off, but there was just something so wrong and sad about it. He didn't even know. It felt like they were forcing something. It was awkward and emotionally charged, but neither knew what to say or what to ask to make things feel normal again – or their version of normal, anyway. Enzo felt like he wasn't letting Danny let go, and that was his whole reason for appearing at that stupid bar.

It was a great night. It was weird, and God, it felt like it was still imbedded in his bones. He'd think of Danny, and his heart would quake enough to shatter his ribs. His blue eyes and his mousy hair; his little cheeky smile; how he went from shy and awkward to confident in the click of a finger. It was freakin hot. He'd never gotten intimate with any of his soulmates but if it had to be someone, he was glad it was Danny.

It was just the first time that he wished he'd had more time with one of these people. By the time their voice faded, he was ready to move on, usually but this time, he had just wanted another night. And he hated it.

It wasn't about him! It never was. What he wanted never mattered. It couldn't because these guys needed his help. That's why he was this way. That's why he was cursed. That's why he couldn't get attached. He came in, made sure they were okay then moved on. That was his life and he liked it. He loved these people. They had fun. And then he moved on, and life went on. He helped another person, and another, and another. A couple of months went by in the blink of an eye. He picked up as many hours as he could and built up his savings up a little. His mum came and slept in his room while he rode the sofa. Her and his dad were fighting. He stopped by at one point, told him to get a haircut, said he was getting 'camper' by the day, took his mum and left. He didn't think his mum had officially or fully told him that he was bi. He didn't know what he knew but if he knew, he felt like he'd hear worse. His already greying hair would turn white and the scowl would be so pronounced, he could imagine it sticking.

Anyway, he was sat on his couch, decided to take a day off since the people on the phones drove him mad yesterday. They were all complaining about the same thing. There was some sort of server issue. Everyone was getting chucked off the website. His manager didn't have a clue what was going on and it was just stressful. It was infuriating. He didn't get a lunch break and he worked three hours overtime. He spent most of today sat on the couch with a cup of tea, debating whether to quit his job and flee the country, while watching friends on Netflix. Well, mostly he was randomly skimming through jobs, while looking for some sort of fanfiction to read. He loved cartoons, movies and TV. He didn't have a lot of time for them but he loved them all the same. He read a lot of fanfictions during college, even wrote a few stories on fanfiction.net but then he met Tim and then all his other soulmates, and he just forgot that he liked them. Weirdly, Danny was the person that reminded him how much he loved fantastical characters and weird stories about crazy cartoons. He just had a cartoonish face –not in an insulting way. He was just cute and easy to read with big, blue eyes that made Enzo think about the summer sky.

Anyway, a whole day of getting lost in weird stories while barely focusing on his TV, and Enzo was drowning. It felt like he was fading into his couch. He'd had seven cups of tea and a pot noodle – he didn't even finish the pot noodle. He was ready for a break from his day off. He felt like he'd spent the past two months on a day off, he'd just been working and going insane, while not being able to do the thing that kept him from going insane. He needed a new name so he could travel and have some fun. He needed someone new or he could go back to Danny. He wanted to text him or call him or something. He really wanted to but he didn't feel like it was fair to him. No, he'd screwed with Danny enough.

One day. One freakin day. He'd been enjoying this whole 'nomad moving about all over the place' life for the past five years. He still called this stupid soulmate thing 'his curse', but it had stopped feeling like that a few years ago. Now, though? He couldn't stop feeling like the universe had screwed him over. Better yet, it'd screwed him and Danny over. It'd made them have a great time and they'd been intimate, and Enzo had never felt that close to another person. He had never even felt that close to Tim, and he had been convinced that Tim was his one and only soulmate. After that, with all the names and all the travelling, everything got floopy and confusing but he was happy and he was okay.

Now? He was hung up on some guy that he had spent one freakin night with. Just one night. One day. The shortest amount of time before that was one week.

At least, that was seven days. Seven days was enough to help a person, enough to get to know someone and have some fun. One night? One night was pointless and frustrating. Danny needed more or did Enzo need more? He didn't know what he wanted anymore. It didn't seem fair from any angle and heck, he missed Danny.

He never missed his soulmates. Why was Danny so different? What was it about him? What was it about the universe? What was wrong with him? Everything in his brain got so jacked up that night. What if he just didn't get another name? What if this was his life now? Oh God, this couldn't be his life now. It couldn't, could it?

Enzo sighed and slumped heavily into his couch, dropping his phone on a pillow before glaring up at the ceiling. The sounds of friends faded around him, as he listened to the sounds of his boiler and the living room light. Was it meant to be that loud? It was like an echoing hum that encompassed this entire area.

His eyes tilted to the clock and a deep sigh retched through him. It read five p.m. Eh, at least the day was nearly over and he could hopefully sleep off his frustration. He slumped further into the couch, tilting his head into his shoulder and closing his eyes.

The room fell eerily silent as a strange, warbling breeze filtered through his mind. Enzo woke up with a shot as his heart pounded through his chest, ears desperately searching for any sound. Nothing occurred to him until he breathed out and one name hit. 'Marlow,' a small, strong voice whispered and Enzo felt his heart ache as it tugged through his chest.

"Right," he sighed to himself, feeling oddly resigned as he grabbed his jacket and chucked on his shoes. He wandered out of his door, locked up, then headed down to the street. The night was already bleeding through the sky, fog ebbing and flowing over Enzo's boots, as he shoved on his helmet and started the long trek to Chester.

He'd gotten better over the years, at finding a sense of his soulmates through their voices. 'Marlow' sounded quite meek and nervous with his little, warbly voice but that didn't necessarily mean he was. He could just be hiding that part of himself or pretending or something. People were weird. He kind of hoped Marlow wasn't out and about doing anything crazy. Enzo wasn't sure he had the energy for that but on the other hand, he could kind of do with blowing off some steam; have a little fun; get out of his head for a while. Yeah, that sounded nice.

One benefit to travelling at this time of day was the sunsets and the stars. It was dark and foggy, but the sky was lit up in oranges, reds and yellows. It was like fire bleeding through the rising mist, stars falling through it and blinking down at Enzo as he trailed down road after road after road, the wind beating through his face and shuffling his jacket.

It didn't take long for him to arrive at 'Rosie's'. A state of dread flooded him, as the base beat through the

138

concrete and piles of students gathered out front in varying states of undress and drunkenness. Two couples were aggressively making out against the walls, and Enzo had to fight the gag when he spotted their tongues fly out their mouths. He could basically smell the vodka flitting off them in wafts.

He locked up his bike and helmet then trudged through the door, wandering through the dancefloor as base-heavy music raked through his eardrums and caused an epic headache. He could barely breathe through the smoke and beer smell.

He hadn't been to a lot of clubs. He'd been to his fair share, but he can't say that they were his favourite place.

Enzo wasn't much of a dancer. He had no balance or rhythm and just generally, didn't enjoy it. It made him feel stupid and unattractive, especially in comparison to all the other people out there who seemed to know what they were doing. Or were they just good at faking it, or were they too drunk to care? Enzo didn't know but yeah, clubs were not his scene and now, he was dreading meeting the latest name. What sort of a name was Marlow anyway?

Maybe this wasn't his scene, either? Maybe he was here with friends? Enzo didn't know and he didn't know what to do. Did he just get a drink? It was *loud* in here. Too loud to hear people's voices. Would he be better off hiding in the bathroom and praying that Marlow popped in at some point? No, that's weird. He did kind of need to go, though.

He sighed, then awkwardly shuffled around the crowds of people before collapsing into the bathroom and basking in the slightly quieter setting. He relieved himself quickly, then stood and leaned back against the wall, enjoying the lack of painful bass music, as his eyes closed once more. The bathroom was small; white tiled and covered in graffiti. It smelt like urine and stale water in here, but Enzo would take that over beer and sweat. Well, neither were good but this was a little more tolerable with the lack of music.

The door then burst open, and a headache speedily slammed through Enzo as the music started up again. A man with long, brunette hair appeared and chucked a pile of water in his own face, revelling in the relief with a wide smile. Enzo silently smiled to himself before a weird, familiar feeling snapped through his chest, and his eyes widened.

Yep, this was Marlow. Enzo wasn't shocked by this, he was kind of shocked by how confident and forthcoming the man was. Evidentially his judgment about the man being meek and shy was incorrect. He was usually the one offering to buy the other a drink. Enzo wasn't too enthused about joining a group of strangers for drinks, but he wasn't about to ask Marlow to abandon his friends, and he knew the man would want answers, so, sometimes, you need to just roll with it.

There was something sad about Marlow, though. There was a sort of twinge in Enzo's heart when the pair linked eyes. He felt something weird pulling them together, something new and heavy. He didn't know how to explain that feeling but maybe it'd lead to an interesting story, at the least.

The pair wandered out of the bathroom and Marlow was quick to get them each a beer. They grabbed a standing table near the end of the dance floor and just started sipping. Well, Enzo was sipping. Marlow was freakin chugging.

"Whoa, slow down man," Enzo said, with his hands out and a little nervous smirk on his face.

Marlow blinked in surprise, then tilted his bottle down and placed it back on the table with a sheepish smile on his face.

"Not a race, you know."

"Sorry, I don't really like beer," Marlow admitted.

"Then, why'd you order it?" Enzo asked.

Marlow shrugged. "It's a single syllable, easy thing to yell across a club bar."

"Smart," Enzo said as Marlow grinned sharply, the red in his cheeks getting darker and hotter.

The boys took another sip before linking eyes and feeling warmth thrash through their chests. Marlow took in a deep, shaky breath while staring over Enzo, his green-grey eyes falling from the man's face to his shoulders, then his hips and feet before linking back to his eyes. Enzo cocked a brow while Marlow opened his mouth to speak, but no words seemed to come out.

"What?" Enzo asked after a moment and Marlow jolted with wide eyes.

Okay, maybe he was a nervous, shy person. Was he just putting on an act when he asked to get him a drink?

"So, you're really my soulmate?" he asked and Enzo lowered his eyebrows with a little nod. "But you're so…" he began, then gestured to Enzo's body, while Enzo fell back in confusion.

"So?"

"Hot," Marlow said bluntly and Enzo scoffed with a wide grin and a deep blush.

"Thanks," he squeaked. "You too."

Marlow rolled his eyes, leaning on the table while giving Enzo a sceptical expression. "Yeah, sure," he stated. "Bet I'm not what you were expecting. Who were you expecting? How am I your…"

"People don't just get one soulmate, Marlow," Enzo replied easily, the words flowing out on reflex. "I wasn't expecting anyone. I just know who they are. I hear your voice and have like a vague idea of where to go, then I come and find you guys –typically to make sure you're okay."

"Us guys?" Marlow asked with a sceptical eyebrow. "And to make sure we're okay?"

Enzo sighed then slumped into the table. "Yeah," he admitted. "I've been hearing different names every few months, for the past five years and I tend to just show up and help you guys through things." Marlow blinked then lowered his eyebrows.

"So, you're like my guardian angel? Or like my genie?" he asked and Enzo grinned gently.

"In a way, I guess, but I don't fly or have magic powers."

"Then what do you do? How do you help?"

"Uh…" Enzo began then blinked. Apparently, he helped by sleeping with them then disappearing the next day when his name disappeared. He would then remain hung up on them but unable to text them, because he was worried about it not being helpful to them. Enzo wasn't sure what he did, but thinking on that; God, had he helped anyone? "You know, I'm just here to help you um… move on? Or just… okay. I need to ask you an awkward question, and you don't have to answer, but…" Enzo paused, then looked deeply into Marlow's green-grey eyes. "What happened to your other soulmate?"

A weird light clicked off through Marlow's eyes as his face fell to a dull, hollow husk. The deep, dark lines under his eyes became prominent in the low lights, as Enzo looked over him worriedly.

"Charlie," he sighed then heavily leaned on the table. "We split up a month ago. He uh… his name kind of faded. He took the house, and uh, yeah…"

"I'm sorry, man," Enzo said simply then placed a hand on Marlow's shoulder, causing a gentle wave of static to rifle through his own muscles.

Marlow scoffed then chugged the rest of his beer, while looking over the club and avoiding Enzo's kind gaze. "Hey, it's all right. I'm all right. It's uh… yeah… but I didn't expect, well…you," he admitted, then shakily gestured to Enzo as the dark-haired man scoffed.

"No one ever does," he stated, and Marlow grinned widely. "So, how long were you and Charlie together?"

"Four years," he replied, and Enzo sissed awkwardly. "Went to Uni together. He uh… he broke up with me, then, um…" Marlow avoided Enzo's eye once more, scraping at the label on his bottle, then staring at the table. "Started dating this guy from his work. I think he's moved in now; I don't know."

"Oh, that's awful," Enzo said, sympathetically. "Sounds like an ass."

"He wasn't," Marlow muttered tiredly then looked over his beer again. "Want another drink?"

Enzo blinked, then looked at the bottle in his hand, realising that he'd taken maybe one sip, or two, while Marlow had finished an entire bottle.

"I think I'm okay for now," Enzo said easily, gesturing to his still-full bottle.

Marlow rolled his eyes, his form shaking a little as he gripped the sides of the table.

"How many have you had tonight, Marlow?"

Marlow jumped, then stared up at the wall in thought. "Uh…" he began awkwardly. "About… right uh… five, then there was uh… the shots and uh… twelve?"

Enzo's eyes widened. "Yeah, I think it might be time to switch to water buddy," he stated, and Marlow scoffed.

"I don't think my friends would like that."

"I think they wouldn't like you passing out or throwing up," Enzo said, and Marlow rolled his eyes.

"I can handle my drink, Enzo."

"Oh, I don't doubt that," he responded easily. "But, just for now, maybe we skip the next drink, okay?"

Marlow looked over Enzo sceptically, his eyebrows lowering as little gulps trailed through his throat. But he reluctantly nodded after a few seconds, eyes sighing as they trailed the floor.

Enzo smiled, relieved, but felt his heart ache as he looked over Marlow. Maybe he'd have to try and take him home? He didn't like the idea of the man having a thirteenth drink and collapsing on the dancefloor or having some form of meltdown in the dark. He looked tired and out of it.

"Hey Marlow, any chance I could take you home?"

Marlow's eyes widened and his head shook speedily. "No, no. I'm okay, I swear. I won't grab another drink for a bit. We're heading to the uh… the science place, when Lexi gets back and those two stop groping each other on the dance floor," he said then flippantly gestured to the big guy and the tiny girl currently swaying slowly to the bump-and-grind song.

Did they know where they were? Or what song was playing?

"Those are your friends?" Enzo asked and Marlow nodded.

"Yeah, we were in the same society at uni," he explained vaguely. "Lexi should be around somewhere. Sure you're okay getting dragged along with this?"

Enzo scoffed then rolled his eyes. "I've been dragged to weirder," he admitted vaguely and Marlow cocked a brow.

"You got some stories, don't cha?" he asked, and Enzo grinned.

"Oh, tonnes," he admitted.

"Then we'd better get going quick – too loud for storytelling in here," Marlow said, then awkwardly grabbed his jacket and chucked it on.

Enzo stared at him in confusion before a tiny, brunette girl appeared and clocked Enzo with a serious look.

"Who's this?" she asked, pointing at Enzo but looking at Marlow.

"Oh," Marlow began with a little grin, then placed an arm over Enzo's shoulders, to the dark-haired man's immense shock.

His eyes went wide while looking at Marlow, then he turned to the new girl with a confused squint. She was young –younger than Marlow, for sure. Her eyes were sharp and clawing; they made Enzo insanely uncomfortable, as they dug into his soul.

"This is Enzo," Marlow explained with a strong, confident voice that threw Enzo through a loop.

Who was this guy? He was shy but confidently offered to buy drinks but otherwise? Enzo didn't know but he got the sense that Marlow didn't know. He couldn't explain it but the grin on Marlow's face in that moment and the stance. The strong, straight sense. It felt like he was watching a character speak, not a person.

Marlow continued, "My new soulmate."

Enzo's eyes went wide as he looked over the new girl.

"Enzo, this is Lexi."

"New soulmate?" Lexi asked him, in deep confusion, scepticism and curiosity lacing every feature on her face. "As in... voice in head? Already know each other... weird sparks? Whole shebang?"

Enzo scoffed then leaned forward on the table, Marlow pulling away and leaning down beside him.

"Yep," he stated simply and Lexi grinned wickedly.

"Ooh, interesting," she said and Enzo squinted at her.

"How so?" he asked.

"I mean, I did guess that everybody didn't just get *one* soulmate given how much people change throughout the years. It'd be kind of insane to think that we just get one shot. I mean, some people..." she began, then pointedly looked at Marlow, as the man jolted back

147

from the table. "... Like Charlie, turn out to be dicks who cheat on their partners then run off with his new manager, taking every goddamn thing their soulmate owns, plus the house."

Marlow sighed and rolled his eyes. "Charlie didn't cheat on me. and he didn't take everything I own."

"He did take the house, though," she argued and Marlow rolled his eyes with a deep sigh.

"His parents gave us the deposit. It was his name on the lease," Marlow explained, purposely looking at Enzo.

Enzo just nodded, then turned back to Lexi.

"You wouldn't cheat on him, would you?" she asked with lowered eyebrows and Enzo jolted.

"I... I wouldn't cheat on anyone, but that's not why I'm here, anyway."

"No?" Lexi asked.

"No, he's just my guardian angel. Here to make sure I'm okay," Marlow stated happily then cocked up an eyebrow with a little grin. "Which I am."

"Yeah, right," Lexi muttered then rolled her eyes before turning back to Enzo. "Can you do me a favour?"

Enzo blinked in surprise. "Uh..."

"Just, don't hurt him, okay?" she asked. "I'm kind of good at reading people and you um..." She squinted deeper. "There's someone else, isn't there?"

Enzo jolted back, then lowered his eyebrows as Lexi grinned.

"I knew it."

"There's um… there's…" he began to explain, feeling his head start to sweat. "Marlow is my soulmate. I'm just here to help him."

Lexi grinned wickedly then folded her arms, while Marlow looked over Enzo sceptically.

"Sure, looks like it'll just be the three of us, anyway. Pretty sure Dennis is gonna have to carry Ashley home," she said, then gestured to the pair on the dance floor.

The small girl was basically collapsing on the big man, as he desperately tried to drag her off the floor.

"Great," Marlow stated, then clapped loudly and gave a wide smile. "Then let's go."

Enzo wasn't sure how they got there, or when he got the colour-changing cocktail but, yeah, that's where the night went. The bar was *rammed*. Enzo, Marlow and Lexi got a table just in front of the bar, where people were hovering behind bar stools and beside booths, desperately hoping that someone would leave. They were like harpies and Enzo was not loving it. He was especially not liking how Lexi was looking at him. It felt like she could read him like a book, and it was making all his insides feel squirmy. He was relieved when she headed off to the bathroom, and Enzo was just left staring at Marlow – Marlow, who'd drank more than his fair share of the shared Zombie cocktail that Lexi ordered, and Marlow, who was currently on his second cocktail while Enzo was on his first.

149

"What happened to not drinking?" Enzo asked, looking over Marlow's face.

Marlow jolted, a shaky smile appearing on his sunken face as he shrugged. "Lexi was buyin... seemed rude not to," he slurred, eyes blinking slowly as he awkwardly stared at the table. "Is there someone else?"

Enzo jolted then stared at Marlow. "No," he replied quickly. "Well, yeah, but that's not the point. My soulmate changes basically every month."

"Why?" Marlow asked tiredly, then slurped at his bath bomb cocktail.

"I don't know," he admitted.

"Must be nice," he slurred and Enzo's eyebrows lowered. "You never get your heart broken; don't get cheated on and left after like..." He sighed, then gulped down another sip. "I mean, I can't..." Marlow began, then looked over himself. "It's not like I was good enough for him anyway," he continued and Enzo felt his heart shatter into a pile of spikey glass. "Or you, you're um..." He sighed, then leaned his hands on the table while staring into Enzo's eyes. "... Too pretty for me."

Enzo's cheeks blushed but he forced himself to straighten, clearing his throat and looking down at Marlow.

"Hey, hey. You can't think like that," he stated. "You're gorgeous, Marlow."

Marlow scoffed and rolled his eyes, leaning back and looking over himself. "I'm weird looking at best, I know and I've gained weight. I have weird eyes and my hair's too long plus, I'm just..." he rambled off, then sighed. "I'm just boring. People get bored and leave. You're gonna leave, aren't you?"

Enzo gulped then stared down at his shoes.

"Not for a little while, at least," Enzo stated gently, and Marlow smiled for a second before his face fell again.

"You'll get bored, too," he muttered, then wrapped his arms around himself as his eyes began watering.

"Marlow," Enzo said sadly, then stood and wrapped an arm around his back.

Lexi appeared at the table in that moment, and Enzo widened his eyes at her. She just nodded and pulled out her phone; hopefully to call a taxi to take them home.

The taxi was quiet. Lexi was in the front, and the boys were in the back. Lexi and Enzo basically carried a sleeping Marlow through the lobby and into his apartment; trudging along and trying to share the load before the pair awkwardly chucked him onto his couch.

Marlow crumbled immediately, while Lexi and Enzo looked at each other and bit their lips.

"It's okay if you need to go. I can make sure he's okay," Enzo whispered and Lexi scoffed.

"I've known you, like, three hours. What makes you think I'm leaving you with my best friend?" she asked and Enzo rolled his eyes.

"I'm his soulmate, just trust me. I'm just gonna get him some water and put him to bed. I've done this a million times," Enzo whispered harshly, and Lexi looked over him sceptically.

"Jeez, you have," she said, and Enzo rolled his eyes once more.

"Stop analysing me and go home. I'll make sure he texts you tomorrow or something."

"You'd better," she stated harshly, then squinted and pointed at him before walking backwards to the door and heading out, shutting it behind her.

He turned back to Marlow and looked over him sadly. His eyes landed on the tear stains down his face, as a gulp retched down his throat. "Okay, Marlow. I'm just gonna get you to bed, okay?" Enzo whispered gently, then leaned down and wrapped the man's arm around his back, before trudging over to the small, blue bedroom. Marlow's full weight fell on Enzo as he gently leaned over and placed Marlow into a lying down position, chucking the quilt over the top of him, before wandering off to grab a glass of water and a large bowl. He placed both on his bedside table, closed his curtains and made to leave once more, not able to see much in this tiny room.

"See? You're already leaving," Marlow joked tiredly and Enzo scoffed.

"I'm just going into the living room," Enzo whispered. "I mean if that's okay? I live, like, four hours from here, and didn't exactly think through hotels before heading to the club," Enzo admitted, surprised at himself. He usually did think of these things but he was apparently out of practice.

"Yeah, it's fine. Blankets are in the cupboard in the hallway and you can steal one of ma pillows," Marlow replied then awkwardly tugged a pillow out from under his head before chucking it at Enzo.

The dark-haired man blinked then took a fluffy, cotton thing to the face in the dark, spluttered then grabbed it and hugged it into his chest.

Marlow let out a loud laugh then sat up, grinning. "Sorry."

Enzo chuckled. "It's all right. Get some rest, okay? I'll be here in the morning."

Marlow's grin fell as he slumped back into bed. "I uh… I wasn't always like this, you know," he whispered then yawned. A waft of vodka-scented air flew through the room. "I used to be kinda functional but you know, I guess I'm just…" Another yawn. "…Broken," he choked out.

"Marlow," Enzo whispered but the room fell to silence as Marlow began to gently snore. Enzo was about to say more but he didn't want to wake him. He'd talk to him in the morning. For now? Marlow needed to sleep. Heck, Marlow deserved to sleep. The guy kept going after twelve freakin drinks! Enzo would've been dead three times over on that.

He gently closed the bedroom door and went in the living room, after heading into the hallway and grabbing a blanket from the top shelf. He slumped onto the grey, fluffy couch. He shoved the pillow behind his head and laid down, eyes gazing up at the ceiling as his phone vibrated and his eyes widened. He tugged it out from his pocket, gulping as Danny's name appeared on the top of the screen. It was just a simple 'good night', but it still made Enzo's heart twang. Maybe he should reply? Maybe he should call him? Tell him about Marlow? Ooh, no, for some reason that caused a grey, constricting feeling to stab through his heart.

'There's someone else.' There always was but why did that cause a weird, black squelch through his brain? Urgh. Danny had really messed with his freakin head. Right, it didn't matter. Doesn't matter. Marlow needed his help. He really needed his help. The guy had no self-esteem and was just beating himself up. Enzo really needed to do something. Well, he needed to encourage Marlow to do something but how do you do that?

Enzo sighed, beer flooding his brain as his eyes closed and his head slumped. He sent a quick 'good night' to Danny then fell asleep, his brain swirling and squishing in distortion.

God, why did he text back?

Chapter 8
MARLOW

Hangovers had gotten much worse since Marlow turned twenty-four. He could drink twelve shots and six beers at eighteen then wake up and get on with the day like nothing happened. At twenty-four, he would be hungover for three straight days with each day presenting new symptoms. He'd be nauseous then tired, then he'd have a headache. He'd be constantly thirsty and hungry but not want to eat. He'd basically be a zombie. Today was no exception.

He groaned when he woke up, a burning knife stabbed through the back of his brain as a wave of harsh, horrid nausea spread through the back of his throat. He groaned as the taste of burning vodka poked at his tongue.

He ran a hand through his hair and grimaced at the grease but couldn't bring himself to care too much between the headache and the nausea and the fact that a cute guy, who was supposedly his soulmate was currently sleeping on his couch.

Marlow's eyes widened at that thought and he darted out of bed, into the living room. His brain and stomach protesting this action severely before he stared down at the sleeping form on the couch, memories flooding the forefront of his mind as his breath hitched and his brain convulsed. "Urgh."

He'd called him pretty. Marlow thought he was pretty but, God, why'd he have to be such a mess when he met someone new? Wait, was Enzo someone new? It sounded like the guy was just passing through. What was he? Why had he just invited a stranger to sleep on his couch? Should he wake him up and kick him out? What should he do? This whole situation was ridiculous.

"Good morning to you, too," Enzo greeted him. He slowly rose to sit up on the couch, the blanket falling to his lap as inky, black hair fell into his pale, perfect face.

"Enzo?" Marlow asked and Enzo cocked a brow.

"Marlow?" he asked and Marlow jolted. "How much do you remember from last night?"

"Uh…" Marlow began then slumped onto the couch beside Enzo. "I uh… well, uh… you were in the bathroom?" he asked, then pointed to him. "And uh… we went to the science place. I uh…" He gulped then stared at his lap. "I called you pretty."

"Yes, yes, you did," Enzo stated. "Thanks, by the way."

Marlow scoffed, face burning. "Yeah, uh… you're welcome," he stammered, and a strange silence hit the room. "I'm sorry," he gulped. "I didn't mean to just drag you into my crap. You don't even know me."

"Hey, we're soulmates," Enzo argued then shrugged. "Dealing with each other's crap kinda comes with the territory."

"Not this quick though, usually,"

"Oh, trust me," Enzo said seriously, while staring at Marlow. "If I get through the first encounter without one of us crying then we're onto a winner. You're one of the calmer introductions I've had."

"Really?" Marlow said, surprised.

Enzo grinned. "One of em chased me down the hall with a bat. She was fun. Another almost hit me with their car. There's been tonnes. As far as I see it, if I don't almost die then we're winning."

Marlow grimaced. "You have low standards, my friend."

"I don't," Enzo responded instantly, then stared deeply into Marlow's eyes, gold irises glinting as Marlow's mouth fell completely dry. "All my soulmates are wonderful, wonderful people. Best people on the planet, I believe."

Marlow rolled his eyes. "Pretty sure you're biased."

"Oh, definitely, but doesn't mean I'm not right," Enzo said with a little smile.

Marlow smiled back, feeling his heart shiver through his chest.

"Marlow, I um… okay, I don't know where to begin here," Enzo began then bit his lip. "But uh… the things you were saying last night?"

A twang stabbed through Marlow's heart as he bit his lip. "Oh, yeah… just um… forget it, okay?" Marlow murmured then stared at the floor, praying that Enzo would drop it.

"You're not broken, Marlow," Enzo said gently, and Marlow's heart flattened through his chest.

"Forget it, okay?"

"No," Enzo interrupted.

Marlow jolted, his eyes tilting back to look at Enzo.

The man smiled at him lightly, then pressed a hand into his shoulder. "You're not broken, okay? I don't really know you but, well uh… I guess I can't say that when I can literally feel the link in our souls."

Marlow gave a little smile.

"I can feel you're a good person, Marlow. You're kind and you're sweet. I can see it."

"Thanks, but…"

"No buts," Enzo said firmly. "You're just going through a rough time, okay? There's no shame in it. That guy broke your heart and you're just trying to find something normal to hang onto. It's okay, I get it, but you need to know that it isn't all on you, okay? Whatever Charlie did and whatever happened, it's not because you're not good enough."

"How would you know?" Marlow asked then collapsed in on himself.

"Because everything is a two-way street, Marlow," Enzo stated and the grey-eyed man blinked up to him.

"Have you um... considered going to therapy? Coz uh..."

"I know," Marlow muttered then sighed. "But my mum would kill me if I went to therapy. She worries about me a lot, and mental health isn't her strong suit. She doesn't understand it, and I just... it's not worth trying to explain it to her."

"I get it but it's not about her, you know,"

"I know." Marlow sighed. "But she'd find out, and my whole family would find out, and they'd all know what a freakin wreck I am, and I just... I couldn't handle the pity and the..."

"I get it," Enzo said sympathetically then squeezed Marlow's shoulder. "But you need to know that you're worth more than you think you are, and the only person who can make you see that is you. You can't keep going like this."

"I know," Marlow whispered weakly, his entire chest concaving as a warbling sigh escaped him. "But I just... I just don't know where to begin, Enzo. I wish I did but it was just ...four years – four freakin years. I was gonna propose and he just gave up. I don't even know if Chester feels like home anymore. So much of my life was linked to him, so much of me... so much of just everything. He was my everything and he left, and I just... it feels like everything is swirling out of control. Everything is nightmarish and confusing, and I don't really know anything anymore. Charlie was the person who stopped me spiralling. He talked me down and now

I don't have anyone who…" He choked out a sob then gulped and stared at his feet. "I don't have anyone who knows me well enough to know that I'm worth something. He was the only person who saw that."

Marlow sighed and buried his head in his hands for a second, desperately trying to hold back shaky tears. His head was banging and his nose was sniffing, but there were no thoughts in his head. His head was hurting too much and swirling in a pool of slowly draining alcohol. Sounds were penetrating his ears in harsh, smoky, confusing beeps and strong gusts of air. It *hurt*. Everything hurt, and Marlow wanted it to stop; he needed it to stop. If this conversation kept going, he knew he was going to be a bawling wreck. He could feel it. Hangovers didn't make him sick, usually. They *always* made him an emotional wreck.

"He's not the only person who sees that," Enzo said gently, and their eyes linked once more as Enzo smiled and Marlow's heart collapsed through his chest. "But it's not everyone else's opinion that matters."

"It's mine, I know." Marlow sighed, then stared at the floor.

Enzo smiled sadly, then followed his gaze. "Have you ever talked to anyone about this?" he asked and Marlow scoffed.

"Apart from Charlie? And now you? No," he stated.

"Really? Not even the overly curious girl from last night or the collapsing couple?" Enzo asked and Marlow smiled.

"No," he admitted. "I love them but no. Dennis would never stop asking me questions or complimenting me, and the pitying looks from Ashley would kill me. I know Lexi knows that I don't have the highest self-esteem, but she has enough respect to know that it's my burden to bear. If I ever got into too much trouble though, I know she'd be the first to point it out. She's not exactly the type to bite her tongue when I'm in trouble."

"So, you know you have low self-esteem?" Enzo asked.

"It's not exactly a secret," Marlow admitted, with a little smile. "Pretty sure I have depression, too, but, well..."

"Your mum will kill you if you go to therapy?" Enzo asked and Marlow nodded. "You considered just not telling your mum?"

"Again, she'd just find out." Marlow sighed, then slumped into the couch. "I'm not good at lying to her, and just..."

"Marlow," Enzo said seriously, and cut off the rambling as Marlow sat and stared into his gold eyes, feeling oddly like he was under a hot lamp. "I understand. My mum's the same way. I don't know how she'd react if I told her that I do have a therapist and have sessions on zoom every couple of weeks."

"Really?" Marlow asked and Enzo smiled with a little nod.

"I got to a bad place about four years ago when I was, like, nineteen. My soulmate had left, college had finished, I couldn't talk to my dad about anything – he doesn't even know I'm bi – and he started drinking and fighting with my mum. It was… it was bad. I was meant to go to Uni, but I couldn't and it just was not a fun time. I started closing myself off and spending days and days in bed, until I heard another voice in my head and, well, my life got very different very fast, and sometimes I just need to slow down and talk." He shrugged while looking gently into Marlow's eyes. "It's okay to need that."

"It really helps you?" Marlow asked.

"I would not be like this if it didn't," he stated and Marlow cocked a brow. "I used to be a lot more closed off."

"That surprises me somehow," Marlow said.

"How so?"

Marlow shrugged. "You're just weirdly relaxed and smiley. You being closed off and emoish is quite a stretch," he explained and Enzo chuckled.

"Not sure I was ever 'emoish', but yeah, I was closed off. It took a couple of months of therapy for me to stop bottling things up," he explained. "I think it could help you, Marlow, and you don't need to tell your mother or anyone. Maybe just have a consultation with someone online, and if it's not for you, well try and find something that is. You deserve to know that you're worth something without someone having to tell you."

Marlow sniffed and a flood of tears trailed down his cheeks, leaking onto his Jack Daniels shirt.

"You're also an emotional wreck when hungover, huh?"

"I'm just a wreck, generally." Marlow grimaced then wiped his eyes, while Enzo smiled and ran a gentle hand up and down his back.

The pair got breakfast after that. Marlow had a shower then Enzo had a shower, and they spent the day watching TV and eating pizza, while Marlow took painkillers and tried to keep hydrated. His head kept pounding and he had moments of feeling like he was going to be sick, but he held it back. They watched Friends and random gameshows, talking periodically about random things, while leaning on the couch.

It was easy and simple. It was like they were just friends. Friends who'd known each other a long, long time.

Marlow spent most of his brainpower thinking about this whole 'therapy' thing. He looked up local ones on his phone and clicked on names to see what they specialized in. He found a few that specialized in self-esteem issues but a few would only allow in-office hours, and Marlow found the idea of that terrifying. All of this was terrifying. It was new territory, and he just had this paranoid 'my mum's bugged my phone' thought, before he locked his screen and pressed it back into the couch with a gulp, his eyes finding Enzo as the man watched TV and munched on BBQ pizza with a glass of Fanta.

How was he so perfect? There was just... he was perfect; his smile and his eyes; his hair and his deep, sexy voice. How were they soulmates? Marlow felt like he was barely a five. Enzo was a solid ten. The guy was so freakin pretty with his freckles and his fringe; his gleaming, perfect skin and those light-brown eyes.

Marlow sighed then looked down at himself. He needed to go back to the gym. He needed to get some more moisturiser, get his teeth whitened again and buy some new clothes. Heck, he needed more underwear. He hadn't bought new underwear in years. He needed to do something. He needed to get a haircut and go jogging or something. He'd been so lazy and lost the past month. Where had the time gone? When was the last time he properly shaved? He was an idiot – a lazy, disgusting idiot. Why was Enzo still here?

He shook his head, then stared at his lap with a little gulp.

"You're spiralling, aren't you?" Enzo asked quietly and Marlow jumped.

"No," he responded instinctively, and Enzo rolled his eyes.

"Stop thinking and relax," Enzo said easily. "You don't have to get anything done today. You've got time, and you're nowhere near as bad as you think you are, so get out of your freakin head and watch the stupid sitcom."

Marlow scoffed. "Where do you get off being so demanding? I've only known you, like, twelve hours."

"I'm your soulmate, Marlow," Enzo stated and Marlow's eyes widened. "I know you a lot better than you think I do and trust me, you need to stop freakin thinking and relax. You're hungover –you're not gonna find a therapist today and you're not gonna get anything else done and that is okay, so just stop thinking and breathe. There's nothing immediate that needs to be done. You're okay and it's okay to give yourself a break."

"You're not Yoda, you know," Marlow muttered.

"There is no try, young Padawan," he stated and Marlow let out a loud chuckle. "Seriously, take a break and stop getting lost in your head."

"Fine, I'll try," Marlow agreed, then stared back at the TV as silence quaked around the pair. He did try. He really did but it was hard to focus when your head was swimming in still-digesting alcohol, but every time he started getting lost, Enzo would pick some inane conversation that completely drew his attention; that made him smile and think of something else. It was refreshing and calming. They talked about movies and TV; pointless things that made him happy. Enzo was good at this. He was good at 'playing therapist', and Marlow found him liking the man's company more and more by the second. They joked and laughed; made references and had fun but something was nagging at the back of his head.

Why hadn't either made a move? When Marlow and Charlie met, the pair had kissed within two hours. Ashley and Dennis made out a second after meeting. If Marlow and Enzo were soulmates, and there was clearly chemistry there. There was an easy, comfortable chemistry that made their cheeks warm and their hearts flutter. Marlow was very attracted to Enzo, he wasn't sure about the other way round. But Marlow was attracted to the dark-haired man, and it wasn't even just about the fact that he was hot. He was kind and sweet and funny, plus, oddly mysterious. There was a lot to like about Enzo.

But there was something else nagging at the back of Marlow's brain. For one, did he want to make a move? It didn't feel right. There was this weird barrier in the back of his head. He'd think about kissing Enzo, and a little gulp would fall through his throat before his mind gently told him to stop. Kissing him felt like a weird invasion of privacy or something. He didn't know. He didn't know how to explain it. He wanted to kiss Enzo. He really did, but it didn't feel right, and it wasn't just about him. Enzo said something last night. Well, Lexi asked him something and he didn't exactly deny it. It was nagging him, but he didn't want to bring it up. He had a feeling that bringing it up would destroy the comfortable, homely bubble that they'd created, and he didn't want to do that, since doing that would likely cause him to cry right now.

But he couldn't not ask when it was gnawing at him. "So…" he began, and Enzo jumped before turning to him. "There's someone else?"

Enzo's bright gold eyes went wide, as a very visible gulp fell through his throat. "No, it's uh… it's not like that," he said quickly. "I um… get a new…" He sighed. "I've never known how to explain it, but I get a new name in my head every few months, and things… yeah…"

"I think you explained that vaguely last night, but I don't think that's what Lexi was talking about?" Marlow asked, with a little squint.

Enzo jolted slightly, then rolled his eyes.

"I'm only asking coz, well, uh…" Marlow then slumped forward slightly. "If we're soulmates, then typically, like, uh… soulmates, you know, do more than just talk about friends and movies and stuff? At least, in my experience anyway,"

Enzo smirked lightly. "I don't do that, Marlow," he said, and Marlow lowered his eyebrows. "Look, um…" Enzo gulped and leaned up, looking down at his feet awkwardly.

Marlow didn't think he could look so small and shy. It was weird. It was a weirdly sharp contrast that made Marlow feel rather uncomfortable.

"The name changes every um… I haven't had a soulmate for longer than, like, four months. I can't just show up and kiss them all, then…" He sucked in a sharp breath and shook his head slowly. "It's uh… it wouldn't be fair. I'm sorry."

"No, I get it," Marlow said slowly. "Do you… um… why are you like this?"

Enzo shrugged. "I dunno. I just have been since I was eighteen. I didn't mind it, but, yeah…"

"Didn't?" Marlow asked and Enzo jolted.

"Don't," he corrected, and Marlow cocked a brow while Enzo shook his head. "Don't mind it. It's weird, okay? But it's been going on for five years and I just show up, meet new people and see if I can help them. It's…yeah." A small, weird smile appeared on his face.

"But no kissing or making out of any kind?" Marlow asked.

"Nope," he said, popping the 'p'. "You're just gonna have to make do with my company for however long you can hear my name."

Marlow smiled lightly. "Sure you're not a con artist or a robber or something?"

"Would I tell you if I was?"

"Good point," Marlow said. "You're welcome to stay here and do whatever the hell it is you do. I'll uh… try and be better, I guess?"

"Don't do it for me, Marlow."

"Yeah, yeah, do it for me. I know, but seriously, I'll look into therapists and stuff. I don't know, but I could probably do with some help on a couple things."

"That's why I'm here," Enzo stated with a smile.

Marlow grinned back, and the pair dissolved back into the TV.

It was hard to say how much time passed after that. Days, weeks, months. Everything blended. Enzo worked a little and Marlow went back to his normal work schedule. He only worked one in four Saturdays a month. Typically, he worked nine to five, Monday to Friday. Enzo used this opportunity to travel back home and grab some things before heading back to Marlow's.

He slept on the couch most days but headed to a little Travelodge on a couple because he felt weird just lodging. They spent a lot of time looking into therapists and sorting Marlow's gym membership. He'd forced Enzo to do a couple of home workouts but Enzo didn't mind. The guy had a ton more energy; especially when Enzo started cooking and Marlow picked at recipes. His friends appeared every now and again.

He'd cried during his first therapy session. They brought up Charlie, and Marlow lost it but he kept talking and got everything out over a half hour consultation. He'd been recommended to at least have sessions every two weeks, and Marlow was feeling better. He was standing taller and smiling more. He and Enzo made jokes and watched TV. They enjoyed each other's company, and life just sort of flittered away. Everything felt normal and relaxed. He didn't really think about Charlie anymore. He didn't even think about Enzo. He was trying to focus on himself; keeping his head straight; focusing on getting healthy. He'd lost a bit of weight and gained a bit more muscle. His skin had cleared up, and his shoulder-length brown hair was now cut above his ears with little bits of fringe floating into his eyes.

He'd thrown out Charlie's jeans, blocked him on Facebook and gotten rid of the key to their old house. He was moving forward and breathing. It'd been weeks since he had a spiral, and things were good. He still heard Enzo's name in his head and still felt static every time they touched, but neither had made a move. It just felt like they were friends; like they'd been friends for years.

It was easy and fun, but Marlow couldn't help but feel like Enzo was holding something back. He didn't know what it was, but every time other soulmates were brought up, Enzo would start to say something then stop himself. It was typically when asked, 'How long do you reckon we have?' He'd start to say weeks or months, then his lips would slam shut, like he wanted to add another thing but couldn't.

One day, Marlow woke up and couldn't get out of bed. The grey cloud started weighing down his bones, and the man was desperately trying to ground himself but couldn't. Hours passed, and he hid under his quilt with a deep, wary sigh, unable to move or push himself to do anything but close his eyes and breathe. He was stuck and sad; life was flooding past the windows, and he was supposed to be at work. That thought caused guilt to weigh his bones down harder, as the grey cloud got denser and louder. He closed his eyes tighter and tried to focus but couldn't.

He was vaguely aware of the door opening; vaguely aware of the light flooding through, when a vague, blurry voice appeared through the grey.

"Marlow?" he asked. "You okay in here? I made tea. It's, like, ten? Shouldn't you..." His mouth slammed closed when he saw the sad lump on the bed. "Oh. Uh... okay. I'm just gonna get you some food, and I'll call your boss." He moved forward and placed a mug lightly on the bedside table.

He grabbed the phone and disappeared from the room, coming back a moment later as the grey lightened slightly. "Okay, Aiden knows, and you're okay to stay home. I've messaged Dr. Mulligan, and he's just said to go through the little distracting things that you guys do, so um ... I don't know what you guys do, but..."

Marlow found himself smiling, but the grey was still flooding every sense, and he could barely lift his head through the darkness.

"Okay, distracting," Enzo began, then clapped and started pacing back and forth. "I always used to do this thing when I started drinking. I was, like, scared I was going to like lose control and say something stupid, then forget. So, uh... and this is about the nerdiest thing you'll ever hear, so bear with..."

Marlow pulled the quilt off slightly, the light from the living room bleeding through his eyelids, as he felt his heart start to calm.

"There's a speech in Lord of the Rings; two towers, specifically, spoken by Samwise Gamgee. I don't know this about you, but um... you like Lord of the Rings, right?"

Marlow grunted in response and Enzo took that as a 'yes', before the man pulled the quilt fully off his face and stared up at Enzo.

"I always used to see if I could remember it, and it, like, kept my head straight."

"The speech that Sam makes?" Marlow asked weakly and Enzo stopped, turned and grinned at the man.

"You know the one I mean?"

"Yeah. Uh... the one during helm's deep?" he gulped out, while Enzo smirked wickedly.

"Yeah. Just think about that scene. Heck, I could put it on, or even, like, find another scene in another movie. I don't know what it is about Lord of the Rings, but it cheered me up and just kinda kept me going when I got to that emotionally drunk stage."

"I can't see you as an emotional drunk," Marlow muttered, then ran a hand over his leaking eyes.

"Can you see me drunkenly quoting Lord of the Rings, though?" Enzo asked.

"Yeah, that I can see," Marlow admitted, and the pair linked eyes with matching, little smiles.

"You okay?" Enzo asked gently.

"Little better."

"You want food?"

Marlow nodded weakly.

"I'll bring it in here, okay?"

November passed speedily, and December came like a rush. The air outside got cooler, the streets got busier, and life inside got cosier. Marlow spent ninety percent of his time wrapped in a blanket on the couch, with a movie playing and a hot chocolate in his clutches. Enzo followed suit, insisting that they get the world's biggest marshmallows to put in them.

"Four months," Marlow muttered one night, and Enzo jolted, hot chocolate spilling over the rim of his mug slightly. The pair wore pyjamas – giant, fluffy ones that severely exaggerated the size of their hips. It'd become routine that the pair watch gameshows on Friday evening when they both finished work.

Marlow had had a day where his brain had felt like it was melting. He was originally planning on calling in sick, feeling a bit of a depressive episode flaring, but Enzo talked him round and made him feel a bit more alive, while Marlow went through some grounding exercises. It wasn't easy and Enzo did tell him that he didn't have to go, but Marlow insisted in the end, stating that he needed to keep pushing himself. Enzo said 'fine' but stated that he was making tea that night. They really were like a couple, or flatmates. It was weird.

"Huh?" Enzo asked, then cocked a brow, dark hair falling over his face as he scrunched his features in confusion.

"That's the longest you've been with one of us?"

"Oh. Yeah," Enzo stated, then took a sip of hot chocolate. "Why?"

"Is that how long you could be here, sleeping on the couch?" Marlow asked and Enzo scoffed.

"I don't know if my back could take that."

Marlow grinned and rolled his eyes. "How old are you again?"

"Haha."

"No, seriously – four months..." Marlow began, and Enzo jolted. "Did you um... have you uh..."

Enzo sighed. "Four months was my longest relationship, and I uh... well, I haven't..." Enzo began rambling, but his face scrunched slightly in frustration at his own voice.

"You haven't?"

Enzo sighed again. "I hadn't kissed one of you in five years."

"But you have now?" Marlow asked, his eyebrows creasing in deep confusion as Enzo's pale face started to glow a bright red.

"Yeah, but uh... that was uh..." he began rambling. "He was an outlier, and it doesn't matter."

"But you have kissed us? Have you um... have you..."

"Yes." Enzo sighed, then slammed a hand into his face while Marlow's eyes widened. "But again, it doesn't matter. It was a mistake and I'm uh... not doing it again."

"It was a mistake?" Marlow asked and felt his heart pang.

"No, no, that's not what I…" Enzo began, then slumped into the couch with a sigh. "It's complicated." Enzo sighed. "I didn't kiss him. He kissed me, and it was…" Enzo's cheeks got pinker, while Marlow gulped.

"Is he the someone that Lexi asked about?"

"Probably." Enzo sighed and a heavy, impenetrable silence flooded the space between them, as sweat started to form on Marlow's brow.

He wanted to ask more but the look on Enzo's face stopped him. He looked sullen, confused and frustrated. He seemed to even be trembling, and Marlow didn't want to make it worse. He got a sense that Enzo needed to talk about this, but Marlow couldn't force it. If Enzo wasn't ready, then fine.

"What happens when your name fades?" Marlow asked and Enzo sighed, his body slumping, as the tension faded and the blush in his cheeks disappeared.

"I don't know. It tends to happen when you're okay without me."

"No, no, that's not what I mean," Marlow corrected and Enzo pulled a sceptical expression. "Like, do you get another voice? Do I? What happens? Am I just soulmateless forever? Or will I, like, be like you? Like, have you infected me with your…"

"My curse?" Enzo asked with a little smirk, and Marlow rolled his eyes. "No, that's not how it works."

"Then how does it?"

Enzo shrugged. "It works differently for everyone. Some of you hear a different name straight away. Others have a few months, but no one is ever left without a voice, and as far as I know, none of you end up a rudderless ship like me."

"A rudderless ship?"

"What else would you call me?"

Marlow opened his mouth for a second, then scoffed. "Weird."

"Cheers, buddy."

Marlow found that he was incredibly used to having Enzo around. The pair even fell out about stupid things. Enzo stopped staying in the hotel and started paying rent because it felt like the right thing to do, so the pair were effectively living together, and Enzo was a little thrown by it. He'd have gone back home if it wasn't four hours away. Well, he did head back on occasion to check on his parents, but otherwise? Well, Chester at Christmas was nice.

Marlow, Enzo, and Marlow's friends went out to the market a few times. They got pulled pork and cake, and just enjoyed the Christmas lights and the cool atmosphere.

A few nights passed into the month, and Marlow started to miss Charlie a little. He still remembered his expression when they watched The Holiday –the way he'd mime the lines without thinking about it; the way his eyes lit up at the market; the way cranberry sauce would dribble down his chin whenever they had hog roast. He remembered everything in gnawing, irritating detail but it didn't hurt to think on it, anymore. It was like he was looking through dulled glass; like his heart wasn't grabbing the feelings. Those days happened and they were great but they were over and Marlow was okay. It was weird but he was okay. He was going to be okay without Charlie.

"His name was Danny," Enzo muttered one day, and Marlow jumped.

The pair had been wandering through Chester market, buying food and staring in awe at the lights and the stalls. A million smells flitted over and through them, making them hungry. They each wore a thick, navy coat, a woollen hat, scarf and gloves. Enzo wore a pair of black skinny jeans with his boots, a black shirt and a tartan red top, while Marlow wore a plain, green T shirt, light-blue jeans and a pair of blue Converse that were slowly falling apart. Neither had spoken in a little while, but Marlow briefly mentioned how much Charlie had loved the market and how strange it felt without him. Good, but strange, and Enzo fell strangely silent while looking up at the stars.

"Danny?" Marlow asked. "The guy who... uh kissed you?"

"Yeah," Enzo whispered.

"What was he... uh... what was he like?"

"Cute." Enzo smiled. "One of those 'lights up a room' kinda guys. Bright, blue eyes, light-brown hair, kind of looked like a Disney character."

Marlow couldn't help the little bubble of laughter that fell from his mouth with that statement. "How did he…" Marlow began, then looked over Enzo's nervous form, as the pair came to a stop and slumped to sit at a picnic table.

"He just kissed me. We were talking and um… he… yeah, and things progressed from there. I was trying to help him get over his ex, then he kissed me, then asked me about me. And it was weird and intense and just… he was *so* different, then we kinda got lost, and, yeah, well…"

"Was that uh… was he your…"

"Yeah."

"How long were you uh…"

"One night."

"What?!" Marlow yelled. "You can have that little time with someone?"

"I didn't know I could until Danny," Enzo admitted, then shrugged. "Told you… he was an outlier."

"And you're still hung up on him?" Marlow asked and Enzo bit his lip. "Must've been one hell of a night," he muttered then nudged Enzo's shoulder.

"It was good," he squeaked.

Marlow looked down at the ground, then smiled back up at Enzo.

The pair had gotten to know each other well over the past few months, but Enzo still seemed scared to open up about this stuff. He didn't like talking about it, clearly, but Marlow seemed to realise that it was less about not wanting to and maybe more about not knowing what to say. This was a weird situation. One night? That was insane and unfair. The glint in Enzo's gold eyes when he talked about Danny was something new; something that Marlow hadn't spotted in him before now; something that Charlie had had in his eye when they had looked at each other. Holy crap.

"Are you in love with him?" Marlow asked and Enzo's eyes went wide.

"No. I uh… I can't be," Enzo stated. "We had one night – that was it. It's always like this. One soulmate at a time. I help them, then I move on. I've been here, like, three weeks now, anyway. You're my soulmate now."

"But we're different and you know it," Marlow argued, and their eyes linked.

It was true. They both thought the other was cute and they had sparks when they touched, but they were more friends than they were anything else. They were friends and roommates. They talked about nonsense eighty percent of their time together and had fun, but after a little while, Marlow had no desire to kiss Enzo or go any further than just chatting and joking. They were friends more than soulmates, and they both seemed to agree that it was better that way.

"So, I repeat – are you in love with him?"

Enzo sighed sharply. "We had one night, Marlow. It's not that simple."

"Did you have a good time?"

"Yeah," Enzo answered wistfully. "But still, it was one night. I just wanted more time. I've never had that before."

"You've never wanted more time with one of us?"

"I just… okay…" Enzo sighed. "You'll see it when my name fades, but by the time it does, you'll feel ready."

Marlow cocked a sceptical eyebrow. 'Ready?' What the heck did that mean?

"I don't know how to explain it but I'm just here to help, and we have a good time but then it ends, and it's fine. I've never left a soulmate and felt like I hadn't had enough time."

"But Danny?"

"I mean, he'll be fine without me. I helped him get rid of his exe's stuff, then we uh… had our night, but…"

"So, you did help him?"

"Yes, but it was just one night."

"You considered that was all he needed from you?" Marlow asked and Enzo sighed deeply, slumping down into his seat.

"Yeah," he reluctantly admitted.

"But it's not about him?" Marlow asked cockily, and Enzo slumped further with a gulp.

"One night's weird," Enzo muttered. "Come on, what person can just have one night with someone who's linked to their soul? I've never had that. It's always been a week or a month, or two or four. One night? It was just wrong. We were together then I woke up and his name was gone. It was… it just… God, it didn't feel right. It's like there's no closure there. But then I heard your voice, and I'm here, and *this*…" He gestured between the pair of them. "Helping you with the therapy and the working out and all that – and you look great, by the way."

Marlow's cheeks started to blush.

"This is what I'm supposed to be doing. This is what's normal."

"This is your normal?" Marlow asked, and Enzo chuckled.

"Meeting random, cute strangers in bars, then helping them through past relationship trauma while bettering themselves, is my specialty," he stated and Marlow rolled his eyes with a little smile.

"But what about you?" Marlow asked, and Enzo shrugged.

"I'm happy. I like doing this. I meet great people, get some good stories, travel to some places. It's been this way for five years. I don't want it to change."

"Are you sure about that?" Marlow asked and Enzo rolled his eyes.

"Yes, I am."

Marlow raised a sceptical eyebrow. "Because it is okay to want more, you know."

"It's not though," Enzo stated, then slumped further into himself. "Coz it's not what's been decided for me."

"You came here to help me get over my soulmate and figure myself out, right? That's what you do?" he asked, and Enzo nodded in slow confusion. "You know you're a person too, right? It's okay to think about what you want and who you are, you know. It's not crazy to want closure, or you know, something more. And it's okay to go for that something more."

Enzo smiled, as a warm silence flittered over them. "Right, thanks, Yoda."

Marlow was starting to come back to life. The world was starting to make sense again. He didn't wake up and automatically check Charlie's side of the bed. He wasn't worried about spending Christmas alone. If he made a mistake, he thought about it for a second then went back and fixed it. He had a moment of beating himself up, then he stopped and grounded himself before slowing his breathing and focusing on what he could do right, rather than what had been done. It was a lot; a lot to remember and a lot to do but talking to Dr. Mulligan every week was helping; working out was helping; being on a schedule was helping; having Enzo around to encourage him on the bad days was helping. Everything was looking up and getting better, until …

Well, Enzo didn't exactly explain what would happen when his name faded. He'd tried but, well, 'It fades quite quickly, but the feelings tend to stay' wasn't exactly helpful.

So, Marlow woke up on December 16th with a sharp ring stabbing through his ears and a weird, liquid sensation flooding his head like jelly. He sucked in breath after breath after breath before everything fell silent. Every voice in his head disappeared and he jolted up in shock, wandering through to the living room with wide eyes.

"Enzo," Marlow said and Enzo was staring at him.

"Yeah, it's gone." He sighed with a little smile.

"So, uh... what now?" Marlow asked awkwardly, then ran a hand through his hair with a little, awkward smile.

It was eight a.m. Marlow and Enzo were in their pyjama bottoms. Enzo's hair was tied up in a little, messy ponytail, and each had tired, slightly sunken eyes. A blanket sat over Enzo's lap as a lopsided smile crossed his face.

"I guess you get your apartment back," he stated, and Marlow felt his heart stop.

"Uh... you don't have to um... you don't have to..."

"Marlow, you'll be okay," Enzo said gently, getting to his feet and walking forward. "It's just time, and you don't need me, you know that."

Marlow rolled his eyes and folded his arms. "I was a borderline alcoholic before you showed up," he argued.

"You were just a binge drinker," Enzo argued back, then chucked a shirt on over his head, tugging out his ponytail in the process, as dark curls cascaded over his shoulders. "And you're fine. You're doing better. The name typically fades when people don't need me anymore."

"Like Mary Poppins?" Marlow asked and Enzo jolted. "Or Nanny McPhee?"

Enzo's eyes went wide. "Yeah," he choked out. "Um... we can keep in touch? I mean, well, please text me, or call me if you're having a rough time and just need a distraction. I am here."

Marlow looked up in surprise with a little smile. "Okay, same goes for you."

"Will do, young Padawan," Enzo muttered, then saluted and disappeared into the bathroom, coming out in his jeans and boots – same shirt though – and his hair was still a mess. "Seriously, though," he continued then properly turned to Marlow with a little smile, gathering his laptop in his arms. "You're going to be okay."

"I know," Marlow stated. "Thanks um… thanks for um… for uh…"

"Yeah, you're welcome," Enzo said. "And thanks for uh… thanks for everything, too."

"I didn't really do anything."

"Oh, you did," Enzo muttered, with a little smirk.

Marlow cocked his brow then shrugged. "Okay," he conceded, then moved forward and awkwardly gathered Enzo in his arms. "See you round, Enzo."

"See you round, buddy," Enzo replied, and the pair pulled back. "Say bye to Dennis, Ashley and Lex for me, all right?"

Marlow smiled and nodded, before the dark-haired man disappeared through his apartment door, closing it behind him.

Chapter 9
DANNY

Christmas was a weird time for Danny. This would be his first year working at a school during this time and he was loving that, but it was forcing him to up his Christmas spirit, and he didn't have a lot of Christmas spirit to begin with. He liked Christmas, sure, but it was just a holiday. The lights were pretty, the movies were nice, the music was fun but there was never anything that drew Danny to this holiday. He used to spend it with his family but things changed when him and Allison got together. They spent Christmas alone together. He cooked, she did the dishes, and they just talked, watched movies and ate chocolate all day. It was just another day, really but Danny loved it. It was nice, calm and chilled. The air was cosy and homely and there was no pressure, but this year?

This year, Danny was going home. He was going to see his parents, grandparents, aunts, uncles – God knows who. People who only knew about him and Allison through notifications on Facebook. He was not looking forward to having to explain that but he had to, didn't he?

The past few months had been weird. He didn't know what to do about Enzo, or about the lack of names in his head. It was silent, and that was *so* spooky. His head hadn't been nameless since he was a kid. He felt like he'd fallen back in time but, well, he hadn't. Enzo was real and he'd discovered that he was bi, and that a person could have more than one soulmate. *So* much had changed in just one night.

Danny couldn't quite believe that it had just been one night. Why had it only been one night? Enzo made it sound like they'd get months or weeks, at least. Why was it only one night? Danny felt like a right slut after that. He'd essentially had a one-night stand – a one-night stand with his soulmate but still, a one-night stand. Danny never thought he could be a person who did that. One-night stands weren't really a thing, nowadays. People found their soulmates and boom! That was it. Well, that was Danny's previous perspective, anyway. What was his perspective now? Well, he didn't know. People were weird.

He did start seriously looking into other people's relationships, though. He worked out that his parents split up right before he was born, then got back together a year later. His friends fought about stupid, stupid things that almost split them up. A few couples he'd known as soulmates in college had split up now, according to Facebook. Things were a lot more complicated than his fairy-tale mindset had led him to believe. Just how long had he hidden behind this ideal soulmate image? It felt like a veil had been pulled off his eyelids.

It didn't matter anyway. It'd been a month and a bit –about six weeks since Enzo came in and blew up Danny's entire view on soulmates; six weeks since, well, Danny's virginity. 2: electric boogaloo. He wasn't sure what to count his first time with a guy as, but he kind of saw it as losing his virginity again. It was a new experience in a lot of ways, and maybe he liked the fact that he was the dominant, more confident one in that scenario. It was a new thing for him, after all. He liked making Enzo feel safe and just having his way with him, making him make those noises and collapse into his pillow. He felt amazing and it was amazing. Every time Danny thought on it, his chest would inflate, and his heart would ache; a smile would creep onto his lips, and a blush would completely envelope his face.

One night. One freakin night. Danny wished they could've had more. He wished he could hear those noises and wake up to those eyes again. He wanted that but one night. Maybe there was a reason.

Danny was a believer in fate. A believer that things happened for a reason, and maybe Enzo and Danny were meant to be passing ships. Enzo was meant to come into Danny's life and flip his world view, and that was it. He was meant to make Danny see things differently, then go back to his reality and keep helping people – the way he had helped Danny. That was Enzo's life. Danny needed to get back to his. He needed to get promoted at school and stop being a trainee. He needed to sort out his apartment and get back into things that he lost when he was stressed about moving and Allison and all that stuff. He needed to re-evaluate who he was and what he wanted. He needed to put himself first, then maybe the silence through his mind would go away, or maybe it wouldn't. Either way, he needed to figure himself out. He needed to be okay in himself and learn to enjoy his own company. Soulmates weren't as important as his own sanity. Enzo had tried to show him that, and Danny had kind of, well... he flipped the lesson, but he still wanted to be secure in himself. He didn't like how shy he was at the bar or how down he'd been the past few months. He'd pulled away from a lot of people and hidden away. He needed to get some air and to start being himself again.

What was the first step in doing that? Obviously, it was organising a bunch of kid's Santa masks and stapling them to a wall in rainbow order. The benefits of being a trainee teacher was getting all the leftover jobs, plus the paperwork, plus the lesson planning, with half the credit and two thirds of the pay. Danny had been doing this for about a year, now since passing his teacher training. It was a small primary school and technically, he was a qualified teacher, but they picked him up from his placement on a 'trainee teacher' salary. Danny worked very hard and he loved his job. He had a class and a lot of work and well, he was living alone now. He could survive paying rent and bills on his current salary, but there wasn't a lot of wiggle room, and his savings had taken a big hit in the past year. He really needed the promotion. Like, yesterday. Hence why, he was currently sorting out Santa masks with the speed of the Flash outside Mrs Davenport's office, peering in nervously every couple of seconds, while he tried to build up the guts to go in.

"Come on, Danny," he grunted through his teeth, while cocking the staple gun. "You can do this. You deserve that promotion. You need the money. This is the last day of term before Christmas. You need to do this..." He glared at the office door, specifically landing on the 'Headmaster' sign, before letting out a shaky sigh and stumbling towards it, knocking on the red-painted wood. "Oh God, oh God, oh God."

"Come in!" Mrs Davenport bellowed, and Danny stumbled through with a little nervous smile. "Ah, Mr Strand."

"Good afternoon, Mrs Davenport, do you have a minute?" he asked politely, fingers trailing his palm anxiously.

"Of course," she stated happily, grinning her classic, overly wide grin, revealing the bright-red lipstick on the front of her teeth. Her deep-auburn hair was currently tied into a little swirly bun on the back of her head. Her tanned skin was glimmering in the dull daylight streaming through the slightly open blinds. She currently wore a glittering black and silver top with a keyhole cut below the neck, but above her chest. She was a big lady; well, not big. She was curvy. Her cleavage currently poked through the keyhole in an awkward, bunched-up fashion that made Danny a little uncomfortable, but he wasn't looking. He just wanted to tell her, or maybe she knew? He didn't know the protocol with this stuff. He thought telling her might make her self-conscious, and he didn't want to do that, so he just took a seat opposite her with a little nervous smile, hand trailing through his mousy hair before his fingers began fiddling with the cuff of his light-blue button shirt.

"So, what's on your mind?"

Danny jolted then gulped, while desperately attempting to look into Mrs Davenport's deep, brown eyes.

"Uh...well... I've been working here for almost a year now, and uh... I am a qualified teacher."

"Ah," Mrs Davenport stated, with a little smile. "You're wondering when we're gonna stop tagging the 'trainee' onto your job title, huh?"

Danny blinked in surprise, then gulped. He knew Mrs Davenport was a good person. She was a good boss. A little demanding and unempathetic about the workload, but she hadn't been a teacher in about twenty years. And she always had a lot of work to do. Danny understood. He had days of being frustrated by it, but he liked his job and loved his kids enough to get past it.

"Well, uh... yeah..." Danny murmured, then ran a hand through the back of his hair. "I love this job and I'm happy here, and I uh... well..."

"Daniel," Mrs Davenport interrupted, and stamped on Danny's rambling with her gentle, demanding tone. "You're a good teacher, and you work hard. We were going to offer you a permanent contract in the Spring term, but since you're here," she said with a little grin, and Danny felt his heart fall. "Well, how would you feel about being a permanent teacher here?"

Danny's eyes went wide and a shocked, slow scoff escaped his slightly parted lips.

"I'd... that'd be... yeah," Danny managed to stammer, a little grin taking over his face, as his shaking form stopped jittering and his heart began to clamber to a normal rhythm.

"Wonderful," Mrs Davenport said with a grin, as she rose to her feet. "I'll have the contract written up asap."

Her hand stretched out to Danny, as the man slowly rose to his feet opposite her. He breathed out slowly, then pressed his hand into hers, their fingers wrapping gently as they shook hands. The weight in Danny's shoulders disappeared as they pulled away.

"Merry Christmas, Mr Strand."

"Merry Christmas, Mrs Davenport," he replied, then awkwardly shuffled out of the office, collapsing back into the closed door with a shocked grin on his face.

The day went by in a happy blur, the grin never leaving his face. He went through the Christmas activities with the kids. They made paper chains and did word searches, talked about the nativity and sang Christmas carols.

Three p.m. hit and everybody shuffled out of the bright, blue room. Danny gathered his bags, his laptop and said 'Merry Christmas' to his fellow teachers, before racing home and collapsing on his couch. He took in a deep breath, before his eyes caught onto the tiny suitcase on his dining table.

He had yet to pack. And he was getting a train in about an hour. His parents were waiting for him; his aunts; his uncles; all of them slowly gathering with wine, food, music and movies. All of them wearing cheesy Christmas jumpers and sparkly earrings; all of them eating enough quiche and cheese-on-a-sticks to kill multiple lactose intolerant people. Everything would smell like those sickly-sweet, cookie candles, and everything would be lit up in rainbow, glittering lights that switched on and off periodically, painting everyone's faces in blues, reds, yellows and greens, while darkness flashed between the colours.

Danny wasn't ready for the questions. Well, he was but he wasn't. He was ready to see his family. He wanted to see them, to be with them, to be surrounded in warmth and love – maybe a little judgment and condensation? But that was just Uncle Barney. Uncle Barney was the family's red card; grabbed a whiskey and pounded them nonstop until he puked in someone's plant pot. It happened at every gathering, but between the pounding and the puking, he was sprouting judgmental nonsense and asking inane, annoying questions that made you want to shoot yourself. He was tall and bald, pale as anything, and always wore purple, circle glasses that exaggerated the size of his very triangular nose.

His Aunt Sophia was married to him. They'd been married for six years. She wasn't as vocally judgmental as he was, but she was the Queen of fake-pity. The Queen of 'Oh, that must be terrible', but secretly thinking 'I'm just glad it wasn't me.' Danny wasn't looking forward to telling them about Allison or about his other news.

He was thinking about coming out to his family today. At least, his parents. He thought they deserved to know, and he didn't want them to be shocked if his next soulmate was a guy, or if maybe he didn't get another soulmate and he was just... Well, he didn't know how to go about dating people if they weren't his soulmate, but he figured he'd have to find a way around that eventually. He was trying not to think on it, but it was a hard line to walk. He wanted to be relaxed about soulmates and not think about it or worry about it but he was about to travel on a train and enter a room full of soulmates, without a soulmate, for the first time in two years. He was going to turn some heads, and he'd been doing well with this stuff for the past few weeks. He'd stopped worrying and focused on work. He stopped himself from thinking about Enzo because thinking about Enzo made him yearn. They'd texted a bit but their conversations were always short and stilted. There was something missing. Danny couldn't put his finger on it, but texting Enzo felt different to talking to him. It felt like there was a wall between them. Well, there was. He wasn't imagining that.

Their night together was amazing but it was just one night. Danny kept thinking it was a mistake to try and make it feel like more. He wanted it to be more, but he knew Enzo was moving on. He knew that Enzo had a new soulmate now. Danny originally thought that Allison's voice would come back when Enzo left, but it didn't. He didn't know how to feel about that. It felt lonely without her name, or without anyone's names. Danny didn't want to rely on his soulmates to feel good, but his head felt empty without a name.

But maybe this was what he needed. He needed a chance to listen to his own voice, for a change; do what he wanted, not what someone else did; do things for him and work out his own stuff. And he had *a lot* of stuff to figure out. He had thought he was straight until a few weeks ago. When Enzo said that people get lost in relationships – Danny was offended by it but now, he couldn't stop thinking on it.

He'd started looking through his flat and finding things that he'd lost track of with Allison. He'd stopped drawing and playing his guitar; he'd stopped doing his dance workouts and stopped properly learning how to cook. There was no time, and if he had time, he spent it with Allison, or he was finishing off lesson plans, forgetting that he was once passionate about learning how to draw; forgetting that he once wanted to learn how to cook, because he didn't like relying on ready meals and canned foods. He could still play guitar, but he'd left it in the cupboard for so long that it'd fallen out of tune and was currently drenched in dust. It was his fault, of course. He should've kept playing and made time to cook, but when you get comfortable, it's easy to lose track of these things – *so* easy. Enzo had showed him that, and he hated it. He hated that Enzo was right. Would Enzo have to sacrifice parts of himself to be with Danny? He didn't want Enzo to do that. Heck, he didn't want to do that again. He loved playing guitar, and he loved drawing. He didn't want to lose anything else. He wanted to keep figuring things out and getting back on track. He wanted to explore more parts of himself, travel to different places, but right now?

Danny gulped, then forced himself into his room, chucking out underwear, socks, shirts and trousers, before grabbing his toothbrush, hairbrush and deodorant. He chucked everything in his suitcase before throwing a deep-blue and white fair isle Christmas jumper over his head. He was only going to be there for a couple of days, then he was heading home and spending Christmas day with a couple of friends from work, but he liked being prepared. He liked having multiple outfit options for no reason. He didn't really care what he looked like around his relatives. Most of them were lovely, and the judgy ones would judge him anyway, especially when he told them that Allison was gone. He didn't know how they'd react to him being bi. The look on Barney's face might be worth just announcing it to the room when he got there.

No, he wasn't doing that. The thought actively caused nerves to stab through the base of his spine. He zipped up his case then wandered around his flat, turning off switches and checking that nothing was going to set fire while he was away. He felt a moment of sadness when he switched off the Christmas lights and the Christmas tree, but he'd be back in three days, and the cosiness would be waiting for him. He hadn't known whether to put up a tree or not this year, but the fake one that him and Allison bought last year was in his cupboard, with the decorations piled on top. Leaving it there when December hit caused an impatient, wrong feeling to press through his heart, so he got it out and decorated it and did the little dance while untangling the lights. He wrapped himself in tinsel when twirling it around the tree, and almost collapsed into it while standing on his couch to place the angel on top. It was just a simple, green tree with white lights on it, silver and gold tinsel, and gold and silver baubles. It was simple, but pretty. Not as extravagant or perfect as the one that Allison decorated last year, but Danny liked it.

It made him feel cosy —maybe made him feel a little less lonely.

He chucked his coat on and did up the zip, pressed a hat over his wavy hair then opened his door and rolled his suitcase out behind him.

He didn't live too far from his parents. It was about a twenty-minute train journey —not too close but not too far, and he didn't mind the journey, even if he was dreading the destination. He slumped in an uncomfortable, scratchy seat, suitcase above his head. He leaned against the headrest, eyes tilting closed as he thought of how to explain everything to his family.

'Okay, Mum, Dad, aunties, uncles, Grandma, Grandad. I know Allison was my soulmate, but uh… she's in America now, and we're over. Oh, and um… I like guys now, too.' Maybe that would work? Maybe it was best to just get it all out there. "No," Danny muttered out loud, with a deep sigh. He needed to handle this one on one; start with the easy and get to the hard ones. Easy? Mum, Grandad, Grandma, cousins. Hard? Uncle Barney, his wife, Dad and Aunt Bexxie. The cousins wouldn't care. Barney would ask a million questions, his wife would offer fake sympathy, his mum would likely be shocked but would then just ask if Danny was okay and move on when Danny said yes. His dad – Danny had *no* clue how his dad would react. He didn't talk to his dad about this stuff, so he didn't have a gauge for it. He could scream or yell or kick him, for all he knew.

His dad wouldn't kick him. God, how would he react though? His parents weren't exactly religious or traditional, but maybe his aunts and uncles were? Maybe someone was in their family. There was always a gay cousin. That was a weird thing he'd heard, and he didn't know if *all* his cousins were straight. He had a lot of aunts and uncles, so a lot of cousins, but most of them were eleven or younger. Some could be gay, or bi, or anything, but there was no news on that, yet. His aunts and uncles and parents and grandparents were straight. Holy crap – Danny was the gay cousin.

This gathering was going to be a disaster. Could he just get drunk and hope for the best? Could he blow it off? Well, he'd obviously have to tell them eventually, and just, okay… it was three days. Danny could handle three days.

The train stopped and Danny grabbed his suitcase, stumbling to the door and wandering out, eyes flickering across the train station in a desperate attempt to find his aunt's tiny, blue car. The train station was small, –two platforms, a little room with some bathrooms, and a place to buy tickets, but that was it. There was barely any parking, and no space to get a taxi. Danny had to walk to the opposite road and stand on the edge of the street waiting for Bexxie. The cool, biting, winter air speedily stabbed through his limbs and numbed each of his fingers one by one. He sucked it in and felt it cool through his lungs, like lemonade bubbling the acid in his stomach. The sky was a light blue-grey through the gleaming, winter mist; clouds shone over the stars through patches of grey and white. There were lights off in the distance, glowing from the small town centre across the road.

Danny both loved and hated coming back here. It felt like home, but it didn't. It made him comfortable, but it didn't. It was this in-between place – purgatory. He didn't love it; he didn't hate it. It was just home; home in ways that Great Yarmouth wasn't. Well, he didn't move too far from his parents when he moved out. He happened to get a training teacher place in Great Yarmouth. He had travelled back and forth for a while, before meeting Allison and moving out there. Everything happened fast.

A little, blue car then appeared before Danny, as he smiled and waved through the window at his short, brunette aunt. She grinned back widely, before parking just in front of him. Danny quickly clambered into the car and placed the suitcase in the back seat.

"Daniel!" she yelled happily, pulling him into a suffocating hug.

Danny smiled and wrapped his arms around the woman's thin frame, the pair pulling out a moment later.

"So," Bexxie began, her grin falling to a gentle, sad smile, as her blue eyes looked over Danny worriedly. "How are you?"

Danny felt his heart clench, and his neck fall numbly against his shoulders as he leaned into the chair with his eyes closed. He was expecting this. Bexxie was an inordinately kind, caring woman. She lived down the road from his parents and was constantly around whilst Danny was growing up. If he were to enter a person in a 'Who knows Danny best?' contest, he'd put up Bexxie, and she would kill it. She could read him like a book, and it scared and frustrated him sometimes, especially when he wasn't doing too well and didn't want to talk about it.

"I'm fine," Danny replied, with a cool smile, looking over Bexxie's red, floral dress and her pale, freckled skin. She'd gotten a haircut since the last time he saw her. Her brunette hair now fell to her shoulders in little, frizzy waves. She looked pretty and smiley, as always. Her cheeks were reddened and beaming – she always looked a lot younger than she was. She was in her late thirties, but looked about twenty-four, with her smooth, perfect skin and bright, childish smile. Danny always thought she looked the same, even after all these years.

Her small, gentle smile fell slightly, as she pressed a hand into his shoulder and gently shook him. "You can tell me, you know," she stated calmly.

Danny grimaced. "I know, but I *am* fine. Can we just go and get this over with?"

Bexxie scoffed before putting the car in drive and speeding off. "It's not gonna be that bad, kiddo," she said, and Danny rolled his eyes.

"Easy for you to say. Where is Carl?" Danny asked.

Carl was Bexxie's soulmate – a shockingly shy, awkward man, who was the same height as her. He was an accountant or a pharmacist, or something. He had circle glasses and a bald, shiny head. Danny had talked to him twice, possibly? Him and Bexxie had gotten married when Danny was a kid. He'd been the ring bearer.

"He's keeping an eye on your mother," she explained, and Danny scoffed.

"You left him alone with her?"

"Of course not!" she yelled indignantly, and Danny let out a little chuckle. "I love him, you know."

"I know." Danny sighed, and a weird silence flooded the air between them as Danny's heart clenched once more.

"Wanna tell me what happened? All I know is um…"

"Facebook?" Danny asked, and Bexxie nodded silently while looking at the road. "There's not much more to tell – she left. She lives somewhere in the US now. New York, I think. I can't hear her voice anymore, but uh… there's uh…"

"Danny?"

Should he just do it? Should he just say it? How did people come out? "Uh… well, I'm okay, but I've just, well, I've uh… worked out something recently. And uh…"

"Kiddo? Whatever it is, it's okay."

Danny sighed sharply, then stared at his shoes. "I uh... I like guys," he stated quietly.

Bexxie remained silent.

"And girls... guys... um... and girls. I'm bi?" he continued awkwardly, then turned to his aunt. To his shock, she was grinning widely, while looking out the window.

"I knew it!" she exclaimed happily, and Danny's eyes widened.

"You uh... you did?"

"Yes, Danny!" she yelled, then turned to him with a slightly less-terrifying grin. "Sorry, it's just with Allison and all that, I just assumed you'd never figure it out."

"Me... figure it... how did you know?" Danny asked in deep confusion, his face lighting up a painfully hot red.

She shrugged while looking out the windscreen, and a little, shaky gulp withered through Danny's pounding heart.

"You talked about guys a bit when you were a kid, Danny. Not a lot, but a bit, and I could see it in your eyes when you looked at boys, that there was something. It's nothing to be ashamed of or anything. You're still you. I'm still proud of you, and if anything, I'm happy for you. I'm not glad that Allison left, but maybe it was for a reason?" she rambled off, then turned to Danny with a raised, knowing eyebrow, as Danny jumped and stared back at the windscreen, his face still burning.

"Yeah… uh…maybe," Danny answered weakly, then stared at his lap. Maybe she did? He hadn't put that together before. Would he have worked it out properly if Allison hadn't left? He hadn't given it any thought while they were together. He'd see a cute guy on TV and think they were cute, but that was it. He didn't know, and he would never have given himself the opportunity to be with a guy while he was still with Allison. He wasn't that kind of guy.

The little, blue car appeared outside his parents' little, red bungalow. The rose bushes by the gate were trimmed into perfect, round clouds, their white and pink petals poking out. A giant oak tree hung over and smothered the property in a deep-grey shadow through the slightly lit-up sky. The pathway to the door was lined with small, grey tiles, a little patch of green on either side.

Bexxie parked opposite one of the bushes, as Danny tugged his suitcase out from the back. She turned to Danny with one last smile, her hand pressing into his shoulder gently, while Danny's heart fell warmly through his chest.

"They'll understand, you know."

"Even Barney?" Danny scoffed out, with a raised eyebrow.

"Okay, maybe not him, but he's the exception, not the rule," she stated, and Danny rolled his eyes.

"Nice way of saying 'twat,' Bex," he said, and the pair climbed out of the car.

Danny dragged his case along the tile floor, Bexxie following behind him, as they speedily appeared before the gleaming, wooden door.

Danny's gaze tilted to Bexxie, who bit her lip and sighed. "You ready for this, kiddo?"

Danny opened his mouth to answer, but Bexxie had already opened the door, and the pair were lost in a sea of random relatives.

A couple of hours passed easily, Danny blending into the background with a glass of wine. No one asked about Allison or did more than hug him and give him kisses on the cheeks, which he just awkwardly smiled through. A few of his young cousins tried to drag him into playing on the Nintendo Switch, but he awkwardly refused and slumped into the couch beside Bexxie.

His grandma sat in the armchair opposite, wearing a long, floral skirt and a large, cream cardigan. Her dark, curly, short hair was tied back slightly, while her bright, blue eyes gleamed in the twinkling Christmas lights and the floating candlelight.

No one had bothered to turn on the main light. The carpet was new, white and incredibly soft under Danny's socked feet. The couch he sat on was about twenty years old; maybe older than him. It was an orange, floral patterned three-seater, with two matching armchairs on the left and the right. A giant flat screen sat in front of it, and the kids were currently playing Just

Dance or something. Danny didn't know and couldn't tell, they were just moving *a lot*.

There were four of his cousins there. Jenny, Annelise, Blaine and Hayden. All held a little remote and were dancing with wide smiles on their faces.

Annelise was the youngest. She was seven and currently wore a pink, sparkly dress with thick, white tights and a plastic tiara in her long, brown hair. She was not doing well at the game, due to jumping about and not paying attention, but she was having fun, so why did it matter?

Jenny was her older sister by about three years. She was desperately focusing on the game, her short, brown hair falling to her shoulders, in a little bob with a matching full fringe. She wore jeans, a hoodie and mismatched SpongeBob socks that looked a little too big for her.

Hayden and Blaine were twins. They were nine, with dark-brown, short hair and bright-green eyes. They both wore button shirts and jeans and were desperately trying to psyche the other out in terms of the game. Neither were winning. No, Jenny was kicking all their butts.

Bexxie was Annelise and Jenny's mother and was currently grinning at them both, specially looking at Annelise who kept turning and posing for her. Carl was sat next to her, nervously sipping his beer, while watching Jenny with a little smile on his face.

Barney and Sophia were sat on dining chairs between the three-seater and the armchair on the left, each looking increasingly uncomfortable while staring at Danny. Barney's purple glasses kept rising up his nose as the man flinched curious eyebrows. His nose was bigger than Danny remembered. It was like a little beak in the centre of his face. He wore a three-piece suit but had discarded the blazer, so he was currently wearing a deep-blue shirt, black tie, grey trousers and a grey waistcoat.

Sophia wore a red, velvet dress that tightly clung to her slim, bony figure. Her deep-brown hair was tied up in a high, slicked-back ponytail. Huge silver, teardrop earrings fell from her ears, appearing to weigh down the lobes painfully as they were highlighted red. Her face was incredibly defined, all her bones appearing as if sculpted through her skin. She looked scary, and if Danny was a kid, he would genuinely think that she was a witch, and she was glaring right at him.

His parents were sat together on the other armchair, with his grandad sitting on a dining chair next to his grandma. The three looked oddly relaxed. His mum was sitting on his dad's lap, with a little, wistful smile on her pale lips. Her mousy hair was tied back in a loose bun, and she currently wore a floral blouse and some grey slacks.

His dad's dark-brown, curly hair was standing up in a million weird directions. His square-rimmed glasses covered his forest-green eyes. He currently wore a blue plaid, button shirt and a pair of black trousers, as well as his old, disgusting slippers that smelt like dog slobber and looked like dribbling fish. The pair were just looking at each other, as the Christmas lights danced over their smiling faces.

His grandad currently held his grandma's hand, wearing his typical suspender trousers and a button white shirt, his half-rimmed glasses on a chain around his neck. They were smiling at each other, nothing but love in their rainbow-lit eyes, and Danny felt a little twinge of envy squeeze his heart while looking at them.

This room was *very* full –almost uncomfortably full. The air was hot and loaded, and loud with the kids dancing and giggling. Danny found it hard to focus on anything, so he just sat and sipped at his wine, praying that nobody talked to him.

"So, Danny," Barney's drawling voice started.

Danny sighed harshly while suppressing an eyeroll. Yeah, prayer never worked for him.

"Where's Allison?"

And… here we go.

Silence hit the room like a boulder. The kids quietened down and turned to stare at Danny. All the adults placed their drinks down and turned to Danny, as the man gulped and stared at his lap. The silence got more and more clawing, as Danny's heart began spinning through his chest. He felt everything within him tense, then relax, in a strange, shivering ache.

Bexxie placed a hand on his shoulder, and Danny's gaze jumped to her gentle, smiling face. A sigh escaped him once more as he turned back to Barney's overly curious expression. His whiskey breath flew through the air and slapped his nostrils, as an inhuman smirk appeared on his bird-like face.

"She left," Danny stated simply. "We're not together anymore."

The silence got worse, as everyone's eyes widened.

"But she was your…" Sophia began, and Danny rolled his eyes at her sharply.

"Soulmate, yes, but she moved away and we split up," Danny said simply, while glaring at her.

The silence suddenly got worse. Danny could almost feel the rancid judgment floating through the hot, heavy air. It stung his skin like radiation, as he took a quick sip of wine and sighed once more.

"But I'm okay, and it's okay. Sometimes these things just…" He shrugged. "… Don't work out."

"But you're *soulmates*," Sophia repeated, and Danny rolled his eyes once more.

"Not anymore, we're not," Danny stated.

"That's not how it works, Daniel," Sophia argued.

"Then explain why her voice is gone," he replied with a little, cocky grin.

The silence then got weird, as everyone gasped and stared at Danny with varying looks of 'Huh?'

"But that uh… you can't…" Sophia began muttering.

"Danny, do you just not hear a voice anymore?" his mum asked gently, while rising from her seat and gently kneeling before her son, concern lacing her light-green eyes, as she looked up at him.

"Uh, yeah…uh, no, I don't," he said, while looking at his mum. "But I'd…uh, there is uh…" Okay, so he was doing this. "There was another voice, and um it uh…"

"You got another soulmate?" Barney asked aggressively, and Danny let out a sharp sigh, while glaring at the floor.

"Yes, but just, okay," he began, then got to his feet speedily, turning to face the room, pointedly avoiding Barney and Sophia.

"So, where is she?" Sophia asked, and Danny felt his heart drop like a penny through the waters of a fountain.

"It wasn't a she," he said quickly, his eyes closed, and the silence no longer felt clawing. It felt positively frozen. It felt like the air in the room had risen then collapsed to the floor in a pile of heavy mist. It was horrific and uncomfortable, and Danny felt his body squirm painfully.

"So, you're gay now?" Barney squawked, and Danny scoffed, opening his eyes as a waft of whiskey breath hit him once more.

"Bi, actually," he corrected, with a little smile.

"So, where's this guy?" Sophia asked, and Danny rolled his eyes.

"His voice is gone, too." he stated. "I wasn't lying when I said there's no voice in my head."

The clawing silence fell once more.

"But I'm okay, and this is okay, and just... yeah." He shrugged, specifically smiling at his mum, as she got to her feet. "Is um... is this okay?" He didn't know what he'd do if she said no, but it made him feel moderately better asking.

"Oh, honey," his mum said weakly, then raced up and wrapped her arms around his back. "I'm so sorry," she muttered.

Danny wrapped his arms around his mum, too. "It's okay, Mum. I'm okay, I promise."

"Really?" she asked, then pulled back from the hug.

Danny smiled genuinely, feeling a little nervous flutter rattle his heart. "Really," he adamantly stated, then turned his gaze to Barney and Sophia, then to his dad, then his grandparents, then the kids, then Bexxie and Carl.

Most of them were smiling or staring in awe. Barney and Sophia were looking him up and down sceptically, but neither seemed up for saying anything else. His dad was giving him a strange, wide-eyed look, that made Danny pause.

"Dad?" he asked, and his dad jolted, shaking his head in surprise. "Are you all right?"

"Yeah," he answered immediately. "Yeah, son."

Danny's eyebrow cocked, but he shook it off when his dad smiled. The room fell back into easy

211

conversation after a few minutes, and Danny collapsed back onto the couch with his mum beside him, wine glasses clutched in their hands, as they laughed and joked about nothing. Danny felt a huge weight lift free from his shoulders as a sharp, slow breath inflated his lungs. He found himself walking from the room after a little while, his attention being drawn to his phone, as he pulled up Enzo's contact and sighed.

Was this meant to happen? Soulmates were decided by the universe. Enzo was picked for him by the universe for one night. They were made for each other for one night. Maybe Enzo was just supposed to get him on track after Allison. Maybe the pair were never meant to be more than passing ships, but Danny couldn't find it in himself to be resentful of that. He loved that night. He needed that night.

And what if he wasn't destined to have another soulmate? What if Allison and Enzo were it for him? Maybe they were. Maybe Danny wasn't meant to have more than those two, but what he had had with them both, he wouldn't trade for the universe. He loved it. He'd do it all over again if he could, and sure, there were no voices now, but it was quiet and it was calm, and there was time. There was always time. He didn't feel it before, but he felt it now. Things had changed, but he was ready to figure things out and keep moving. The universe didn't get to dictate everything. It was maybe there to point him to the right people and in the right direction, but it didn't get to decide everything. From now on, Danny was going to take things the way he wanted to.

He pulled up Enzo's contact once more, typing out a quick 'Merry Christmas, Enzo.' The corners of his mouth lifted into a little smile when the reply bubble appeared.

'Merry December 16th, you weirdo' came the reply, and the mousy-haired man scoffed, before wandering back into the living room.

Chapter 10
REBECCA

Screw men. They all suck. They're all annoying and loud, they just eat your food and fart in your bed. They tell you off for stealing their hoodie, then they bloody leave and act like it was all your fault. He freakin took the blender! That was her blender. Her grandma bought them that blender, and he never used that damn blender. He just took it to be petty.

Rebecca glared at the coffee maker, standing in her office in her black skirt suit and wedge-heeled shoes. A pair of skin-coloured tights covered her thick, muscular legs, and her long, black hair was currently tied in a high ponytail. Her skin was pale, and glittering in the daylight streaming through the window, but her face was sunken and pissed. She was the queen of resting bitchface. Her workmates reminded her of this a lot, but today? Today, she was seething. She didn't even know why she came into work.

His voice was gone. Keith's voice was gone. Her soulmate had completely and utterly disappeared. They'd broken up under a week ago! It'd been four freakin days, and they'd been together for three years, and now, his voice was gone. She didn't even know that could happen! He was her soulmate, and she wasn't sad. No, she was angry. Why would the universe do that? And what was she supposed to do now? Just go through life without a soulmate?

That sounded good; that sounded freakin great. Guys sucked and dating sucked, and everything was hard and frustrating and annoying. Dating was a waste a time. Soulmates were a waste of time. She was better off by herself, and she was buying another freakin blender when she got home today. Keith was not having that goddamn blender. What else had he taken? Where had he gone, actually? He didn't know anyone in the city! Was he couch-surfing with one of Rebecca's friends? He'd better not be.

Eh, it didn't matter. She wasn't seeing him again, anyway. Maybe she could go to a bar tonight and find a nice man to hook up with, then she could post it on Instagram and piss off Keith or make him feel as bad as she did. Had her voice gone, too? Probably. It didn't matter anyway.

The New Year had been weird. Her and Keith had broken up before the clock struck midnight. He'd grabbed his stuff, stealing the bloody blender, and darting from the apartment. It'd been four days since then, and he'd blocked her on everything. She was just trying to message him about the rest of his things but no, he was gone. Maybe she'd burn them – burn his stupid jumpers and those goddamn manga books that he never read.

It was her first day back at work. She didn't think 'Oh, my soulmate left me on New Year's' would get her out of the first day. It might've done, but she needed to get out of the flat anyway.

She was on lunch now, but the coffee machine wasn't working and it was driving her mad –mad enough to pull out her purse and storm out the office to find lunch elsewhere.

She appeared in town centre and headed straight to Gregg's, grabbing a cup of black coffee and a sausage roll, then angrily slumping onto a bench, while glaring at the jewellery store opposite. There were barely any people here. It was the first Monday in January. A lot of people didn't start work until tomorrow or the day after. Rebecca was just unlucky on that front.

She worked as a complaints manager for an energy company. She basically spent days being yelled at by people. She'd note down the complaint and report it. The other managers would fix the issues and she'd call those customers back to explain, and that was it. It wasn't the worst job in the world, but it wasn't the best. She didn't hate it on most days but today, she just hated everything and everyone – men especially.

Any man that got into her path was just asking for it.

"Huh hm," a deep voice muttered, and Rebecca was instantly irritated, feeling all the blood pop through her veins like party poppers.

She tilted her gaze up to the man before her, her eyes going wide as her head fell even more silent. A gust of heavy air inflated her skull and caused her ears to ring, as a sharp piece of static nonsense flittered behind her eyes and gave her a headache.

A moment passed, and she resisted the urge to groan while staring at the tall, dark-haired man in the light-blue jeans and deep-orange jumper. He was just smiling at her with folded arms and a deeply casual air about him. A deeply smug, casual air that made Rebecca's blood boil.

She stood up speedily, as the static faded and the air gusted out. Her fists clutched her sausage roll and her coffee before she stomped off and her mind fell silent. The world fell silent. The music blaring from above faded, and she stopped in her tracks with a deep, deep gulp, as something started rising through the back of her mind and footsteps started petering behind her. 'Enzo' a deep voice whispered, and Rebecca felt her heart clatter to a heavy stop, as the man appeared beside her.

"Okay, Rebecca," he stated, and her eyes flashed to him dangerously.

"Don't," she said, then put her hand out.

'Enzo' blinked in surprise, then put his hands up in surrender, while speedily walking along beside her.

"Look, I know this is a lot, but…"

"Don't. Just don't," she growled. "Just leave me the fuck alone. I've gotta get back to work."

She then sped off into the distance, while Enzo stopped still and watched her go, blinking at her back in confusion.

Good. She didn't want to talk to him anyway. Who the hell was he? He couldn't be her soulmate. Keith was her soulmate, but why could she hear his voice? Didn't matter –doesn't matter. He was just a stranger; an annoyingly attractive stranger with a nice, deep voice that kept echoing through her head.

She got back to the office and rode the elevator to the sixth floor, tossing her sausage roll wrapper in the bin as she stumbled over to her desk and chucked on her headset. She didn't even think for the rest of the day, her mind getting completely lost in other people's complaints. A man ranted to her about how his contract price had gone up without warning, a girl talked about how her power kept going out, and a few talked about signal and Wi-Fi, which wasn't even their company's fault. Before Rebecca knew it, it was four p.m., and she was gathering her things to go home, her mind blissfully empty, aside the dull, whispering voice stating 'Enzo', which she shoved down through her brain with ferocity.

She got her bag, chucked on her coat then raced out the office, taking in the cool, evening air with a light, awkward smile, as she sighed and closed her eyes. Her headache faded to a dull roar, as she made her way over to the bus stop.

Her office was in the town centre, and she lived in a little borough, about twenty minutes away. The buses were pretty few and far between currently, but she didn't mind the journey home. She liked the quiet but not too quiet nature of it. She hated getting home and her house just being silent. It'd only been four days, but it felt like lifetimes passed in the silence.

The bus showed a few minutes later, and Rebecca chucked in her earphones then slumped into the backseat, leaning on the cool window and peering out with tired eyes.

Streetlamps, trees, houses, little shops and fish and chip shops sped by, as she got lost in her music and breathed. The bus wasn't too busy. There were four, maybe five people on here. There was an older couple with a giant golden retriever, a lady with a baby, and a teenager with more piercings than skin on her face. There was another person; another person on the end of the bench where Rebecca sat; another person that was causing the nerves in Rebecca's body to stand on end. Her heart started to cave in painfully, as the voice she'd been drowning out kept getting louder and louder and louder. She grunted, then glared across at the dark-haired man, tugging out an earphone, then catching his light-brown eyes, her breath hitching in the process as frustration tugged at her veins.

"You stalking me or something?" she asked with a raised eyebrow, and Enzo rolled his eyes while looking at her.

"Kinda didn't have a choice when you ran off earlier," he muttered, and Rebecca scoffed.

"Well, I don't know you, and you followed me home. I could easily call the police," she stated, and Enzo's eyes widened.

"You wouldn't," he breathed.

"What makes you think that?" Rebecca asked coolly, already typing a '9' on her phone.

Enzo scoffed in deep shock, a frown falling on his face as he shuffled over to her. "Look, I don't know what's going on with you, but you don't wanna do that," he said evenly, sitting a couple seats closer to Rebecca.

A weird, begging twinge floated through his golden irises. She looked at him and gulped, her hand falling to her lap as a weird, warm, familiar rush flooded her heart.

A smirk appeared on Enzo's face, and Rebecca felt annoyance twinge once more.

"You know what I am, don't you?"

Rebecca scoffed, then tilted her gaze outside, thankfully recognizing the street, clicking the button and standing up.

"No," she said firmly. "Coz you can't be, and I'm not yours, and I'm not interested, so…" She then leaned into his face, as the bus lurched to a stop. Enzo blinked dumbly while staring at her. "Go home, Enzo."

Enzo scoffed, and Rebecca stepped off the bus. He let her get a few steps ahead, then followed her off. The doors clicked shut behind him, as she began walking down the street to her little house.

"See, you made a mistake there," Enzo stated easily, before Rebecca managed to get her earphone in.

Rebecca growled under her breath. "Oh yeah?" she asked and Enzo grinned.

"You revealed that you knew my name," he stated, and Rebecca stopped, turning to him with a sharp glare. "You feel it too, and you know it."

She rolled her eyes and folded her arms. "You're not my soulmate. Keith is."

"And who is Keith?" Enzo asked, and a sharp stab of boiled rage invaded her heart.

"None of your business."

Enzo scoffed and rolled his eyes pointedly. "You're quite aggressive, you know that," he said, and Rebecca let out a deep puff of angry air.

"You're quite frustrating, you know that," she retorted, and Enzo grinned.

"It's been said before," he said, and Rebecca rolled her eyes.

"I'm not surprised," she stated. "Now leave me alone," she demanded, then began walking off. "You're not my soulmate. I don't want a soulmate. This whole 'soulmate' thing is bullshit."

"Whoa, okay," Enzo said, and leaned back in surprise while walking alongside her. "Unfortunately, that's not how these things work."

"Why won't you just piss off?" she asked, and Enzo rolled his eyes.

"Coz I can't," he answered honestly.

"Oh, you absolutely can," Rebecca replied. "I will, and can, call the police. Why can't you just leave without being dragged away in a bright-blue car?"

Enzo shrugged. "Coz I'm intrigued as to why you're so determined to get away from me, when I'm just here to help you," he answered, and Rebecca lowered her eyebrows, stopping in her tracks and turning to the man.

"Help me?" she asked.

"Yeah," Enzo admitted. "You obviously have some issues with this soulmate crap. I'm here to help you with them."

Rebecca spluttered, warmth spreading like honey through her heart for a moment, only to be stamped out by frustration.

"Help me with them? Just who do you think you are?" she asked.

"Like it or not, I am your soulmate," Enzo replied. "Keith's name is gone, isn't it?"

Rebecca jolted, and she felt her eye twitch.

"Taking that as a yes. I'm here to help you move past that."

Rebecca scoffed, then rolled her eyes fiercely. "What makes you think I need, or even want, your help? I don't even bloody know you."

"Oh, you do, and you know you do," Enzo stated easily with a little, cocky smile. "Just trust me. Just trust me for ten minutes. That's all I ask. If I don't help you in that time, or if I don't have the answers that you're looking for then fine, chuck me out."

Rebecca looked over the man, feeling waves of frustrating but comforting warmth float through her veins, as she stared into his golden eyes. Her teeth jutted through her bottom lip, as her gaze fell to the ground.

"If I do trust you for that time, and you do fail in convincing me of anything, then you'll leave me alone?" she asked, then tilted her gaze back up to the man.

"You have my word," he stated seriously, and Rebecca nodded.

"Okay, then come on," she muttered.

She led the stranger to her small, red brick house and dragged him in, locking the wooden, blue door behind them.

They appeared in her small, cream living room, Enzo instinctively taking off his shoes and putting his jacket on the hook. Ten minutes – he had ten minutes.

Rebecca kept her shoes on but did chuck her coat and bag on the hook, as she led the dark-haired stranger to the couch.

He sat down immediately. Rebecca sat on a cushion away from him and desperately attempted to not roll her eyes.

"So, ten minutes – go," she demanded, her eyes glaring into Enzo's.

"How do you feel about soulmates?" he asked, and Rebecca cocked a brow.

"This is how you want to use your time?" she asked, and Enzo nodded with a knowing smile.

Rebecca just sighed and stared across the room, content in letting this idiot waste his time so she could just chuck him out and be rid of him. "I feel like they're full of crap."

"Why?"

"Because there's no guarantee that you'll have anything in common, or that you'll get along. You could be linked to someone you hate forever, and there's just no logic to it. I don't want all my relationships to be chosen by some universe thing that knows nothing about who or what I deserve to be with." Rebecca ranted, pointedly glaring at Enzo with that last statement.

The man's smile fell.

"People are always fucking changing, too. Keith changed. I hated who he became in the end. He was just an angry dick who never listened. That didn't change because we were soulmates. He was an asshole, and I'm glad he's gone."

"Then why aren't you happy to have a new soulmate?" Enzo asked, and Rebecca rolled her eyes.

"Because I don't *want* one. I don't want to just be constantly shackled to another person; having to change things about me to fit what they want; having to move places to make them happy. I don't want to *have* to love someone just coz the universe says 'Hey, this guy is your soulmate.' No, screw that. I get to choose, and I choose no more dating assholes who don't appreciate me, who don't see how hard I freakin try and just what I bring to a relationship, which is *everything*. You think Keith ever put any effort in with me?" she continued to rant, her eyes twitching as Enzo's brown eyes grew wide. "No. No. Fuck no. The guy never cared. He just left – on New Year's! Do you know how crappy that was? He was my soulmate. I thought he was gonna propose, or we were gonna get a better place, but nooo, he just grabbed his shit and left. Soulmates are bullshit, Enzo. I don't care what you have to say about it."

Enzo opened and closed his mouth, but no words came out, Rebecca found the anger in her head getting hotter and hotter, while looking over his freckled face.

"I get that," he muttered after a minute, and Rebecca jolted with a little, doubting smirk. "And I get that you're angry right now. Leaving on New Year's? That's a crappy thing to do."

"Right?" she scoffed out, having not been able to talk to anyone about this before now. "He was such an asshole, as well. He took the goddamn blender! We

225

were together three bloody years. I'm never getting that stupid time back. Like, just what was the point? He never deserved me. My mum was right. I just shouldn't date people. People suck."

She folded her arms, while Enzo looked over her curiously.

"So, you're not sad at all that he left? You're just angry?" Enzo asked awkwardly, and Rebecca nodded in a 'duh' fashion. "What happened with you guys?"

Rebecca scoffed. "What didn't?" she asked. "Met when we were nineteen. Had sex on the first date. Moved in a month later and met each other's families a week after that. We were like best friends, just talked about everything. My friends were *so* jealous, coz Keith was freakin hot. The dude could've been a model, but nope, he also happened to be a goddamn genius, so he studied to be a doctor. He was always stressed, always too busy for me, so I picked up the slack. I cleaned, I tidied, I cooked, and for a little while, I didn't mind it. But then he stopped talking to me, and then he stopped wanting to go out. We hadn't had a date night in six weeks when he left. He pulled away and I tried to get him back, but after a little while, it just wasn't freakin worth it," she ranted off, then snapped her mouth closed, turning to Enzo curiously. Why the hell was she telling this random stranger all this crap?

"Oh," he muttered after a second.

"That wasn't even the worst bit. We were supposed to move last year, but he got a place on a stupid course up here, and it wasn't even a choice – we had to stay. He completely dictated our relationship – all the decisions – and just expected me to go along with it coz we were soulmates. He never once asked what I wanted. He wanted to go to this school, so we stayed, and just..." she continued to ramble, then growled and shoved a hand through her hair. "And now I have to tell everyone that we split; that he left and that his voice is just gone. My family are going to think I'm such an idiot. My mum will just be all 'I told you so' and 'You should never have dated that man; he gave me uppity vibes – you were never gonna be enough for him.'" Her eyebrows lowered at that last statement, her mother's shrill voice stabbing through her mind in a burst of painful red, as her blood started to heat up.

"What would you have wanted?" Enzo asked, and Rebecca's gaze snapped to him furiously.

The man placed his hands up placatingly, while Rebecca rolled her eyes.

"I don't know, but we both agreed when we moved here that it wasn't permanent. It was until he finished his bachelor's. He finished it a month ago, and where are we?"

"Still here?" Enzo asked, and Rebecca laughed humourlessly.

"I never liked it. I hate it. All the people are rude, my job sucks and the hours are crazy. I finished my degree a year ago now, and I'm nowhere near close to doing something I want to do, and it's all Keith's bloody fault," she grumbled, then gritted her teeth while glaring at the floor.

"Sorry, but how?" Enzo asked, and Rebecca snapped her gaze back up to find him looking at her curiously.

"Haven't you been listening?" she asked, then sighed sharply. "We moved here because of him."

"Where did you want to live? What do you wanna do? Why does being here prevent that?" Enzo fired off rapidly, eyebrows lowering periodically.

Rebecca felt an angry sword of fire penetrate her heart. She stood up, only seeing red, her eyes twitching and her head pounding. Enzo's eyes widened in fear, as a shaky gulp fell through his throat.

"He wanted to do his course here, but his course. The guy worked for a year at a hospital, for free. Guess who had to work so we could pay rent?" she ranted, her eye twitching and voice rising, as Enzo began to collapse into himself. "We moved here, and he was still studying. When he wasn't at school, he was reading about school. He never had time for anything, and his loans barely paid for anything, so guess who had to work again? And you think I had time to even think about going for a master's, or starting my career and going into something I had *no* training for, when we needed money?"

Enzo opened and closed his mouth, while Rebecca breathed in air like an exhausted gorilla.

"No?"

"No," she confirmed with a sharp sigh, then slumped back in her seat.

"But what's stopping you now?" Enzo asked, and Rebecca slumped further.

"This place is leased, and I'm used to my job now, and there's no point in moving when that idiot's gonna come back any day," she stated.

"Why would he come back?"

"Coz we're soulmates, or whatever," Rebecca grunted out. "I don't want him back. The guy can go jump off a cliff for all I care, but you know, we're stuck, so, yeah ... there's no point."

"Rebecca, that's not how this works," Enzo stated slowly, a genuine, kind tone in his voice that made the rage in Rebecca's blood start to curdle.

"Of course, it's how it bloody works," she stated aggressively, and Enzo rolled his eyes.

"See, that's what everyone th…"

"No, no. I don't care what you say here. Soulmates are soulmates. Keith is coming back because he *has to*. I don't care whose voice I hear. I've heard his voice for *years*; put up with his crap for *years*. I love that useless idiot, and he is coming back," she ranted off, then stood and glared up at her tiny clock. "Ten minutes."

Enzo sighed sharply, then stood. "Fine." He glared at her before trudging over to her door. "I get it, Rebecca. Keith asked a lot of you, and I get that it doesn't seem worth it now, but I'm here, and the universe gave me your name for a reason, and I think it's to prove to you that… well…"

"You're not my soulmate, Enzo," Rebecca said bluntly, then went to the door and opened it. "You won't ever be. Everyone only gets one, and mine's coming back, so just…"

"Rebecca," Enzo stated simply, placing his hands out once more.

"Don't," she replied, and Enzo placed his hand on her shoulder as a weird, warm, familiar flash flooded her body and she shivered. Both closed their eyes for a moment, before Rebecca growled, "Get out."

"You know you feel it, too, and you know you and Keith weren't right. I know there was a lot going on in your relationship, and you don't have to stick with someone *just* because you're soulmates. It's not how it works. If you're not happy, then get out – it's that simple," he said, and Rebecca snarled, slamming the door and appearing directly in Enzo's face.

"It's not though, is it? My parents are soulmates – been together thirty years. My cousins and my sisters – even my freakin niece. Wanna know what it's like to tell your family that you're not marrying the guy that the universe picked for you?"

"Better than marrying him then being miserable forever," Enzo growled out, anger rising slowly and steadily through his limbs, as he glared back. Rebecca was tweaking his last nerve on this crap.

"It's not though!" she yelled. "Because it's not my goddamn decision. Three blasted years! I heard his voice for three days, then it was gone. The guy just walked out on me. He just freakin left."

"Then why do you have to stay and wait for him?"

"Because he's my soulmate!"

"Okay, we're going in circles," Enzo muttered, then sighed, placing a hand on his head to block the headache.

"Yes, we are, now get out," Rebecca fumed, then tilted her gaze to the door.

"Rebecca, you know that you have every right to decide what is good for you and what isn't…"

"Urgh, you're giving me a headache," she grumbled, then glared at Enzo. "Yes, I know that. I'm not a moron."

"Then why wait for him?"

"Because he's m…"

"And if you say because he's your soulmate, then I will break something in this room," Enzo threatened, before she could get out the rest of her sentence.

She sighed sharply through her nose, then headed back to the couch, slumping down on it with an eyeroll.

"Three years. It's hard not to love someone after that long," she admitted. "One night – one wrong night –that's all it took. So many things were right before then."

"What happened?" Enzo asked quietly, not moving from beside the door.

"He left," she stated. "He just gave up. I'd been trying to get us back on track for a long time, and he just didn't care. He gave up and moved on. Then his voice was just…"

"Gone," Enzo finished for her, and a stone-dead silence flooded the room, as anger faded through Rebecca's bones and disappeared into the couch.

Enzo gulped, then appeared at her side, placing a hand on her shoulder once more. "Look. I know it's hard, and I'm sorry, but I can help," he stated slowly.

The calm, warm flush flooded her heart as she tilted to look in his eyes.

The pair were maybe an inch apart, possibly two. Close enough for Rebecca to smell Enzo's deodorant. He smelt fresh and clean, like washing powder or generic shower gel. His hair was cascading around his face and causing little, curled shadows. His eyes seemed to glow gold in the low light of Rebecca's apartment. His face was soft, gentle and sweet, with little freckles over his nose. Rebecca felt the moisture in her mouth disappear while looking over him.

Her heart began trying to penetrate her chest, as she gulped and desperately tried to bring any moisture back, her head swimming in the wonderful warmth and the heart-quaking tension. Her limbs turned to jelly and she just tumbled forward, eyes closing and the room disappearing around her.

"Whoa, whoa, whoa," Enzo stated quickly, then retracted his hand and stood up, as the pair widened their eyes. "That is not what I meant."

"Then what did you mean?" Rebecca demanded, embarrassment quickly dissolving into anger, as she stood up strongly and looked over Enzo.

The pair were about the same height, with Rebecca being maybe an inch taller.

"I thought you were in love with that Keith guy," Enzo stated in confusion, and Rebecca rolled her eyes sharply.

"You come here and tell me that you're here to help with this bullshit soulmate thing, and that you are my soulmate and that you feel the same way I do. You're a stranger, Enzo."

"But I'm not."

"Exactly!"

"That's just how this soulmate thing works, you know that," Enzo stated, and Rebecca let out an angered breath.

"You know how all this sounds, right?" she asked, and Enzo lowered a confused brow. "It sounds like a come on. Heck, it feels like one – with the shoulder touches and the calling out to me – you're just coming onto me." She shrugged, and Enzo rolled his eyes while folding his arms.

"I don't do that," he stated evenly, and Rebecca cocked her eyebrow.

"I know a come on when I hear it," she argued, and Enzo's eye twitched.

"That's not what this is," he argued, his tone slightly rising. "And even if it was, why would you want to sleep with a stranger if you're waiting on someone else?"

"Coz he's not here, is he?" Rebecca argued sharply. "He hasn't really been here for a long, long time."

Enzo's eyebrows lowered further. "What's that mean?" he asked, and Rebecca scoffed through her nose.

"It means that he hasn't been here," she repeated.

"No, no, Rebecca," he stated, and she felt her breath catch. "What does that mean?"

She jolted slightly.

"You slept with someone else, didn't you? That's why he left."

"No, that's…" she began, then sighed angrily. "He was always… he was… and there was this… urgh, why do I need to explain myself to you? Get out."

Enzo scoffed, then slowly shook his head at Rebecca. "Okay, so you have the nerve to rant about how you're too good for him and about how much you did for the pair of you, and then he pulls away, and I get that that sucks, but it doesn't justify being unfaithful. If you're unhappy, just leave," he ranted, and Rebecca rolled her eyes.

"He's my soulmate," she stated. "There was no 'leaving'."

"There is, if you're kissing other guys," he argued, with a raised eyebrow.

"Get out," Rebecca growled once more. "You have no idea what I went through for him, and what I did for our relationship. I screwed up once; do you know how many times he screwed up? The man was an asshole."

"But you cheated," Enzo argued back, and Rebecca felt anger begin to choke her.

"He cheated. He pulled away. He stopped talking. He stopped trying, and just expected me to."

"So leave!" Enzo yelled. "Don't cheat. I get that it sucks and that it's hard, but…"

"You don't get it, though," Rebecca argued. "This wasn't my fault."

"It was," Enzo growled out. "He may have closed the door but you locked it in chains and threw it in the ocean. He shouldn't have pulled away, he should've talked to you but still… it just doesn't give you the right to cheat. You were unhappy, break up."

"He's my soulmate."

"Not anymore," Enzo argued back, and the anger started pressing up through Rebecca's nose and shoving through her brain in a red-hot trail of sludge.

"Get out," Rebecca repeated, and scoffed in shock. "You have no right to judge me on this. You don't know me, and you don't know my relationship. I worked *hard* for us. I made *one* mistake. He made thousands."

"Your mistake was different."

"It wasn't," she stated, then glared through the ground. "He should've stayed. He should've tried."

"When you gave up?" Enzo asked, with a raised eyebrow.

"I tried for years. What did he do?"

Enzo scoffed and shook his head.

"What?"

"Sorry," he muttered. "You're so self-involved, you know that? Do you have it in you to think about what he was going through? Or what you did to him? Did he catch you? Is that why he left?"

Rebecca opened her mouth then closed it, while glaring through the man.

"Taking that as a yes. You broke him, Rebecca. Whether he did talk to you or not is irrelevant. You broke him, and that was *your* choice. You weren't happy? Talk to him. I don't care how much time he didn't seem to have. Find a moment and grab him. You're *really* not happy, then leave. You don't cheat on someone you love because you're just hurting them."

"And what do you know about that?"

"I know how much it hurts to be betrayed by someone you love. I've seen it; I've felt it. It's like being stabbed through the heart. I get it that him pulling away sucked and that your relationship wasn't easy, but you have to know that what you did was wrong," he stated, and Rebecca scoffed.

"Get out," she repeated. "And leave me alone. Ten minutes – that was the deal."

"Gladly," he growled, then marched to the door, opened it and stormed out, slamming it behind him as silence quaked over Rebecca.

The name 'Enzo' flooded through her head still, as she glared at the ground.

Chapter 11
ENZO

Five years of doing this and Enzo could honestly say that he'd always liked his soulmates. He always understood them; always helped them; always figured out ways to make them feel better; always had patience and stood by their side. He loved his soulmates. They were different people, with different goals and different smiles, but they were all beautiful and kind and wonderful.

He didn't doubt that Rebecca had tried, but something in him snapped when he found out that she cheated. Heck, something in him snapped when he heard her call this whole soulmate thing 'bullshit'. She talked about trying in her relationship, made it sound like this was all Keith's fault, and she just didn't see it. She genuinely didn't. She shattered her soulmate's heart, then had the nerve to blame the universe and him, but never herself. There was nothing Enzo could do for her, if she didn't see what she did as wrong; if she saw herself as flawless, then tried to kiss him while being in love with someone else. Enzo couldn't help her. It was all on her. *She* needed to see that she was wrong, and she needed to figure it out. Enzo didn't have the patience for her crap. She was self-centred and frustrating. Her attitude on soulmates was killing him.

It was killing him more because he felt like this whole soulmate thing was ridiculous. He felt that people had so many preconceived notions, and so many people stayed in unhappy relationships because the 'universe' picked people for people. If Keith wasn't Rebecca's soulmate, would she have cheated? Probably not. She would've broken up with him, and that would've been that – maybe. But she didn't seem to see that she cheated, and that was a problem. She didn't seem to see that *any* of this was her fault. She just kept calling the guy she loved an asshole, then spoke about how hard she had tried, how much he didn't talk and how that justified cheating on him.

Enzo wasn't a hundred percent sure what made him feel so righteous on this matter. It may have been Marlow, or any of his other soulmates. He'd been witness to a lot of people walking out. His parents fought like hormonal, possessed teenagers on the best day. Enzo was pretty sure that they hated each other. He'd never asked, but the pair barely spent any time together; never hugged or held hands around him or kissed. The only time he saw his mother was when she stayed at his to hide from his dad. She never talked about it. She came; she ate; she slept. They watched TV, sometimes, she never looked happy, but if Enzo asked, she was fine. She was always fine, but Enzo knew it was a lie. It was obvious. He hated seeing her like that, and he knew that it was his dad's fault. He felt the urge to go and scream at him sometimes, but he didn't. His dad was just sad, and he was kind of a jerk, but he was still Enzo's dad. It was all a scrambled mess in Enzo's head, and it didn't matter. It wasn't his relationship.

Rebecca was right to kick him out, and Enzo was one hundred percent sure that she wouldn't let him back in. He didn't have any right to judge her on her actions or her words. He hadn't been cheated on before, but he knew what it did to people, and it wasn't justifiable in his head. People can always talk about things and figure things out, or they can just break up. It's not easy. It's never easy, but it's better than shattering a person and making them doubt how worthy they are and how much they can trust other partners. Open relationships and casual relationships are a thing, but if you haven't set those limits, then you're just being unfair to a person who loves you, and a person that you love. It sucks, and it hurts.

It caused a weird twist in Enzo's gut, and a strained wisp of black frustration stabbed through the back of his head. He didn't get it. He genuinely didn't get how people could do that or how Rebecca couldn't see that she was in the wrong, and if she didn't get it, then Enzo had a hunch that him telling her was not going to do anything more than anger her.

She needed to do this alone. Enzo just didn't want to deal with it. It was more than that, but he had felt his whole-body tense angrily around Rebecca. He had felt it get worse when she admitted to cheating. He'd never felt that with one of these people. He'd always liked them. His soulmates were salt of the earth, sweet, kind and wonderful in their own ways, and Enzo loved them through and through. He'd defend them to holy hell, but Rebecca? She was stubborn, angry, frustrating and argumentative, and every part of him was tense around her. He didn't like how she had treated him on the bus or in town. He understood how she must have felt with a stranger approaching her –not exactly a great opener – but she obviously felt that he was her soulmate, and she just chose to walk away! And all things considered, creepiness aside, that hurt. It hurt and it was rude. Why had the universe paired them together?

Enzo didn't have a clue, but he hated the universe for it. It'd been a *long* time since he wanted to curse the universe –curse all this soulmate crap. In what universe would him and Rebecca be happy together? No universe. That was it. She was abrasive and pessimistic and just plain … *gah*! She might be nice underneath all that crap, but she still cheated on her soulmate. She needed to better herself and fix her attitude, and Enzo wasn't the person to fix it. He was done.

One day, and he was done. Normally, he'd try a little harder. A few of his previous soulmates had been more reluctant to accept his help, so he wasn't shocked by it. He was hurt by it, but he kept trying. He was patient, and they let him in. They didn't argue with him, walk away, or say that he was coming onto them then

241

kick him out. He'd argued with all his soulmates in some capacity, except for the ones who were sad or excessively drunk. He'd argued with them, but he'd always been able to reason with them. Rebecca felt beyond reason. Not just that. He didn't want to help her. He didn't want to go back there. Had he ever felt that before? He'd never felt that before.

She made him feel worthless and awful; frustrated and angry. She made him feel just plain stupid. She made him worry that he'd accidentally come on to every soulmate that he'd ever met, or just been creepy and frustrating. Did none of them want his help? Was he doing the right thing? Why was he like this if it wasn't to help people? Why couldn't he just have a normal soulmate and fall in love like everyone else? Why was he cursed to just meet a new person every few months? Was he ever meant to end up with anyone? Did he even want that when he could potentially end up with someone like Rebecca? Maybe Rebecca wasn't that bad deep down, but today she was a self-involved asshole who didn't seem to care that she'd hurt a person she loved, when he hurt her first. She was a child – a spoilt, selfish child – and Enzo was continually frustrated by her.

Whoa, wait. He didn't want to end up with anyone. He wanted this life, didn't he? God, what did he want? He didn't want to be like Rebecca. He never wanted to be like that. If he ever got to a place where he was that complacent and unhappy yet was still waiting for his other half to come back, then that'd suck. He didn't want to be with someone just because they were his soulmate. That's why his parents were together and why so many of his other soulmates were together. He'd seen a cacophony of unhappy people together because they thought they had to be. He never wanted that, but was that all that soulmates were? There had to be soulmates out there who were happy together. There *had* to be, right?

Enzo was cynical about this crap. He preferred being alone. He wanted to leave and move on, but he didn't want to believe that there was no purpose at all to people having soulmates. Just because he wasn't meant to have *only* one, and just because his parents were miserable, didn't mean that nobody worked out, right?

It was hard for Enzo to see relationships as anything but pointless, with the people he'd met and the relationships he'd heard about. People sucked, and it was hard to argue otherwise when you spent your days travelling about and hanging out with people who'd lost their soulmates in one way or another, or who had never met and would never meet them, so why did what Rebecca did to her first soulmate jab a hole in Enzo's heart? Why did Allison breaking Danny's heart hurt him? It wasn't that he didn't care or that he didn't understand; he loved all his soulmates.

Marlow once talked about getting cheated on, and he felt anger rise through him like heavy foam. It hurt him. His mum talking about his dad hurt him. He hated people he loved getting hurt. It was a weird part of him that he didn't acknowledge properly. He didn't want to. If he did, he'd always be sad. His soulmates were always hurting. He was there for them, not the other way around. Well, maybe Danny was different, but that was one night.

It was all complicated and convoluted, but he'd never walked out on one before; never walked out on them before his name faded. He never thought that they'd be better off without him, but maybe he should've been thinking that. Maybe his role was pointless and everyone would come to their own conclusions eventually – post-soulmate – without him. Maybe his curse was just a curse.

The drive from Rebecca's felt like it took three days, when it only took about an hour and forty minutes. She wasn't far, but Enzo's mind kept drifting and drifting, her shrill voice repeating 'Rebecca' through his head like an echo. He could still feel where she was; he still felt the tug on his heart and he hated it. He hated it more than he'd hated anything. It was so incredibly frustrating; frustrating enough that Enzo really wanted a freakin drink when he got home, and he never drank out of frustration. It was a thing that his dad did, and he didn't want to be like his dad.

Regardless, he got home and unlocked his door, before wandering into his kitchen and grabbing a cider, He popped it open and took a sip in much needed relief.

"Oh, welcome home," a familiar voice stated, as the light in Enzo's small, white kitchen turned on.

He felt his heart jolt as his eyes tilted up to meet the newcomer's. "You know this is my flat, right? I gave you a key for emergencies," he muttered, then raised a brow as his mother rolled her eyes.

She looked better today. Her skin was pale, but less pale than usual. She had a little colour in her cheeks, but the bags under her eyes could win a competition. She wore a little mascara and some smudged blusher on her freckled face. She was a young mother; slim and tall, with short, black hair that sat atop her head in a small swirl. Today she wore a red, floral, button dress, tights and a pair of lace-up, blue boots. Her eyes were a piercing green that glowed in the low lights of Enzo's kitchen.

"Excuse me, I am your mother," she stated, and Enzo scoffed. "Don't think you have any rights to tell me not to be in your living space, when you lived in me for the first nine months of your existence."

"Jesus, okay," Enzo stated, with his hands up. "Stay as long as you want, but please, never mention that again."

His mother smiled, then tilted her gaze to the cider worriedly. "What are you doing home? I thought you had a new name?" she asked in confusion, and Enzo sighed sharply, taking another sip and relishing in the fruity taste of his berry cider.

"I did," he muttered.

His mum opened her mouth to ask more, but Enzo just raised his hand. "I don't wanna talk about it."

A weird silence hit the room, as Enzo's mum watched him chug several sips of cider before placing it on the side.

"You need to stay the night?"

"Please," she begged gently, and Enzo smiled.

"You know where the bed is. I'll sleep on the couch," he sighed, and his mum smiled.

"I'm the lodger here."

"You're also my mother," he said, taking another sip. "And you are much older..."

His mother scoffed with a wide, outburst of shocked air. "I demand you sleep on the floor, for that comment."

"I'm not sleeping on the floor in my own flat," he replied, then wandered through and out the kitchen before turning on the TV. "Besides, I'm not working tomorrow, so wanna watch some TV? We can order something; I haven't had tea yet. Have you?"

His mother sighed, smiled sadly then shook her head, a look of weary frustration on her pale face, as Enzo offered a small, sympathetic smile. He didn't know what had happened or what had been said. She may explain later, but it didn't matter. Enzo wanted to distract her, and Enzo needed distracting, so TV, cider, and takeaway sounded ideal. If they talked, they talked. If not, Enzo was dissolving into fantasy worlds with his mother, then sleeping on his couch, while cider made his brain forget Rebecca, his current hazy feels about soulmates and his freakin curse.

His mother sat happily watching the TV. A few hours passed, and neither of them talked. They ordered pizza, turned on a show about Merlin and Arthur and magic, and just got lost. Enzo had a cider, then two, then three, while eating a large margherita pizza. The food, plus the alcohol, made him feel sleepier and sleepier, until his eyes closed and the world around him faded. He was mildly aware of a warm, fluffy thing being placed on him and the pizza box being taken off his lap, but not really. His mother shuffled out of the room after turning off the TV and tidying up. She headed to the bedroom and fell asleep in Enzo's warm, little bed.

They did this a lot. Enzo wasn't a fan of his mum being upset, and he wasn't a fan of how closed off she was about his dad, but he understood it. He never pushed her. If she wanted to speak, then she could, and if not, Enzo was there anyway. He didn't want to talk about his thing, but he couldn't stop thinking about it. His parents were a classic example of soulmates who just weren't meant to be. He'd met *so* many people who just expected their relationships to work out because the universe 'said it would', and then when it didn't, they were shattered. Enzo had seen enough of that to know that. Maybe soulmates just weren't worth it? Maybe it was better to decide your own feelings and your own things; maybe it was better to not let the universe dictate how you feel. Where would Enzo be if he decided to trust his instincts and do what he properly wanted?

Danny asking how he could say that, ached through his head. 'You need to know that you're important too.' 'You're just… perfect.' A myriad of quotes, that Enzo's heart remembered with increasing ferocity, flooded the back of his head, as he tossed and turned in his sleep.

He'd talked to his soulmates about varying things. They always asked why he is the way he is. Some asked how many soulmates he'd had, but most of them seemed to take Enzo seriously when he said that he was there to help them. He didn't mind it. He wanted it that way.

Marlow was different, but Marlow was different because of Danny. Everything had started with him, and Enzo hated it. He hated all of this. His limits and his feelings on soulmates were so simple – so cut and dry – and he was happy with that.

Or was he just telling himself that? He loved all of them. He always knew that he loved them. They all caused his heart to skip beats. They were all kind, funny and great, and he'd never denied how much fun he'd had, with any one of them. He wanted to help them and be there for them, and he never left without knowing they were okay. He loved what he did for a reason. He just had moments of feeling lonely and moments of wanting someone to vent to, but they were just moments. He never needed anyone. Heck, he never wanted them. He wanted his own company. He wanted to do his own thing and exist and just move forward, without someone else to worry about.

But was he moving forward? Just, dammit. He'd been doing the same thing for five years; working the same job; he hadn't even come out to his dad. Was he moving forward? What did that even mean? He had savings, but tonnes of them were wasted on hotel rooms and fuel for travelling about the country. He had wasted a lot of money on 'rent' at Marlow's. He wasn't worried about money, but he'd be remiss to say that he didn't wish he had more. He had enough to get by, and if he needed more, he worked more. It was simple, but was he happy? Was this what he wanted? He'd never sat down and thought about it, until now. Soulmates were always this ridiculous thing that seemed too perfect to work – too perfect to work, according to every other soulmate that Enzo had had. All their relationships fell apart on the basis that people didn't think they needed to try because they were soulmates. Maybe his curse wasn't a curse. Maybe soulmates were. They were an excuse for people to not try. Soulmates made people complacent. They'd gotten over the hump and found them, and then they were just waiting and slowly falling apart, until someone gave up or cheated or ran off.

Were relationships even worth it if they lead to things like what happened to Keith and Rebecca? Charlie and Marlow? Danny and Allison? Enzo's parents? And *tonnes* of other people in the world. What made people want to have another person with them?

Why would Enzo want that? Did he want that? Everything ended in heartbreak, even when the universe decided that you were meant for each other, or the universe paired you with people who weren't right for you or weren't good enough for you. Enzo would bet money on Allison and Charlie not being good enough for Danny and Marlow.

That wasn't fair. None of this was fair. All of it was complicated and infuriating, and he could still hear Rebecca's stupid voice in his stupid head!

He woke up groaning, back protesting his half-sat-up position, as he chucked his beating head into his hands. Everything hurt. His stomach was lurching pizza through his throat, and his head was pounding so hard he could feel his brain shoving the eyeballs out their sockets.

Hangovers at eighteen? Yeah, they're fine. You have a bit of a headache, at most. Enzo didn't really know what a hangover was until he was twenty-two, and now he got hungover after two drinks. Headache, nausea, fatigue – the whole nine yards. He hated it, and there was no cure. He'd just feel like crap for a day, then it'd be over.

His headache was not helped by Rebecca's voice quaking through his brain and making anger infest his bones. He wasn't going back there. He'd jump into Mount Doom before heading back there, but that didn't stop the fact that she was still technically his soulmate, and he was going to keep hearing her voice until the universe decided he'd had enough. But he wasn't going back, and he wasn't helping someone who wouldn't admit that she was wrong to cheat on the man she loved.

It wasn't that Rebecca was beyond help. She was probably – maybe – a nice person beneath her anger and self-involved nature, so she would come around at some point. Maybe she'd apologize to Keith and those two would figure things out? Maybe she'd just lose Enzo's voice, and that'd be it for her. It wouldn't be it for him.

His mum left in the morning. They had a silent cup of tea and a muffin, each smiling at each other awkwardly, while Enzo kept a strong grip on his head to hold back the banging headache. Then she kissed his cheek, thanked him for letting her stay and left. Enzo said that she was always welcome, then he hopped in the shower, Rebecca's voice stabbing through his ears like a stupid, painful plague that made him want to rip off his freakin ears. The hangover wasn't helping, but the voice was just... urgh.

Should he go back? He felt guilty walking away. He'd never done it before, but this was the first time that he felt this gut instinct, like this fire and anger and just... she didn't need his help. She didn't want it, and it wouldn't help her in the long run. She was stuck on this idea that nothing was her fault and that she'd done everything in their relationship, with her other half screwing up everything and basically throwing her into the arms of another man. Enzo knew that there was a lot more to the story and people didn't cheat for no reason, but it was up to her to figure it out, and Enzo wasn't going to hold her hand when she didn't want him to. It was her choice for him to leave, as much as it was his. He couldn't stop himself thinking about her though, and he hated that. The voice in his head was increasing his blood pressure and making his headache about a billion times worse.

So, he decided to sit on his couch, shove in some earphones and listen to some random, loud music that popped up on his Spotify. It worked – kind of. It worked even better when he'd had some painkillers and gotten rid of his headache. He fell asleep on the couch quickly, then did the same thing every day for a week; waking up to Rebecca's voice, getting mad and telling her to shut up, then shoving in his earphones, taking some painkillers and falling asleep on the couch. His back was in bits, but he didn't care. His mum had showed up at some point, Danny texted, his boss called, but Enzo was out for the count. The man would sooner jump out a window than talk to *anyone*.

He just wanted her voice to freakin fade! He wanted to move onto the next one! Why wasn't it fading? Why did he get weeks with her and only a night with Danny? What was wrong with the universe?

It took ten days –ten days of Enzo listening to enough heavy metal music to cause a long-lasting ring through the back of his ears. Ten days. He hadn't shaved. He hadn't showered. He hadn't worked. He hadn't messaged anyone. He'd barely slept, but she was gone. It was gone. Enzo had never felt this level of relief.

He woke up and breathed out properly for the first time in over a week. He looked at his painkillers and just walked past, before hopping into his shower and washing away ten days' worth of agonising frustration. He wilted completely in the water, breathing calmly to a gentle, slow, normal rhythm.

Silence. Freakin, blessed silence. He could breathe and relax; watch things; talk to people. He should probably reply to Danny and his mum. Oh, and his boss. Crud, what if she'd fired him? Enzo started to feel shaky, as he flipped his phone over and dragged it up from his bedside table.

His eyes closed, and a breath floated out his mouth. A stabbing ring rattled through his ears, as the silence got louder and windier. It felt like candyfloss pressing through his eye canals, and Enzo's eyes slammed closed in agitation.

The silence got louder, growing to the volume of a wind tunnel that Enzo currently stood in the middle of. The stabbing ring got harsher and sharper, jabbing through his eardrums and releasing the air, while making his brain squeeze and squish uncomfortably.

"No. No. No. No," he sighed desperately, and shook his head, closing his eyes tighter with a deep, guttural groan, his fingers sharply pressing through his temples.

'Kelsie.' A small, kind voice whispered through his mind. The wind faded as the ringing stopped, and Enzo's eyes snapped open, his body slumping in frustration as he glared up at the ceiling.

"You really can't give me a break, huh?"

Chapter 12
KELSIE

It'd been six years since she first heard her soulmate's voice and name – 'Arlene.' She had an accent – a strong one – but Kelsie was never good with accents. When she first heard it six years ago, she spent every day at school trying to find her. She searched Arlene's on Facebook, trying to see if she could find videos with audio; see if she could recognise her voice, but nope – nothing. Six years, and she'd never met her soulmate. She had a feeling that she never would but kept telling herself that everyone was destined to meet their soulmates. It would happen any day, and there was no point in trying anything with anyone else because, well, she'd meet Arlene, and then whoever she was dating would get hurt and it would suck.

She was twenty-four years old. She had never kissed a girl, never been on a date and never had sex, but she was okay. She wasn't lonely. She had great friends and a good job. She was set up and ready for Arlene, for whenever the universe dictated that they meet.

"Hey, Kels," a kind, gentle voice stated, but Kelsie's head was up in the clouds, staring at the ceiling. "Earth to Kelsie? Hellllooo?" the voice continued, shaking a hand in front of the pale girl's face.

Kelsie jolted immediately, the swinging chair tilting back, until she caught herself and awkwardly jolted to the ground with a small scrape.

"Oops, sorry."

"Cara, dude. You could've freakin killed me," Kelsie exclaimed then playfully glared up at her friend. Cara Montez. Twenty-four, Cuban, gorgeous, best friend, roommate and absolute, -freakin-menace. Her long, brown hair was cascading around her face in wavy curls. Her eyes were a deep brown, her lips a dark pink. Today she wore a grey sweatshirt with some form of anime character on it. Kelsie had no clue what it was, but she knew it was one of Cara's favourites. Her jeans were lightly torn at her knees, and her boots had tiny splashes of mud on the sides, the laces slowly falling undone.

"Don't be dramatic, Jones. At most, you would've gotten a concussion, and maybe that would teach you to stop swinging on these stupid, cheap chairs."

Kelsie smirked lightly. "I've worked here for three years, and I have fallen off these chairs about a dozen times. I'm not learning anything."

Cara rolled her eyes and folded her arms, as Kelsie got to her feet.

"I am not driving you to the hospital when you crack your head open," Cara stated.

"Oh, yes you are," Kelsie argued easily. "I need someone to hold the pieces of my skull together."

"Well, find someone else – not sure we're at that place in our relationship."

Cara and Kelsie caught each other's eyes and smiled, a weird flush of warmth flooding around them as they blushed and gulped, then stared down at their feet.

"Uh, anyway, Thompson wanted to talk to us about something. Think we've got a new project, and he wants us to head it up."

"Any clue what it is?" Kelsie asked.

Cara shrugged. "Nope, but we should go find out, before the man comes over here and drags us out by our ears," she stated, and Kelsie smirked.

"Okay, lead the way, Montez," she said, then did an air hostess 'there's the exit' gesture, as Cara rolled her eyes playfully and lead the pair out to their manager's office.

Kelsie met Cara when they were twenty-two, both just out of school and starting work at a small animation studio in London. They were both terrified, with Kelsie being the more visibly afraid on day one.

Cara bought her a cup of tea, sat with her at lunch and from then on, they were scared together. Cara smiling and keeping Kelsie steady on days where she got in her own head, Kelsie reminded Cara to take things more seriously when Cara forgot. They had it easy together, laughed and joked like an old married couple. The office called them 'work wives' sometimes. It didn't help that they'd moved in together last year when Kelsie's apartment fell through.

Cara was unfairly gorgeous; she was one of those people that looked like she'd walked off a billboard. Her make-up was always perfect, her hair was always shiny and flowing. Kelsie had moments of forgetting Cara was a real human then she'd ramble about anime for three days and Kelsie would remember she was a nerd.

They loved each other. Kelsie didn't know what she'd do without Cara. They were a package deal, they were a team. Her job was a dream but Cara made it more than that.

Both had never met their soulmates. Cara's was called 'Jamie.' She had an American accent and Cara barely talked about her. She lived abroad and meeting her was improbable. Kelsie had never really heard her talk about it though. They'd talk about soulmates for a moment, Kelsie would go into a ramble about what it'd be like to meet Arlene one day. She'd ask about 'Jamie' and Cara would clam up. It was a thing they had in common but Kelsie did feel a tad alone in her attitude to soulmates, maybe everyone didn't think they were as fantastical as they seemed to be.

"The show's about a lesbian superhero, like Spiderman but female and her love interest is her best friend. It takes place in this fictional city called

'Reflecity' where people get powers when they show inordinate amounts of selflessness. It's about the difference between good and evil, follows the two girls as they navigate what it means to be a hero and discover what it means to be good... they discover that good isn't easy and evil isn't so cut and dry. The creator worked on similar projects but this is her first solo... she specifically requested you two be placed in charge." Thompson explained, daylight beaming off his bald head as Kelsie fell back in surprise.

"Us?" She asked, gesturing to Cara and her as Thompson adjusted his bowtie and stood up from his desk.

"She wanted the episodes to be authentic to the character's journey in terms of sexuality..."

"So, she's playing the lesbian card?" Cara asked abruptly and Kelsie gulped.

"No." Thompson stated calmly, obviously too adjusted to Cara's bluntness after working with her for two years. "She wrote this show based on her own journey, the main characters are based on her and her best friend. She's watched shows animated by you both and is aware of your writing ability. This show is very important and personal to her, she chose you two as she believes you will do it justice."

"And we will." Cara stated proudly while Kelsie tried to process what was happening.

"Great, I've emailed you both the concept and a few CVs of the animators I believe would be good for this project. Get back to me with a team and an initial pilot outline before the end of the week." He demanded, Cara nodded and dragged Kelsie from the room.

They appeared back in the break room and collapsed into the chairs, Cara pulling out her laptop and excitedly opening her emails as Kelsie blinked and tried to process that discussion.

Their own project? Cara and Kelsie were heading up a show, just the two of them? They oversaw a team and a new show that had potential to go major like a lot of the other shows did and not only that, it was an LGBTQ+ show? Kelsie was frozen in the importance of this. She wanted to do it justice but it felt like... like, a lot.

"Hey." Cara whispered through her panic, cutting it off and taking her hand as Kelsie jumped back to reality. "This is gonna be awesome, Kels."

"I know but what if... what um..."

"No, no. No doubting yourself, kiddo. You're an amazing animator and a great writer. You could kill this in your sleep." Cara stated, as if those were objective facts and Kelsie felt her back straighten slightly. "Besides, it's just the initial stages... we get the team together and come up with a plan. No panicking because we're in this together, okay?"

"Okay." Kelsie gulped, small smile flooding her lips as Cara squeezed her hand. Warmth elapsed them for a moment before she pulled her hand back and stared over the laptop screen.

They shared a lot of moments like that. Cara tended to be Kelsie's confidence and faith when she started to doubt her abilities, she was always the one who reminded her of her own skills and achievements. Cara had a lot of faith in Kelsie. Too much, in Kelsie's opinion, but the pair fought for each other, pushed each other and Kelsie always found herself spluttering when moments of honest admiration passed between them.

She never really knew what to make of their relationship. It'd always been so easy, she'd never had that with anyone before. Their friendship went from strangers to acquaintances to best friends in about three cups of tea. She was grateful for it but constantly found no explanation for their inexplicable link. They loved each other, cared about each other instantly and Kelsie's world with Cara in it became bright and abnormal in the best ways.

Some days, Kelsie wanted them to be soulmates but knew that was impossible. People only get one, right?

Kelsie smiled, her face blushing slightly as she turned to stare at the floor. "Yeah, we uh …" she began before a strange, squelching feeling fell through her brain, and her sharp, green eyes jolted up. A cold breeze flooded through her suddenly silent head. She stared across the room, her mouth falling dry and eyes going wide.

A tall, dark-haired man appeared in a grey T shirt with a red, flannel shirt tied around his hips. A pair of deep-grey jeans sat around his slim legs, and a pair of beat-up, black, lace boots sat on his feet. A matching beanie covered the back of his head. His sharp, light-brown eyes locked in on Kelsie, and the entire world froze as their eyes met.

"Enzo," Kelsie said aloud, in time with the deep voice in her head.

"Enzo?" Cara asked, then cocked her brow as Kelsie shakily got to her feet.

"I um …" Kelsie began, feeling her heart start to pound through her chest.

"Kels, are you okay?"

"Yeah… uh… yeah, uh… fine. I just gotta go to the bathroom," she announced, then pushed the glass, breakroom door open and raced over to the reception, while Cara watched her in confusion, then shrugged and continued to scroll through CVs.

Kelsie appeared by the rounded, office check-in desk. Peter sat behind it with his headset over his short, blonde hair. His blue eyes were glittering and friendly, while he animatedly talked to someone on the phone, but the man leaning against the desk from the outside was the one that had grasped Kelsie's attention. He just stared at her, his bright, brown eyes glistening gold in the dull office lights, as they both caught their breaths and gulped.

"Uh… Kelsie?" the man questioned, his deep voice rattling around Kelsie's head, as her eyes widened in shock.

"Enzo," she stated, and the room fell into horrific silence, as the dark-haired man nodded, a sharp sigh falling through his pale lips.

"Let's uh… get a coffee? Yeah?"

All Kelsie could do was nod numbly, while following the pale, freckled man out of the building.

Enzo grabbed them both a tea as they entered the small coffee shop in town, each claiming a little couch of their own and wrapping their fingers around their warm mugs.

"So… uh this is… I'm assuming this is new for you?"

"Which part?" Kelsie gasped out, cocking an eyebrow. "Meeting my soulmate? Getting a new soulmate? Discovering that I'm maybe not as gay as I thought I was?"

Enzo's eyebrows lowered in surprise. "You're a… you're a lesbian?" he asked, and Kelsie slowly nodded as Enzo's eyes widened. "Well, that's new."

"What the hell's going on, Enzo? I've had a soulmate for the past six years. Her name is Arlene, and she lives somewhere that isn't here. She's supposed to be like… we're supposed to meet one day, and that's supposed to be it, so what the heck is this?" she asked, then gestured between the two of them, a weird, warm familiarity spreading.

"Uh… yeah … okay, it's a long story. You got time?"

"I just ditched work, so yeah. My roommate will cover for me, hopefully," Kelsie stated firmly, then took a sip of tea.

"You don't just get one soulmate; no one does." he stated, and Kelsie felt her heart quicken. "It's normal, and it's okay. Nothing has to happen between us, coz, well, obviously... well, I'm assuming that you're not attracted to me?"

"Not into guys, but you're cute. And it's like, you feel like... familiar? Like there's this weird heat between us?"

"Yeah," Enzo agreed, with a little nod. "That's how soulmates feel; like it feels like we already know each other. Like we're drawn together. Can't say I've had a soulmate who wasn't attracted to my gender before, though, but the universe has been making some mistakes lately. Well, I don't know; it doesn't matter. Point is, we are soulmates. My soulmate changes every few months, and I show up and try and help. God, I was better at explaining this before, but from what I can tell, your soulmate is from overseas and you've never met her, right?" he rambled off.

Kelsie blinked in surprise, then cocked her brow. "Yeah. But we will meet one day – that's like the rule of soulmates, isn't it?" she asked, in genuine confusion, feeling a swell of disappointment and relief flood her stomach when Enzo bit his lip apprehensively.

"It's um... it's not always a guarantee, Kelsie. A few people do meet their soulmates, even when they live far, far away. Like I've heard of people meeting their soulmates on holiday. But it's just…" Enzo looked up and sighed. "Finding your soulmate isn't a guarantee. It sometimes doesn't happen for people."

"Oh," Kelsie stated dully, and the world gained a cold, grey sheen as her gaze fell to her mug.

"I'm sorry, but uh … soulmates are weird, Kelsie. I don't know how to explain them. I mean, the universe set me up with someone a month ago who was just not good; she wasn't good. Well, she might've been, but, yeah. And then, you seem great, but you don't like dudes, so it makes me think that soulmates are about more than just being attracted to the other person, but I don't know. Well, I know they're obviously more, but, you know, I've never been set up with a lesbian before, and I've heard some uh…" He gulped, then stared down at his tea.

"You ever heard of people forging their own soul connection?" Kelsie asked suddenly, words slipping out before she fully had time to process them.

"People… uh… people doing what?"

"Forging their own connection. It's um…" She gulped, then glanced around the little, pink coffee shop. "Something I read about. People who like… uh who lose their soulmates. Like they die or something and, well, they're lonely, so they start dating. There are these apps for people whose soulmates aren't around anymore. I think they were supposed to be for grieving or something, but people started meeting people and dating and, well, falling in love and just..." She gulped down a wad of nervous saliva. "After a while of them dating and falling for each other, their... um... their name fades, and the person they've been dating appears, and it's like, um..."

"They *became* soulmates?" Enzo asked in shock, and Kelsie nodded slowly with a smile. "Is that real? That happens?"

"You haven't heard of it before?"

"No," he admitted, then shook his head, shock overtaking his gentle features, as the light of the café caused the freckles on his face to glimmer.

"It happens. I've read about it, and my aunt did it. My uncle died a long time ago, and she was lonely, so she started going to this support group and met my uncle Sean, and they uh... they fell in love and had another kid and got a house, and it um... I don't know when it happened, but she told me that, one day she woke up, and she heard his name in her head, and he heard hers, and it was..." Kelsie gulped and stared at her knees. "... Amazing, and when she told me, I started reading about it, and there are like tonnes of stories."

"Why have you read so much about this, Kelsie?" Enzo asked, and the dark-haired girl jumped, meeting Enzo's eyes with a bewildered stare.

"Wha?"

"It's just that, earlier you were talking about how certain you were that you'd meet your soulmate one day. Arlene? Right?" Enzo asked.

Kelsie awkwardly nodded.

"So why would you worry about forging your own connection and like um… I thought you believed we all get one?"

"No, I uh… I think that's a tad nuts," she said, and Enzo's eyes widened.

"Right, that's a change of pace."

"I mean, think about it. How can people be linked to each other at *all* stages of their lives?"

"That's what I've been saying!" Enzo shouted happily.

Kelsie choked out a laugh. "So, seriously… own soul connections. Why do you…"

"There you are! Seriously, Kels. Ditching work to get a drink with a tall, dark stranger – little cliched, ain't it?" a new voice loudly exclaimed, causing Enzo and Kelsie to jump.

A short, tanned girl appeared before them, hands on her hips and a serious, slightly amused scowl on her face. Kelsie immediately gulped, feeling her cheeks light up, as Enzo watched over her with a bemused, curious expression on his pale face.

"Sorry, that was my fault," Enzo quickly stated, and Cara's gaze snapped to him curiously.

"And you are?" she asked, her deep-brown eyes glaring through him curiously.

"Enzo," he replied, then placed a hand out to her. "Guessing you're the roommate?"

Cara blinked back in surprise and gripped Enzo's hand. "Cara, and yes. You talked about me?" she asked, turning to Kelsie with raised eyebrows.

Kelsie jolted, running a hand through her hair before collapsing in on herself. "Uh… yeah uh… did you cover for me?"

"Didn't have to. We're supposed to spend the whole afternoon looking through CVs and going over the show concept. Thompson hasn't even been out of his office. I just went in and handed over the candidates we're gonna interview and emailed the show concept to myself. He said we could work on it from home, as you finished that scene earlier." She stated then shrugged. "But you're gonna have to explain this later." She pointed between the pair of them.

Kelsie jolted.

"I'm gonna head home. Meet ya there?"

"Yeah… uh see ya!" Kelsie called awkwardly.

"Nice to meet you, stranger," Cara said, then saluted the dark-haired guy.

Enzo smiled. "You too, Cara."

Cara smiled, turned on her heel and left the café, as Enzo turned back to his blushing soulmate.

"Ah, I get it now," he stated, with a cocked brow, as Kelsie shuddered and stared down at her mug.

"What?"

"You like her." His eyes tilted to the door then back to Kelsie, as a sly smirk appeared over his pink lips.

Kelsie jumped. "Well, yeah, course I do. She's uh... my..." Kelsie began, then turned to the door. "My best friend."

"Right, so all this 'forge your own connection' crap has nothing to do with how nervous you got when she appeared? How you're blushing and can't even look me in the eye?"

"No," Kelsie immediately defended, then looked Enzo in the eye for a second, before turning back to her tea.

"It's okay, Kelsie. Cara seems great; why wouldn't you want to go for it?" Enzo asked genuinely.

"Coz um..." Kelsie gulped, her eyes tilting back up to Enzo. "What if I'm wrong? What if my aunt's wrong? And like, what if I meet Arlene, or Cara meets Jamie? I don't wanna lose her. What if we start dating and we just fall apart? It's not worth it. It's not worth the risk; plus, we have soulmates. Wait, do I still have Arlene?"

"Uh... yeah, probably. I can't say for certain. Some people get their name back when I'm gone; some don't have a voice for a while; some get a new one straight away, but no one is ever left 'soulmateless'," Enzo explained. "But still. You even said it yourself that you don't think people get just one, and, well, I'd say I'm proof of that. Well, I guess I kind of am. Maybe we're like 'friend soulmates'. Would that make sense?"

"I guess."

"Anyway, yeah, doesn't matter, even if you don't 'forge your own connection'. It's been six years, and neither of you have met your soulmates. You're allowed to date people who aren't in your head. There's no law against it. People fall in love all the time, Kelsie. It's okay. Soulmates aren't the only people you can date."

"But if you dated someone you loved while having another person's name in your head, and then you met that person in real life and felt this," She gestured between the two of them. "Could you deny it and go back to your partner; *only* thinking of them and being with them? And could you keep going and dating them while thinking that one day, you could just randomly walk down the street and have your entire world blown up by one stupid voice? Could you do that? Just keep going; keep not thinking. Isn't it selfish? And just, awful? There's too much on the line here, and like, it's just…" She collapsed into herself once more. "I don't wanna hurt her."

"Kelsie," Enzo said sadly. "Okay, I get it; I do. But, how long have you been in love with Cara?"

Kelsie cringed and stared through the floor. "Feels like decades." She gulped, and they linked eyes once more. "About two years? Two and a half?"

"Kelsie, I get that it's complicated, but you've been waiting six years for Arlene. Cara is here *now*."

"But what if she doesn't like me back?"

"Oh, she does," Enzo stated firmly. "I'm always amazed at how people don't see it. She likes you; you like her. Don't let stupid soulmates get in the way. You might form a connection – you might not – but you'll never know if you don't try. Do you really want to just spend your whole life waiting for someone you might not meet, rather than go for it with someone who already likes you and is *here*?"

Kelsie made to open her mouth but couldn't.

"Kelsie, I've had a lot of soulmates, and I'm just telling you what I think. If you love someone, regardless of whether you're linked, or meant to be, or whatever you should tell them and be with them."

Enzo gulped down a breath while staring at his fidgeting fingers, and Kelsie couldn't help but think he looked lost, like he was talking about something else.

"It's always going to be a risk – always – but whatever happens, haven't you waited long enough?"

Chapter 13

Enzo had left after that. Him and Kelsie got a muffin each, then left. Neither spoke much after Enzo dropped the 'haven't you waited long enough?' bomb. He'd given her his number and told her to text or call when she needed to; that he was there to help, and Kelsie trusted every word out of his mouth with her whole heart. She kind of hated it. She hated the idea that this is what having a soulmate felt like. It was like you trusted and loved someone from the get-go; no control; no thinking; no choice. Enzo was a guy. Kelsie was not attracted to guys and that hadn't changed since hearing his voice. What the heck, universe?

Kelsie wasn't cynical when it came to soulmates. All her family were soulmates, legitimately – all. If you counted her aunt who forged their connection and Kelsie did, because she could see it and feel it when her aunt and uncle were around. Her parents were soulmates; her siblings had found theirs; all her work friends were soulmates. There was a reason that Kelsie thought meeting Arlene was inevitable. Heck, she still thought it was.

Her mind wasn't clear and her heart was still aching. She didn't know what she wanted, how she felt. It was like the universe had blown up fundamental pieces of her thought process. Soulmates were so permanent and important, they were inevitable. Arlene was inevitable. She had to be, didn't she?

What if she wasn't? Heck, if Enzo could be her soulmate then maybe soulmates weren't all they were cracked up to be. After all, Enzo was a guy and friend soulmates being a thing seemed to make sense. If people could become soulmates, then who's to say that anything isn't possible when it came to them. Maybe Kelsie had more control than she thought. Maybe Arlene wasn't as inevitable as it seemed.

But what about Cara? Was Enzo right? Did they have feelings for each other? Were they meant to be together? Could they forge their own connection and did it matter if they did if soulmates were so all over the place anyway?

'Haven't you waited long enough?' Two and a half years of being in love with a person was a lot. Being in love and holding it back, thinking about what it'd be like to kiss her and hug her, hold her hand. She stuffed these feelings deep down, hid her dreams and her hopes under a pile of 'but I'll meet Arlene and then lose her.' She never, ever wanted to hurt Cara. Cara was beautiful, wonderful and Kelsie would take a bullet for her in a heartbeat.

'Haven't you waited long enough?' She had. She'd waited long enough but how could she do this? It felt like this would be a mistake, that she'd lose her best friend and that Arlene would pop up and Kelsie would have to go. How she felt about Enzo was terrifying, it felt like she'd lost control. She loved him without knowing him because the universe decided it. Maybe she didn't want that? Maybe she wanted to make her own decision, be in love with a person she chose. A person she knew, maybe she wanted that more whether they were soulmates or not. Was that so wrong?

But what about Jamie? Cara hadn't talked about her for months but Jamie was Cara's destiny, not Kelsie. A part of her twinged jealously at that thought but it was true. If Jamie appeared, Kelsie would be shattered. All of this was risky, it was big and important. Kelsie didn't know what she wanted when she shakily unlocked their flat and headed in.

Their flat wasn't huge. They had a tiny, open second floor with one small, square room. It was Cara's bedroom, and it was on full open display, with Kelsie's bedroom downstairs being opposite the kitchen. They had one bathroom and one shower. Their kitchen and living room was a small, open floor room, with a little dining table on the left side by the window. It was a cheap building in an awkward corner of London. It took the pair of them three underground trains to get to work and to get home, but neither complained. They each had tablets and took opportunities to work from home when they could.

Crap, the project! Oh god, the thing they needed to work on together. That'd be so freakin awkward if Kelsie told her what was going through her head right now. She couldn't tell her, could she? Crap, crud, no. Kelsie's heart felt as though it was leaping through an obstacle course, up and over hurdles and through hideous, dark tunnels. She could feel it shaking through her chest and rattling her ribs. Her breaths were coming out in cold, weak streams. Her head was spinning, and she just couldn't get a grasp on reality. Why was this such a big deal? What was this? She could just walk away, say and do nothing; keep life the same way; keep going. Cara was still there, and Kelsie was still there. They were still best friends.

'Haven't you waited long enough?' Enzo's voice quaked and echoed through her head, as she winced.

"Howdy stranger," Cara's voice stated, and Kelsie jumped out of her skin, her eyes wide, and her earphone slipping slowly from her ear.

Cara smiled, before getting up from the couch and appearing opposite Kelsie in the kitchen. "Whoa, sorry kid. Didn't mean to make ya jump."

"You didn't uh… there's um…" she began stammering, then gulped, before sucking in a strong breath and forcing their eyes to link. "There's something I need to tell you."

There. Decision made. Let the universe dictate whether it was stupid or not.

Cara's deep-brown eyes widened in surprise. "Okay, colour me intrigued," she stated, then gestured dramatically to their blue, two-seater couch.

Kelsie gulped and visibly shook, before placing her phone on the kitchen counter and walking over to join Cara.

It was a small couch, and Kelsie always chose the left side. Cara always sat by the window. The TV was in the dead centre against the back wall, and each had a shelf beside it full of DVDs and games. Kelsie's was mainly full of books, while Cara's was ninety-nine percent games and manga. They watched a lot of the same shows on Netflix, but Kelsie could only name two animes. Cara had tried to educate her, but it did not work. The couch leant against the kitchen island, and a large window shone light over it, highlighting the ridiculous number of stains on it. It was an old couch when they'd bought it, but the girls were artists, so it was basically drenched in ink, chalk and paint.

Kelsie settled into the familiar spot, trying to relax, but finding herself unable to. She sat up straight, and Cara followed her stick-like posture while staring at her best friend worriedly. She'd tied her hair up in a little scrunchie and changed into her sweatpants since getting home. She still wore the jumper, but her feet were bare, and her rounded face was on full display, with little wisps of wavy hair falling into her gleaming eyes.

"Kels, are you okay?" she asked slowly, and Kelsie jumped, a little gulp falling down her throat.

"Yeah."

"You don't sound so sure," Cara chuckled.

"No, it's just I… I just don't know where to begin here," she began, and Cara stared over her, a warm, confused clench pressing into her heart.

"Wanna start with the guy at the coffee shop?" Cara asked, eyes squinting, while Kelsie nodded.

"Sure um… okay. You know my soulmate?"

"Arlene, yeah." Cara stared blankly.

"Right, well, um… You know how, like, everyone is under the impression that we all just get one?"

"We all do get just one, don't we? I mean, I remember you mentioning your aunt. The one who got, like… Didn't she become someone else's soulmate?" Cara asked, tilting her head curiously, as Kelsie blinked in surprise.

"Yeah. I told you about that?"

"Yeah, though you were kinda drunk. It was the night that we started on that project, and the studio was nominated for some awards, and we were celebrating with that bottle of champagne," Cara explained, then felt her face blush hotly as Kelsie smiled.

"Right, uh…" Kelsie gulped, then stared down at her fingers. "Did I say anything else?"

"Not really," Cara admitted, with a little smirk. "You said I had pretty eyes and that you thought me

277

speaking Spanish was cool, then you fell asleep on my lap," she stated, then shrugged.

Kelsie cocked a brow. "I said your Spanish was cool?"

"Yeah," Cara laughed. "I didn't know you liked it until that night, but, yeah. I just... I don't know; teased you a little with it, and you fell asleep."

"Is that why you've been speaking it more the past couple months?" Kelsie asked suddenly, and Cara jolted.

"I um... I've been speaking it more?"

"Yeah, like before, you just spoke it when you were on the phone with your nan but the past couple months, you've been like... There's, like, those nicknames you've been using. I don't know. I can't think of any specific samples, but you have been speaking more of it," Kelsie stated. Why couldn't she think of any? There were tonnes. Cara called them out when they were heading to bed. It made Kelsie paranoid, like she was insulting her subtly but there was a tone. Cara had a purring tone when she said those words, a tone that made Kelsie weak in the knees.

Cara shrugged. "Right, probably then," she admitted casually, then glanced out the window as a weird silence hit. No emotions seemed to cross Cara's face and Kelsie's paranoia hit tenfold, what was she thinking? How did Cara feel? Why did she speak more Spanish? What were those nicknames? Dammit, what was going through her head?

"Anyways, yeah, um… the guy in the bar was my um…"

"That guy was Arlene?"

"What? No. No, that was Enzo, and he is my… Well, okay, just to state for the record: I am gay, but Enzo is my soulmate," Kelsie rambled off.

Cara chuckled then slowly noticed the serious look on Kelsie's face.

"Seriously?" she asked, and Kelsie slowly nodded. "How uh… what? How is that possible?"

"I honestly don't know. He just explained that he gets a new soulmate every few months and like, goes around and meets them, helps them, and well, uh…"

"So, he's like Mary Poppins?" Cara asked.

"I guess," she answered. "But anyway, he's kinda got me thinking about soulmates in general, and uh… okay." She tilted her eyes to Cara's, feeling her heart fall back through her ribs. "How do you um… how do you feel about Jamie?"

Cara blinked in slow surprise. "Uh… right? We haven't really talked about that in a little while," she gulped, then turned and faced away from Kelsie. "She's gone."

Kelsie's eyes widened. "She's what? She's dead?"

"No, no, no. Well, I don't think, anyway, but I haven't heard her voice in about four months," Cara admitted and Kelsie gasped lightly.

"What? She like… she, like, what?" she asked in slow shock, feeling her heart drop through her like a stone through a river.

"Yeah. I woke up one day, and my mind was just blank. It was weird."

"Why didn't you mention it?" Kelsie asked gently.

"Coz it wasn't worth mentioning. It's not like either of us know our soulmates, and apparently you have a guy now. It wasn't important." Cara explained, then shrugged with a light, awkward smile.

"For the record – I'm not dating Enzo," Kelsie stated and Cara choked out a laugh.

"Yeah, I kinda guessed that. So, what did he get you thinking about?" she asked slowly, as the pair tilted to face each other, each leaning into the couch cushions.

"He … well uh… he's had a lot of soulmates. He was talking about them getting in people's ways and stopping them going for things, and just, um…" Kelsie began, then straightened her back and steeled herself with a gulp. "How long have we known each other?"

"Uh…" Cara began, then lowered her eyebrows in thought. "Honestly, I struggle to remember a time before I knew you, sometimes," she smiled and a little warm rumble shook through Kelsie's heart.

"Same here," She admitted, and the pair linked eyes as the warmth in the room hit tenfold.

"Why?"

"Just, um…" Kelsie began. "I…"

She moved closer, as Cara's eyes widened. The pair sat half-a-foot apart – probably less – as Cara straightened her back and shuffled forward, her eyes linking with Kelsie.

"Kels, just hold on. I uh…" Cara began, and Kelsie cocked a brow, as the girl slowly and shakily sighed. "I care about you a lot. You know that, right? I'm not always the best at, um…" She gulped, then looked down at her lap. It was strange, seeing Cara like this. She looked small and scared, vulnerable enough to make Kelsie feel frightened. She was stunted, almost but her mind was pushing through Enzo's words, trying to stay focused despite how much her hands were sweating. "At uh… Well, I tried once. There was, like, the night with the champagne. You were being cute and cuddly and honest, and just saying things that I hadn't. You see me in a way that I don't think other people do. And I tried to tell you how I felt, but I couldn't find the words, and I couldn't make myself move. I was um… I was scared, but that night still changed things."

"How?" Kelsie squeaked with wide, worried eyes.

"That was four months ago, Kels," Cara stated easily. "The night that her voice faded."

The room plummeted into a shaky, warm silence that shook through Kelsie's bones like an earthquake.

"You mean… I uh… the voice… I did that?"

"I don't know, Kels," Cara admitted.

Kelsie didn't know what to make of that. She didn't know what to think, what to feel, where to look. She was stunned, frozen and caught completely unaware.

Jamie was gone. Kelsie being all drunk and cuddly made Cara lose her soulmate, how? How did that make sense? Were soulmates just nonsense? "What are your feelings?" Kelsie blurted, squinting her eyes. "You said you wanted to tell me how you uh…"

And all the words fell back through her throat when Cara fell forwards and pressed her warm, soft lips onto Kelsie's. Their eyes clicked closed, Kelsie's glasses began to slip as their noses tapped. The warmth in the room echoed and swam around them, as Kelsie held back a gasp and felt the corners of her mouth tip up into a smile.

Kelsie wrapped her arms around Cara's back, and her head started to happily spin. She just couldn't remember a time when she had felt like this. Her heart felt light; her head felt amazing; her body was buzzing; the air was buzzing. The world felt beautiful and warm as Cara's hands fell to her waist, and the pair pulled back to look into each other's eyes, leaning their foreheads together as they caught their breaths.

"Sorry, I totally interrupted you. What were you saying?" Cara asked, and Kelsie grinned.

"You're such a dork,"

Cara winked proudly, as Kelsie tilted her head back.

"So, what does... what did that..."

"It means, I like you, Jones." Cara sighed and Kelsie blinked slowly, words hitting her but not quite processing. "I have for a long time now? It's just this soulmate stuff that's been like... messing with me?"

"Really?" Kelsie asked and Cara nodded slowly.

"I know all your family are soulmates and I just... I didn't want to get in the way of you and Arlene."

"There is no me and Arlene."

"I know but there could be and you're *so* certain that there would be." Cara sighed

"I know." Kelsie whispered, looking at her lap.

"That night four months ago changed a lot for me." Cara admitted and Kelsie's gaze jolted back up. "I didn't really know how I felt or how you did until like... well Jamie got out of the way."

"Did you really never care about soulmates?" Kelsie asked and Cara shrugged.

"I mean, not really? My family isn't like yours. My parents were an arranged marriage and my brother met his girlfriend at school... no soulmates but they love each other as if they were."

"Really?" Kelsie asked, surprise whirling through her. Cara had never talked about that before.

"Yes, really. Soulmates don't run the universe, you know."

"I know." Kelsie gulped. "But if you felt this way, why not say something before?"

"Four months ago, you kissed me on the cheek and told me that I was pretty." She stated and Kelsie's face burned. Cara smirked at her and Kelsie felt herself collapse. "I went to bed and Jamie's name fell away, my head's been silent ever since. I didn't know what it meant or how to feel and you still had Arlene so it was... it was as though no obstacles were taken away."

"So, you've been holding back for this long?"

"What about you?" Cara asked. "What are your feelings? What are you thinking?"

Kelsie's mouth flopped open for a moment then snapped shut, gaze falling back to her lap as a strange silence settled. "I don't know."

"It's complicated, ain't it?" Cara smiled lightly and Kelsie looked up, watching her brown eyes sparkle and her cheeks light up.

"You're so freakin beautiful, you know." She blurted and Cara blinked slowly, cheeks lighting up brighter. Kelsie's hand traced Cara's cheek, their foreheads falling together as Kelsie fought the headache behind her eyes. "It feels like I'm cheating on Arlene." She admitted and Cara scoffed sadly, eyes falling to her lap. "I know that's ridiculous and like, I've never met her and I..."

"No, it makes sense."

"Soulmates are weird, Cara."

"I know." Cara admitted and Kelsie shuffled back slightly, looking over her best friend in the gentle lights. Her eyes were wide and sad, her skin was glowing through the fading daylight. She was angelic and impossible, Kelsie had seen it before. She'd never let herself notice. Hated herself for thinking of anyone but her soulmate. Her soulmate that was one soundbite in her head, a person that she wasn't even destined to meet. She was just a name. A name in the back of her head. Cara was real, she was realer than anyone with her bright smile, the passion in her voice and the twinkle in her eye.

"You like... automatically love and trust them when you meet them like the universe decided... yep, this is it. This is what you want, deal with it but how does it freakin know?" Enzo popped up in her mind's eye, the familiarity around him and the infuriating comfort. It felt like she'd heard his voice for years and there was something so... wrong about that. It was a relationship built on one fact, it was a foundation based on one stick of wood, they didn't know each other, yet they loved each other. Cara and Kelsie knew each other. They'd lived together for a year, it was impossible to not know someone after that amount of time.

"Wow, okay."

"No, seriously. How can the universe dictate how people feel? How can it decide that we wait for people that we might never meet when the people we do meet are..." Kelsie stared through Cara's warm eyes and something shuddered through her heart. "Perfect."

"What? Me?" Cara asked playfully and Kelsie smirked.

"Yes, you. You dork."

Cara smiled and Kelsie dared anyone to say it wasn't the most beautiful thing in the world. "So, what do you wanna do?"

"I wanna stop waiting." She sighed.

"Me too." Cara breathed shakily.

"And I... want to kiss you." Kelsie admitted, face burning.

"Me too." Cara stated steadily, her tone certain and stubborn as the pair leaned back into each other.

They kissed and it was perfect. Magical. Wonderful. Everything Kelsie had ever wanted. Enzo's voice petered out slowly and she was lost. Her best friend holding her steady and keeping her alive as they pulled away and breathed each other in.

"This is crazy." Kelsie breathed.

"Yeah, the best things usually are." Cara stated with a fond smile and Kelsie dived back on her, kissing her until the day faded away.

Chapter 14
ENZO

'Formed their own soul connection'. It was a phrase that Enzo was completely stuck on – a phrase that had flooded all four corners of his mind.

"Formed their own soul connection," he muttered, while staring out the train window, his eyes glazing through the deep, black sky, the stars twinkling through his gold irises.

He'd taken the train to London when Kelsie's voice appeared. He would've taken his bike, but his mum had ranted at him for an hour about how it'd get stolen, so he got on a train and headed south. The tug on his heart got sharper, the closer and closer he'd gotten to London. It snapped to a stop when Enzo appeared in Euston. He then shoved his earphones in and wandered through the streets. He found a giant animation studio, and the voice got louder, the pain in his heart got sharper and Kelsie appeared.

She was cute –very cute. She had big eyes, pale skin, little glasses and a pretty dress. She was about a foot shorter than Enzo. Everything felt the same, as it always did; warm, familiar and instantly comfortable. He always loved that feeling when he first met his soulmates. Kelsie was sweet and kind. She was obviously smitten with that Cara girl, and Enzo didn't know what to do with that.

How could the universe match him with a lesbian? It just got him thinking that maybe he'd lost a little faith in his curse since Rebecca; lost a little faith in what he was doing. Was he never meant to be paired with anyone? He always felt like he was matched with people who he could end up with, but Kelsie was an outlier, and Rebecca was an outlier. At least Kelsie was a nice outlier. Kelsie was cute and sweet, and maybe Enzo had helped her? He'd like to think that Kelsie had gotten her shit together and asked Cara out, despite the names in their heads. Maybe they would 'form their own connection', but even if they didn't, Enzo just got this feeling that they'd be happy together. Soulmates were pointless, after all. The universe couldn't tell you who would make you happy; you had to decide.

These thoughts had been killing him for the past few hours. He couldn't shake them. Were soulmates completely and utterly pointless? Was there nothing worthwhile about them? Did the universe know nothing? Were there no happy people who'd ended up with their soulmates? There had to be people. They couldn't be pointless. The universe had paired Enzo with Marlow and... Danny. But Marlow wasn't a romantic soulmate, either. But Danny? Maybe the universe got Danny right? But why did the name fade? What the fuck was happening? Everything had been screwed up since Danny kissed him. He wasn't meant to kiss these people. He wasn't meant to end up with them. He was meant to befriend them, help them and move on. Why was he never meant to end up with them? Why was this all temporary? Was this what all soulmates were meant to be? In which case, what was the point? People could just find people on their own, without this added 'the universe picked us' pressure. Why was there this pressure? Was Enzo right all along? A part of him didn't want to be right about this.

He wanted to be wrong. He wanted soulmates to mean something. He wanted them to be meaningful. He wanted to know that soulmates could end up happy and together, but why did he want that? He never had any proof of it. He's just spent his whole life helping people who'd lost someone who was supposed to stay by their side forever. He'd spent his life travelling around the country, picking up the pieces of these people and getting them to move forward. Getting them to keep going without a part of their freakin soul. Was that what soulmates were? What were they? What was the point? People were okay by themselves. Enzo had proven that time and time again, but maybe being alone wasn't all it was cracked up to be.

You could be alone and be happy within yourself. People didn't need to be with other people to be happy and secure in themselves. But having someone by your side when things went wrong, having someone by your side when you wake up, having someone to vent to, having someone tell you you're attractive when you're not feeling attractive, having someone just be with you because they wanted to be with you –that's what Enzo wanted soulmates and relationships to mean. He wanted to want someone, and for them to want him. He wanted people to have soulmates who stuck by them for more reasons than just the universe saying they had to.

Relationships were about people. They were about two people getting each other and compromising, finding things in common and driving each other mad, laughing at stupid jokes. It was people supporting each other through hard things, and just making sure the other was okay – making sure they knew that they were dealing with things together. Enzo wanted to believe in relationships. Not soulmates, maybe, but people wanting each other. It was about wanting. Not needing. Enzo wanted to want someone.

His phone buzzed suddenly, drawing Enzo's mind back to the present, as he stared down at the tiny device in his hand. A text popped up saying, 'Hey Enzo, I told her. Well, I tried to, then she kissed me! And well, we haven't fully talked it all out yet, but she kissed me! And I think your voice is fading, but I can't tell. Her voice is gone, and I don't know what that means. It's all up in the air, but she kissed me, and now she's falling asleep on my shoulder, and I'm so freakin happy! Thank you so much, Enzo. It's Kelsie, by the way. xx'.

Enzo smiled while reading the message, as he focused on the name in his head. It was quieter. It felt less powerful as it boomed through Enzo's brain. 'Kelsie'. It'd be gone tomorrow; Enzo could feel it. He had no clue how to reply to Kelsie, but he had a hunch that Kelsie wouldn't care, so he just sent a quick 'That's amazing! Xx' then placed his phone back in his pocket, a heavy sigh escaping him once more as he pulled the phone out again.

Danny's contact flashed up, messages scrolling down the screen, as the dark-haired man sighed and brushed pieces of fringe out of his eyes. He hadn't texted Danny in a couple of weeks, not since Danny had texted saying 'Merry Christmas' over a week before Christmas.

Enzo never knew what to say to him. He wanted to say so much, but he could never type anything. All their conversations had lasted two minutes, but Enzo's heart fluttered when Danny's name appeared on his phone. He hated it, honestly. Danny felt like he was getting a big 'screw you' from the universe, because Danny was so freakin perfect, and Enzo missed him. They'd spent one night together, months ago, and Enzo missed him. He missed everything about him. He missed his smile and his laugh, and the feel of his body against his. He missed the wistful looks in his beautiful eyes. He missed his kindness and his heart. He wanted that in his life. Why did the universe take it away?

Maybe Danny was Enzo's Cara? If soulmates didn't matter, then what was to stop Enzo from running into Danny's arms and just letting go of all this soulmate crap? What was stopping him from going back and continuing their night together? He wanted to. He really did, but something in him was telling him that that was wrong; that he'd just get another voice and he'd just have to move on. They weren't meant to be but soulmates were crap anyway, so what was the point? But this was all Enzo knew. What would he do if he wasn't doing this? He'd just be reliant on Danny, and he didn't want to be reliant on Danny or anybody. Danny deserved better; everyone deserved better. People needed to be secure in their lives and their jobs and who they were, while having a partner who was there when they needed to be. That was how it worked, right? Because that definition felt wrong. Enzo didn't know what people wanted or needed. Maybe there was no such thing as a perfect relationship, or a relationship that wasn't at least, somewhat, symbiotic. Maybe all relationships were difficult and frustrating, and there was nothing worth putting up with another person forever for. That couldn't be right, could it? There were happy people out there. There had to be. There had to be soulmates who made it, and people who weren't soulmates who made it work. People like Kelsie's aunt and Danny's parents. People who fell in love and stayed happy; kept communicating and making things work when things got hard. Relationships took effort, and that's why people got so complacent when they found their soulmates. Enzo didn't want to do that to Danny. What could stop him doing that to Danny? What did he want? Crud, he didn't know what he wanted. He just wanted things to be simple. He'd give his left arm to get his brain to feel less jumbled and heavy. He wanted things to make sense again. Would things make sense with Danny?

Enzo was so wrapped up in his own head that he almost missed his stop, and when he almost missed his stop, he saw a train to Great Yarmouth. He saw the platform and felt his mouth go dry, and a sharp, static sound quaked through his brain.

His eyes couldn't stop tracing the bright, orange 'Great Yarmouth' that continually flashed before his face, as the rest of the world went silent.

"Uh…"

Chapter 15
DANNY

Coming out to his family over Christmas may have been a mistake.

Not because they weren't accepting, and not that he wouldn't do it again, but because his parents hadn't stopped talking about it. Bexxie had sent him links to every gay dating app and site she could find. Every. Single. One. Most of them were just porn, and Danny didn't have the heart to tell her. Well, he also just didn't click on the links.

It'd been three weeks since Christmas. Three weeks, and every conversation with his mother had started with her asking if he was seeing a new guy. His dad asked what it was like to fancy guys and to think about guys, and how he knew he was into them. Danny had expected him to shut down and just avoid the topic all together, so this was a surprise; not an unwelcome one, but a weird one that Danny was still adjusting to. Bexxie and his mum weren't a shocker at all.

School resumed normally. He signed his contract, and his pay went up. The paperwork got a bit more and the class load got heavier, but Danny loved his job and the kids loved him, so what else was there to say on that?

He was currently teaching a year five class, so it was a classroom of nine to ten year olds. This school didn't have assigned teachers for assigned classes, so Danny was moved around all over the place. It was a small school, but every teacher had a speciality, so they tended to focus on that. Danny didn't mind, though he struggled a bit in remembering all the new names, but he eventually came up with little nicknames and acronyms that worked. Well, not on everybody, and he still got it wrong sometimes. He was half tempted to do the substitute teacher thing and have everyone make little name stands, so he wouldn't embarrass himself anymore.

"Sir?" a little red-headed girl asked gently, and Danny's head whipped around from the board to face her. Her freckled hand was up in the air, and an awkward, curious look appeared on her face as she gulped and tried to stare Danny down.

Danny had a quick moment of trying to remember her name, before panicking and remembering that he'd dubbed her 'Red', and she didn't seem to mind.

"Yes, Red?" he asked, with a little smile.

The girl grinned at the nickname, then dropped her hand, her light-green eyes glistening in the daylight streaming through the window.

"Is it true that you have a boyfriend?" she asked.

Danny froze, his jaw dropping slightly. He felt his stomach swirl and quake, as phlegm flew up and blocked his nervous throat.

"Where did you hear that?" he managed.

'Red' just smirked. "My mum said she saw something on Facebook. Prefer... uh..."

"Preferences?" Danny asked, and 'Red' nodded proudly, as the man rolled his eyes.

He remembered Red's mother. She was one of those overly curious mothers who asked a lot of questions. She had talked to Danny for hours last month at parent's evening because she was worried that Red wasn't progressing in the 'right way'. It was frustrating, but he admired how much she cared about her daughter.

But now, she was stalking his Facebook? He didn't even change his preferences. Wait, did he? How else would she know?

Danny's eyes turned to the rest of the class, glancing over everyone as they blinked and stared at him with wide, curious eyes.

"Mr Strand!" one of the louder, bigger boys yelled, then put his hand up.

Danny just gulped and pointed to him.

"I thought you had a soulmate?"

Aw, crap.

"I did," Danny admitted, and the students gasped, while Danny's heart warbled to the back of his chest. "Okay, okay. Everyone, quiet."

Red placed her hand in the air again, and Danny reluctantly pointed to her.

"I thought soulmates were forever," she said.

Danny gave a small, sad smile. "Yeah, I thought that, too," he admitted with a sigh, while glancing around the confused, worried class.

"Are our soulmates not going to last either?" Red asked with sad, green eyes, as the whole class stared at Danny with glassy eyes.

Danny's heart clenched. "No," he said quickly. "No one's saying that." He turned his attention to the class. "Your relationships with soulmates last as long as you work on them."

"What does that mean?" Red asked.

Danny smiled, then sighed sharply and leaned back on his desk chair. "Okay, so you know when you're learning something, you have to practice, right?" Danny asked, and the class nodded. "So, like when you learnt to read, you went over words and letters until you could form sentences, then paragraphs, then stories. It took practice and work."

The class nodded once more as Danny smiled.

"Relationships are like that. Everybody is different. Some people have different hobbies and different beliefs, but you're all special in your own ways, and when two people find each other, it's all about finding the right balance and practicing until you get things right."

Red placed her hand up again. "Then what happened with you and your soulmate?"

Danny shrugged. "Sometimes things just don't work out and that's okay, too." he stated, and the big kid put his hand up again.

"So, you do have a boyfriend?" he asked.

Danny smiled. "No, no, I don't, but I am interested in men *and* women," he stated, and the class gasped once more before bursting into piles of excited conversation. "Okay, okay, quiet down."

"But you don't have a boyfriend?"

"No, I don't."

"But you did?" Red asked and Danny froze, his gaze turning to the floor.

"Uh, okay. Time to get back to the lesson," he stated then forced the kids to focus on the map on the board.

The lesson went by shakily after that, and Danny found his head drifting, his eyes widening when golden eyes and dark hair flashed through his swirling mind. His heart wavered and his mouth overflowed with saliva, but he shook off the thoughts every time, reminding himself of where he was and the fact that him and Enzo had had one night, and that was it.

So much time had passed, and it still didn't feel like one night. Well, maybe it did. It just felt like that night triggered so much. Danny thought of relationships and soulmates in such a different light now. He used to see them as perfect, but they weren't, and he was starting to see the beauty in the imperfections. People had to work hard at their relationships to make them happy. They had to be patient and understanding and try new things. They had to make sacrifices and figure things out as they went. It was all a jumble of things. Every relationship was different. Every soulmate was different, and Danny thought it was amazing.

He was a bit remiss in thinking that he wanted to know this when he met Allison, but he'd come to realise that he didn't want that anymore. Allison was a part of his past, and the more he thought on her and who they were together, the more he realised that he was a different person now and that they wouldn't fit anymore.

Bexxie's point about how this happened for a reason still plagued his mind. Him and Allison weren't meant to be because Allison held him back from seeing a part of himself that he was still figuring out. Thinking about guys still felt a little wrong to Danny. Not that it was wrong, but it was one of those things that he kept forgetting. He'd think of himself as straight then have to correct himself. It was just going to take a bit of time. He maybe should've waited to come out to his family, but his impulses had kicked in when Sophia and Barney were glaring, and he had just wanted to get it over with. He wasn't doubting his feelings, who he was or who he fancied. He knew very well that he was into girls and guys. He'd just been 'straight' for so long, that his mind was still trying to fully envelope the idea; like trying to add a new tab to who Danny was as a person.

He'd joined a few apps that Bexxie had sent and signed up to a couple of websites and created profiles, but he wasn't really looking to date yet. He just wanted to get used to the idea of putting himself out there again, but everything about those apps and sites felt wrong. There was something sharp and heavy in his heart when he looked at the people on them. He didn't know what it was or what it meant but he just clicked off the site when he felt it.

His teacher friends and his school friends had taken him out to the bar a few times in the new year. His Christmas was spent with his old school friends and he loved it. He fell asleep on Amy's couch and had woken up with a hangover and a backache, he loved it. It was lively, warm and perfect. It finally felt completely and utterly like Christmas, and Danny didn't miss Allison once. He just kept thinking about how they should've done this every year, and his friends agreed.

He'd missed them. They'd drifted slightly when Danny started dating Allison, but he was trying to fix things. He was making plans with everybody, picking up his guitar again, starting workouts and just existing. He was smiling more and relaxing into himself again, but he did feel this odd pressure to start dating. Well, he wanted to wait for another voice, but he didn't. He wanted to meet people, but he didn't. He was lonely, but

300

he wasn't. His brain and heart were still a confused jumble that caused aches through his body.

His friend, James, had taken him out to meet people, but Danny just went out to get drunk and have fun. It was a good night, even with James forcing Danny to talk to random guys every half hour. He just made quick conversation, smiled, got a free drink, then made an excuse and went back to his table. He kept explaining to James that he didn't want to date yet, and James had said, 'So? Just sleep with em. No one's saying 'date.' And Danny had slowly said that he didn't want that either. He wasn't the 'sleep with and move on' type. It was something that he knew about himself. Enzo was an outlier on that, but, well, he had slept with him. Had he moved on, though?

The school bell rang out, and all the kids disappeared as Danny cleaned his board and started gathering their workbooks in his backpack. He headed home quickly and collapsed onto his couch, phone falling into his hand as he sighed.

There were four new links from Bexxie, and an invite out to be 'wingmanned' by James. Danny was tempted to throw his phone across the room. He appreciated his family and his friends wanting to help him with this, but he didn't need the help. Well, maybe he did but he just didn't want to date anyone right now. He wanted to figure himself out and relax; not think about dating or living with someone. He wanted to get to a place where he didn't feel lonely, where he didn't notice the quiet echoing around his flat. He felt better, sure, and he was more accepting of how him and Allison had split and the fact that him and Enzo had had one night but his heart still had a hole in it. He needed time.

Danny's sleep-addled brain sent rapid-fire messages to Bexxie and James saying that he wasn't ready to date. Both replied immediately with a thumbs up, while Danny rolled his eyes and deleted the dating apps on his phone. It wasn't like dating nowadays was that simple since most people met their soulmates at eighteen and were just with them forever. There weren't a lot of apps, and the bars that James had been taking him to were singles bars. There were two in Great Yarmouth, and they were typically full to the brim with sad, lonely people who just wanted to hook up to feel something. Honestly, Danny didn't like being part of that crowd. He didn't like people looking that sad or feeling that lonely. Those bars reeked of heartache and Danny didn't want to be a part of that. He wasn't ready to date, but he didn't want to just hook up with equally heartbroken people who he didn't feel a connection to. He just wanted to feel normal again. Life had felt so up in the air for such a long time, and Danny felt like he was just finding his feet.

He sighed deeply then sunk back into his couch, silence echoing around him in a heavy swirl. There was no new name in his head but Danny was used to that now. He couldn't remember a time where he could hear another voice in there. The silence felt normal, but it also felt clawing and weirdly inevitable. It felt like he was waiting for something that wasn't coming. It felt like he was waiting for something important – something fundamental – and just wasn't getting it, but he was also dreading the idea of getting a new soulmate. He wished he wasn't dreading it, but he was. It was all so freakin complicated and frustrating. Danny knew better when it came to relationships now, but soulmates were still a ton of pressure, and he hadn't been alone that long. But he was learning to appreciate his own company; watching things that he wanted to watch and doing things that he wanted to do, without having to ask for the approval of another person.

Danny was a romantic at heart. He'd been excited to get a soulmate, but that hadn't panned out how he wanted it to, so he didn't want that again, yet. He knew now that relationships were harder than they appeared, but he wasn't ready to dive back into one. His life was his life, and he wanted to enjoy it. Was that dumb? Would he regret that idea? Could he really think this and want this while having the memories of Enzo cuddling and kissing him flooding his brain?

A deep sigh escaped Danny, as he shoved a hand into his face and picked up his phone, staring through his fingers to find Enzo's number. He clicked it and stared through the digits while pulling up the messages. He hadn't texted him since December 16th. He'd wanted to but couldn't find a reason.

He clicked the text box and watched the cursor flash but couldn't find anything to type or anything to say. They weren't soulmates, and Enzo had probably had four or five since Danny, which hurt to think on. Wait, was he jealous? He quickly rolled his eyes at that thought and placed his phone face down, into the couch.

Yeah, this was good. This was what he wanted. He wanted to be alone. He wanted to figure things out, adjust to not being straight. He wanted to have the flat to himself. He wanted to enjoy having more money, due to his promotion. He wanted this, but bright, gold eyes and long, dark hair haunted his head and warmed his heart.

No, no. He wanted this. He needed this, but his eyes unconsciously fell to the door, then to his phone, as a light, hopeful flash darted through his heart.

He shouldn't just text Enzo, right?

Chapter 16
JEREMY

Jeremy had been sitting on the roof for three hours. The frosty air was biting at his soft, pale skin, as he stared up at the bright, glowing moon. Everything felt so far away and simple up here. It was just cold. The sky was clear. The stars were bright and shining. The moon was glittering and full. Everything was simple and beautiful up here when nothing else made sense.

Jeremy spent a lot of time up here. He dragged his tiny, single quilt and a pillow up through the Uni halls, unlocked the roof door with his old, first year ID, propped it open with the brick then appeared at the edge and slumped into the cool, concrete ground, his pillow barely covering his butt, while the chilly breeze darted up his loose, space invaders pyjama trousers. The floral quilt wrapped around him easily, making him look like a little, pink marshmallow.

It warmed his skin easily, creating a little, snuggly barrier between Jeremy and the night air. It was the first time in a long time that he'd come out here alone.

The little, plastic table was still out from their date. The legs wobbled when the breeze washed over it. He still remembered her red dress and denim jacket; her black hair tied up in a curly side ponytail. He remembered the twinkle in her deep-brown eyes, her perfect skin glimmering in the sunlight, the smell of her vanilla perfume, the brightness of her smile and the lightness of her laugh. Everything about Vanessa was embellished into Jeremy. She was a piece of who he was.

She was the first person that he'd come out to; the person who'd taken him shopping for boxers and men's clothes; dragged him through Primark's men's section taken his hand and told him to breathe. She was there when he got his long, deep-brown hair cut off, she was the first person he called when he had his first clinic appointment. She was there through the beginning of his hormones – the frustration and the anger – she was there when his chin hair started to grow and Jeremy cried happily for six hours. She was there through the dysphoria. She was his support, his backbone, his everything. She made him feel attractive, reminded him who he was when he was losing it. She was a freakin saint but it was too much, wasn't it? It was too much to put on one person. She'd seen him in pain, seen him hating his body and doubting everything about himself. She'd seen him completely crumble and lose it.

He could still see her face when he had told her, the shock on her lips and the hurt in her eyes. He watched her entire body collapse like one of those thumb, string toys that fell when you hit the button. He watched her start to cry; watched her dark, pretty eyes well up and explode into streams of glittering liquid. He couldn't move or breathe. It felt like every part of him· was shattering and melting, but he was trying to do the right thing.

Jeremy and Vanessa had been together for two years. Two years of dysphoria and binders; two years of doubting himself and hating his body. Two years of therapy and denial and frustration. Two years of his body not matching his mind or his heart. He hated it. He'd have days of feeling okay and feeling happy, then he'd look down at his chest and start to panic. Vanessa would then come and remind him of who he was.

He'd had appointments with therapists. He'd been voice training and forcing his posture to be straighter to hide how his waist went in. He'd been on testosterone for a long, long time. He was used to it now but in the beginning, it was like fire shooting through his veins. His brain would fog in hot frustration and he had zero control over it.

He had days where he felt like he was just pretending to be a boy; where it felt like he was fooling himself, but he wasn't. He was Jeremy. Vanessa saw that. She heard that. She knew his name before he'd said it out loud to anybody, and now? Everything was changing. Now, he was going in for operations –top surgery, then bottom surgery. It'd been years in the making, and after next week there would be no more binders, but he was scared. Terrified. Every time he thought on it, his heart would beat so fast that it'd start to hollow out his chest. It'd been years in the making, and he wanted this, so why did it feel like that? It felt wrong, and he couldn't stop thinking about how his body was going to change, and how he wasn't going to be the person that Vanessa fell in love with, and it was stupid. He knew it was stupid. A part of him would scream whenever he had those thoughts, but he couldn't help it. What if she didn't love him anymore? What if she didn't want to touch him? What if this was just too much, and what if everything fell apart? He couldn't handle that. He loved her, and he just didn't want to see that look on her face when his body was different – when he was different. It was all too much, and he got scared, so he told her that it was over. It was like he'd ripped out his own heart.

"Jesus, it's freezing out here," a deep voice suddenly stated, and Jeremy's eyes went wide as the roof door clicked closed.

He jumped to his feet, his little, pink quilt wrapped around his shoulders like a thick, puffy cloak. The moonlight ghosted over the rooftop, as Jeremy turned and caught eyes with the deep-voiced stranger.

Everything froze when the moonlight gleamed through the man's glittering, light-brown eyes. They almost seemed gold in this light. The breeze fell dead through the cold air, and the voices in Jeremy's head faded through the back of his mind, as a sharp, high-pitched noise stabbed through both of his eardrums like a long, burning needle. His breath caught and his heart stilled, while he glanced over the pale, tall man. He had dark, feathered hair falling in a waterfall around his face, bright, brown eyes that gleamed in the dull light, and freckles that glowed like a constellation over his nose. His body was lean and tall, but his posture screamed 'I'm freezing. What am I doing out on this roof?' His arms were folded over his chest, and his entire form was shivering. He wore loose, blue jeans, a deep-brown jumper over a black and white checked shirt, and brown, lace-up boots. He looked about Jeremy's age, maybe a couple years older. He couldn't tell in the dull light, but it didn't matter. What mattered was how everything and every voice in his head faded when their eyes linked. Where did Vanessa go?

The stabbing, high-pitched noise got harsher and stronger, as a heavy breeze began inflating Jeremy's brain. He could barely breathe through it. His heart felt like it was bursting; like every ventricle and every bit of blood in there was expanding and stretching and bleeding down to his feet. It hurt, it ached, it was hideously heavy, and Jeremy didn't have a clue what to do. He didn't know what any of it meant, until a deep voice whispered 'Enzo' through the back of his brain, and the world completely stilled. Silence dropped like a stone through Jeremy's mind, as the quilt collapsed from his shoulders and his jaw dropped open.

"Whoa, whoa… don't drop that," the stranger said quickly, then sped forward and wrapped Jeremy back up in the quilt, as the helpless boy stared.

"You're uh… you're uh…" Jeremy stammered.

"Okay, Jeremy – breathe," Enzo stated, and Jeremy's aquamarine eyes got wider, his slim, small form falling back in shock.

"You uh… you know my… you heard…" Jeremy continued to stammer, his head starting to swim in the frozen breeze as all the breath got trapped in his throat. His vision started to darken and blur, as his heart stopped and his body lurched.

"Whoa," Enzo gasped, then rushed forward and gripped Jeremy's shoulders through the quilt. "Jeremy, calm down. Breathe, okay? You're okay. It's okay."

The words swirled around Jeremy's head in a pained, buzzing whirl until everything fell glassy and cold. Jeremy's body clattered into Enzo, the warm quilt engulfing them both. Jeremy's eyes slammed shut, as he let out a gasp.

He woke with a start, gasping in breaths heavily, as the moonlight swooned over him.

"Whoa, whoa," Enzo repeated, his hands pressing into his shoulders and his thumbs running over the sleeves of Jeremy's old, white T shirt.

The feeling of foreign, freezing fingers pressing into his skin is what finally shook Jeremy back to consciousness, and the man slithered back from the touch with a backwards crab crawl, hyperventilating the whole time as his quilt collapsed around him.

"Jeremy, calm down," Enzo pleaded, as Jeremy crawled his way into the building ledge and stopped.

His back bumped awkwardly into the concrete as he shuddered and groaned, his butt collapsing properly into the ground when Enzo appeared before him once more. He crouched and smiled gently, while Jeremy desperately tried to catch his breath.

"Okay, okay. I get it. I get that this is a *big* thing but Jeremy, please just breathe."

"I'm... breathing," he gasped through long, tough breaths.

"Barely," Enzo replied. "Just close your eyes for a sec, and I'll explain, okay?"

A gentle, warm, familiar wave flowed over Jeremy and delved into his muscles before nestling into his bones, but that just made his heart beat faster, and his breathing get harsher.

"Jeremy, seriously. Close your eyes and count backwards from ten. Focus on your breathing and think of nothing else, okay?"

Jeremy looked back and forth between Enzo's bright eyes, before gulping down a breath and nodding, his eyes closing.

Ten. Nine. Eight. Seven. He continued to count down, his heart getting slower and the grip on his quilt getting lighter, as he did. Six. Five. The blanket fell properly around his shoulders as his hands completely let it go. His eyes closed tighter, focusing on the light flowing through his closed eyelids. Four. Three. Two.

"One," he gasped out, then opened his eyes as his heart started to beat normally, and the warm tendrils flitting around Enzo gripped around his heart, falling to a pool of warm goo in his stomach. "Who are you?" he managed to gulp out, while squinting his aqua eyes curiously.

"Based on the panic attack, I think you already know," Enzo stated, then sat on the floor and crossed his legs.

"So, you are uh…"

"Yeah," Enzo replied, and Jeremy felt a sharp stab through his heart, as his brain heavily fogged.

"How?" he squeaked.

"That's uh… a long story," he muttered, then looked over the cold, night sky. "Any chance we could go inside before I explain? I know I'm wearing a jumper, but I forgot my coat back home."

Jeremy gulped and nodded, while Enzo got to his feet, leaned a hand down and proceeded to drag the guy through the roof exit. Jeremy took the lead, the pair walked down the stairs and into his little dorm room.

The fire door slammed closed, while Jeremy draped his quilt back on his bed, covering the pillows and the little teddies on the end. Enzo wandered through slowly, taking in the small, rectangular space. The walls were plastered with posters: Lord of the Rings; Superman; How I Met Your Mother. There was a wall with pictures of shots, and another with tropical cocktails. The tequila sunrise pulled Enzo's eye, as Jeremy slumped onto his bed and patted the space beside him.

Jeremy hadn't let his eyes leave the stranger. He watched as the light-eyed man slumped down, quilt quaking beneath the pair like a gentle wave.

"Okay, so you have questions?" Enzo asked, and Jeremy gulped.

"You're my soulmate?" he asked and Enzo nodded.

"And before you say it – people don't get just one," Enzo stated. "I hear new voices every few months."

"You get a new soulmate every few months? And what happens to your…" Jeremy began, then glanced at the picture on his nightstand, devastation squeezing through his heart in a wad of boiling phlegm. It was her on her 19th birthday with a stupid, plastic crown on her head and a bright pink, floral dress that wrapped around her curved figure perfectly.

Enzo caught Jeremy's distraction, then followed his gaze with wide, sad eyes. "Your old soulmate isn't gone. Some people hear their voice again when I leave," he said slowly, catching Jeremy's sad eyes as he gulped and shakily stared at the floor.

"I uh… I don't understand," Jeremy replied. "It's only been two weeks."

"Yeah… uh… I'm sorry, dude," Enzo stated, then bit his lip, turning to look at the picture on Jeremy's bedside table. "So, who is she? What happened?"

Jeremy began shaking, while staring at the photo.

He couldn't tell him, could he? It didn't feel right. Something about all this felt wrong, but he hadn't talked to anyone about this, it was starting to claw through his brain and tangle his thoughts. His heart was pounding and rattling through his ribs, and he still felt this warmth and familiarity about Enzo. It felt like he knew him. It felt like he'd always known him. The man made his heart warm and his head swoon, and he hated that. Only Vanessa was allowed to make him feel that. Vanessa was his soulmate. She'd always be, right? That's how these things worked. Where had she gone? Could she still hear his voice? What was happening? She couldn't be gone! Jeremy didn't want her to be gone. She couldn't be. Jeremy stared at the photo, feeling his vision start to blur and his heart start to ache. It felt like a part of him had been ripped out. She couldn't be gone.

"Whoa, whoa, Jeremy," Enzo said slowly, and pressed his warm hands back into his shoulders. "It's okay, it's okay. You're okay."

"Is she just gone? Is she not my soulmate anymore? I don't uh... I don't understand this. I still love her, Enzo. She um... she's not gone, is she?" he asked, while panic quickly built through his veins and flooded his eyes, tears pouring down his cheeks and onto his white shirt.

"She's not gone, Jeremy. She's just... this just... Okay, this would be a lot easier if you told me what happened."

"We broke up two weeks ago," Jeremy said blandly, while looking at the ground. "I could still hear her voice. She still lives in the dorm down the street. We'd been together two years since she heard my real name and recognised my voice while I headed to a lecture."

"Why'd you break up?" Enzo asked gently, and Jeremy stared at the carpet.

"I uh…" Jeremy began, wriggling awkwardly as his binder tightly compressed his ribs. "All right, I'm trans," he admitted, while hiking up an eyebrow and looking up at Enzo, a small gulp falling through his throat.

Enzo just smiled lightly, rubbed his shoulder and nodded to let him know that he should keep going.

"I uh… I've been on hormones for a few years now, and I've had therapy. I got a loan for surgery, and that's happening next week. Top surgery. Everything's changing, Enzo. She's known since the start, and she's seen…" He gestured to his chest and his lap. "My body's been changing slightly for years, but this is it. This is it, and I'm gonna look different and feel different, and she's not gonna… What if she doesn't like it? What if I don't like it? What if she looks at me differently? I couldn't handle it. I can't handle it. I love her, and she's just perfect and just…"

He crumbled, his breath getting stuck in his throat as his binder constricted tighter. It felt like a freakin elephant was standing on his chest. "I couldn't handle it. I can't… She's perfect. If she stopped loving me or looking at me the way she did before, then I just… I'm gonna be different. It's all gonna be different, and I didn't want us to change."

"So, you ended things?" Enzo asked, and Jeremy nodded numbly. "Coz you were scared?"

"I ended things because she already has so much going on. She works this crappy job at the coffee shop on campus, and she hates it. She's studying engineering, so her course load is crazy. She shouldn't have to deal with me when I'm recovering and can't move. I don't know what I'm gonna end up looking like. My whole body is going to be a mystery, and it's just too much to ask of her. What if she doesn't like it? She's used to me now, and I just... God, it's so freakin complicated."

"You're not happy in your body right now, right?" Enzo asked, and Jeremy scoffed.

"No, I'm not happy in it," he stated bluntly.

"Then you're doing the right thing, and the people who love you will support it. I'm sure... uh..."

"Vanessa."

"I'm sure Vanessa supported you, too," he said plainly, with a little smile.

"She shouldn't have to just... I've been changing for years, and she's just been forced to adjust, but this is just *huge*. She's straight, you know, and she's never been with a... uh... someone who has a uh... She's just so freakin patient and kind, and this is just too much to put on a person. She shouldn't have to just be stuck with me. It's not fair."

"She wasn't stuck with you, Jeremy."

"We're soulmates. We're meant to be together – had to be together. It wasn't her choice," Jeremy stated.

"It was," Enzo replied, and Jeremy's gaze snapped to him, confusion flooding his puffy eyes. "See, Jeremy, this is something that people don't get. We always have a choice, soulmate or not. You broke up with her – that was a choice."

"Because she has too much, and I just…"

"But still, it was your choice. Soulmates aren't permanent unless you make them permanent and you work at your relationship. Things can always go wrong, and people are always changing. It's okay." Enzo stated. "Soulmates are decided by the universe, but it's people's jobs to make them stick, and a lot of them are terrible at it. Some of them have bad luck, and some just screw up. Everyone's different and people don't always end up happy, but you always have a choice."

"I don't think Vanessa felt that way," Jeremy sighed, and stared down at his lap sadly. "She's just always been here and had to adapt, and it's just a lot to put on a person."

A sharp, smooth yawn escaped his throat as he awkwardly shuffled and laid down on his bed, the binder loosening slightly as he gulped down a breath.

"I get it, I do, and I don't want to tell you what to think or what to do here, Jeremy," Enzo said calmly, while staring through his fingers. "But if I cared about someone even half as much as you care about Vanessa – soulmate or not – then I'd have to talk to her."

A light snore escaped Jeremy, and Enzo jolted before staring at the guy, a little smile flooding his features as he awkwardly wrapped the quilt around his snoozing, pale figure. The skin around his eyes was a light red. His arms had landed in a heap above his head, revealing a little skin between his hips and his belly button. His lips were puffed out, and air floated out of his mouth in little wisps.

Enzo slowly stood up from the bed and switched off the light, glancing over the picture one last time, before tiptoeing over the floor and gently closing the door behind him.

Chapter 17
ENZO

Why was he doing this? He didn't know why he was doing this, and he knew leaving the dorm was a dumb idea. He didn't have a key! How was he supposed to get back to Jeremy? He'd just effectively locked himself away from the guy when the guy obviously needed someone to talk to. So why did he leave?

Oh, he was freakin playing matchmaker. He'd already played matchmaker once. He hadn't done this before in the past five years, then he had done it twice in the past two weeks. Just what the hell was going on with the universe?

Enzo just knew that Jeremy and Vanessa should be together. Jeremy was just scared. A lot was changing, and he was worried that it would change them. But Enzo could feel how much he loved her, in every word he said, and he just couldn't sit still and give his usual 'focus on bettering yourself and not on relationships' speech. He was so used to that speech, and this was the second time that he didn't have to use it. Relationships weren't as important as a person's own sanity, sure but when people loved each other and were obviously meant to be, and weren't just together because they were scared, then, well, they needed to be scared together and figure things out together.

Since when was that Enzo's attitude? He really didn't know when any of this had changed in his head, but he hated it. Jeremy obviously wanted Vanessa. It was now Enzo's turn to see if Vanessa wanted him, and he would put good money on her still wanting Jeremy.

So, he entered the little, red coffee shop labelled 'Student U' in blue and yellow lights, gave a silent prayer that he'd see a familiar face behind the bright, glass counter. The entry bells rang above his head, as he appeared in the small, empty space full of old-fashioned couches and small, round, glass tables.

Two figures stood behind the counter: a tall, thick, pale man, with a bald head that gleamed in the low, orange lights, and a short, black girl with long, dark, curly hair tied back in a high ponytail. She smiled sarcastically as Enzo entered. The bald man smiled too, then disappeared into the back as Enzo slowly approached the counter. She wore a grey jumper, blue jeans and a burgundy apron with a little coffee cup logo on the front. Her deep-brown eyes were bright and gleaming, but she looked tired. Her eyes were surrounded in dark shadows, and Enzo felt himself wilt as he leaned on the cool glass.

"What can I get you, sir?" she asked politely and Enzo smiled.

"Actually, hi... uh... are you Vanessa?" he gulped.

Vanessa's eyes widened, before she cocked a brow and folded her arms over the name tag that Enzo had not noticed before.

"Who's asking?" she asked.

"Right, sorry. Kinda forgot that that would be creepy. Sorry," he rambled off. He was used to people knowing his name before they talked! This was weird.

"Hi, I'm Enzo, and I'm a friend of Jeremy's."

Vanessa's hand fell to the counter with a hard slam, a sharp breath falling through her throat, as she stared through Enzo's bright, golden eyes.

"Is he okay? What's happened?" she asked quickly and Enzo jolted back, putting his hands up in surrender.

"He's fine. I think he could do with talking to you. Reckon you could leave early?" Enzo asked, and Vanessa fell back once more with a gulp.

"I uh... I'm not really supposed to, but just uh...one sec," she replied, then put up a finger and quickly wandered through to the back.

A few moments passed, and Enzo heard two heavy, frustrated sighs before a deep *'Fine'* echoed through the wall. Vanessa appeared behind the counter again, her hair down, apron exchanged for a long, cream, fluffy coat.

"Is he at his dorm?"

Enzo just nodded slowly, and she bobbed her head firmly.

"Let's go, Enzo." She walked quickly around the counter and darted out the door.

Enzo blinked in shock, then zoomed after her with a little smile. That was *way* easier than he thought it was going to be.

They arrived at the dorm building. Vanessa pulled out a key, unlocked the door and led the way in. The pair headed up the stairs and down the hall to Jeremy's room. Enzo was not sure what to do here. He felt the need to be here, but he felt like he was intruding. It was one of those catch-22 situations. He wanted to go but he felt like he should stay, so he ended up lurking by Jeremy's door, while Vanessa lightly knocked and walked in to hover over his bed. He stood opposite the tiny bathroom, while Vanessa moved Jeremy's desk chair over to his bed then turned on his desk lamp.

"Hey, dummy, what'd we say about sleeping with the binder?" Vanessa asked quickly, and Jeremy sleepily chuckled before slowly sitting up, painfully groaning and pressing a hand into his stomach.

"To not do it?" he responded gruffly, while blinking and looking up at Vanessa.

An easy, tired smile crossed his blushed face, until a shock of realisation struck him, and his aquamarine eyes fell to a deep green, grey. His eyes stopped on Enzo, and the man jolted then smiled awkwardly, before folding his arms and raising his eyebrows expectantly, miming the words 'Talk to her'.

Jeremy jolted, then turned back to Vanessa, rubbing a hand over his chest as he slowly turned to sit up.

The pair faced each other silently for a few long moments, each blinking and shakily breathing. Vanessa leaned forward and clasped her hands together, while staring deeply into Jeremy's eyes. The air around them felt hot, heavy, sparky and full of tightly coiled tension, that started strangling Enzo's oesophagus.

"Hi," Jeremy stated quietly and Vanessa cocked a brow.

"Hi, are you okay? This guy kinda came and dragged me out of work so we could talk," she stated, then gestured to Enzo, as the dark-haired man fell back in surprise.

"Yeah, uh sorry about that," he said, and the pair turned their gazes to him.

Vanessa stared pensively at him, and Jeremy looked on with wide, sad eyes. They blinked at him silently for a few seconds, then turned back to each other.

"So, are you okay?" Vanessa repeated.

Enzo sighed in relief, feeling like he should leave, but not being able to.

"Yeah... I'm uh..." Jeremy began, then looked at Enzo and gulped. "Well, uh..."

Enzo smiled gently and nodded.

"There's um... there's something I should say to you, and I..."

"Jeremy, I know. Enzo just kinda came up, and I know I shouldn't be here, and I shouldn't still have your key. Do you wanna take your key back? I don't really know what to do here. I still have a bunch of your stuff, too. And the posters, and, yeah," she rambled off quickly, her confident, steady posture falling, as her shoulders slumped and her eyes slipped to the ground.

Enzo felt his heart grind to a halt as cool, dusty tension settled through his veins.

"I uh... I don't want it back," Jeremy awkwardly admitted, while rubbing his hands together.

Vanessa just blinked up at him. "You want me to just throw it out?" she asked.

"Vanessa, I..." Jeremy began, then gulped, rubbing a hand down his tight chest. "I'm sorry."

Silence flooded the room in an uneasy wave.

He closed his eyes tightly, then opened them and stared back into Vanessa's eyes. "I... uh... I wasn't honest with you when we broke up. I um... Sorry, I don't know where to..." he began, feeling his heart start to warble through his chest. Breathing started to feel like he was pushing air through a blocked straw.

Vanessa jumped up from her seat and started rubbing circles down Jeremy's back, while slumping onto the bed beside him.

"It's okay, it's okay; just breathe," she soothed, and forced out a few slow breaths through her small, rounded lips, as the pair linked eyes once more.

Enzo watched on in slow shock, as the heated tension in the room fell slightly in a comforting wave. Jeremy's voice got quieter through Enzo's head, as the sparks around the couple started to burn through his corneas. It was so weird. There was something so visceral and charged about the air around them. There was something so bright and magical about the way their eyes twinkled, and their cheeks burned. There was something so kind and unguarded about how they looked at each other. Enzo could see this was hard for them both. It was clear in their awkward, hunched posture and the nervous, gulping breaths but in their eyes, all he saw was love and respect, and it made his heart burn.

Jeremy's breath calmed down, and he smiled at Vanessa. "I missed you," he admitted, before he could think better of it.

His eyes fell to his lap, as Vanessa pulled her hand back with an awkward, little smile that fell when she stared down at her lap too.

Jeremy's gaze turned to Enzo, and he just nodded, miming the words 'Talk to her' again, while dramatically tilting his head.

'What do I say to her?' Jeremy mimed back, then dramatically tilted his head to Vanessa.

'Just talk!' Enzo replied.

"Okay, it's like a silent movie in here," Vanessa stated, turning to look at both boys while raising her eyebrows at Enzo. Her gaze then fell back on Jeremy. "What's going on?" she asked gently, then turned back to Enzo. "And uh …who are you? No offense, but I just haven't seen you on campus before, so are you like a college friend or something?"

"Uh…" Jeremy began dumbly.

"It doesn't really matter," Enzo replied awkwardly and Vanessa cocked a brow. "Yeah, I'm just an old friend. I'm just here to…" He looked at Jeremy with wide eyes. "Help," he added, with a shrug.

"Okay," Vanessa stated sceptically, then cocked an eyebrow at Enzo. "Mysterious – I like it."

Enzo grinned.

Vanessa turned back to Jeremy. "What did you want to say?"

"I'm sorry," he repeated.

"Yeah, yeah. I got it. Me too, but what else?"

"Why are you sorry?" Jeremy asked, in squeaky confusion.

"I um…" She ran a hand through the back of her curly hair, twirling through a strand as she leaned forward and avoided Jeremy's aqua-grey gaze. "Just when we broke up… it was weird, and I know you just… you were just… I was just clingy and annoying, and I was all stressed from work, and we hadn't been on a date in a while, and I just know that you have *a lot* going on. I'm sorry for being so angry and tired and just…"

"Whoa, what?" Jeremy said quickly, then pressed a hand into her shoulder, with a little, shocked smile. "You have nothing to apologize for, Ness. I uh… it wasn't about that. You're perfect; you've always been perfect. Just, okay…" Vanessa blinked back in surprise, as Jeremy let out a shaky, awkward breath.

"Right, so my surgery is next week. I was talking in therapy about um… about…" Jeremy began, Vanessa rubbing a hand down his back once more. He closed his eyes for a second, smiled, then turned to stare down at his clasped hands. "Okay, so with the testosterone and the voice stuff and just… I don't know; even like the subtle things like me trying to stand taller to make my waist less in. And me working out more, so my chest was more toned and my hips were less rounded and curvy, and I just… Okay, my body's been changing. I've been changing for years. You knew me when I was wearing those like long, sweater dresses and tights, and I'd cross my arms over my chest every day and live in sports bras, coz I just hated my body."

"So, like before you came out?" Vanessa asked with a cocked eyebrow, and Jeremy gulped.

"Yeah, but it's like my body's been changing a lot, and I've been changing a lot, and every time that's happened, I just kept thinking on how I wasn't the same person that you fell for; the same person who you heard the voice of two years ago."

"Whoa, whoa. Just coz you gained a bit of muscle and stood straighter?" Vanessa asked, and Jeremy collapsed forward slightly, elbows falling to his knees.

"I know it sounds dumb, but I'm not the same person, am I? And my body's gonna be changing a lot after the operations, and I'm gonna look different. My body's gonna feel different, and it just kept scaring me that you'd be nice and supportive, but you wouldn't be attracted to me anymore. I just couldn't shake it, and I didn't want you to have to lie, and I just…" Jeremy rambled, collapsing further into himself.

"Jer, you know I don't care about that stuff, right? I just want you to be comfortable in your body. That's all I want, and I couldn't give a crap what you look like or what you feel like. And yes, you have changed, but just…" She sighed and gave a little smile, turning Jeremy's face to hers by tilting his chin up and to the right.

Jeremy blinked but looked into her eyes, his face blushing harshly.

Vanessa smiled. "In the best ways, you're more comfortable in yourself, and confident and cool –well, cool in that dorky, awkward way – but I'm attracted to who you are, not what you look like. The fact that you're freakin adorable is just a bonus."

Jeremy smiled, his gaze falling to his lap.

Enzo also smiled, his eyes turning to the door as he properly debated leaving.

"But it's just gonna be a lot, and with the draining and the healing… I haven't even properly investigated bottom surgery, but it's supposed to be invasive. The results vary, and I just don't have a clue what I'm gonna end up looking like. I was thinking about going for the keyhole surgery, but I think I'm gonna get the double incision one, coz that's what Mr Grover recommended. But then there are the uh… the…" He pointed to the bottom of his chest. "… The scars, but he said it was the safer and the results are better. I don't know, and I'm too scared to look up bottom surgery coz I don't know if I want to get it, but if I don't get it, then I'm just..."

"Whoa, whoa. Calm down, Jer. Breathe," Vanessa stated quickly, then pressed a hand into his shoulder. "It's okay; it's okay. You don't need to make these decisions right this minute. You've got time, and you just have to do whatever you're comfortable with. If you want the double incision, go for it. If you want the keyhole, go for it. It's your body."

"But what about the scars?" Jeremy asked, and Vanessa shrugged.

"It wouldn't matter to me," she said with a smile. "Scars or not, you're still Jeremy."

He smiled. "Are you sure you want this?" He gestured to himself. "Coz I know I screwed up, and I'm sorry for hurting you, and I um..."

Vanessa smiled gently, then ran a hand over Jeremy's cheek, their eyes falling on each other as the heat in the room got hotter and happier. Anticipation slapped Jeremy in the gut when Vanessa leaned forward and slipped her warm lips onto his.

That was when Enzo left. He opened the door silently then wandered out into the hall, closing the door slowly before walking down the stairs and out the front of the building. Jeremy's voice faded through his head, as he grinned in the silence and stared up at the half lit-up Uni halls.

His heart was warm and his head was spinning. The world felt light and magical, as the moonlight settled through his bones and a calm breeze shook through his hair. He slipped a hand into his jean pocket then walked over to his bike, wavering before slipping a leg over and settling onto the seat. His eyes did not leave the building, as he sighed and chucked his helmet on.

They were going to be okay – Enzo could feel it. They were happy, adorable and wonderful, and they were going to be okay. Jeremy just needed to pull away for a second and figure himself out. He was scared, and Enzo was just glad that he'd been there.

Also, what was going on with his soulmates? What happened to having months with them, or weeks? He'd had ten days with Rebecca's stupid name, then about twelve hours with Kelsie's, and now eight hours with Jeremy. What was it? Why was time going so quick? Was it because he helped them? Because that's what he'd been doing with the others too. He'd helped all his soulmates, right? Was he meant to set them up with their old soulmates and then move on? Because that didn't feel right.

A sharp sigh escaped Enzo as he turned on his engine. A little squeak flew through his ears, getting sharper and harsher as his eyes widened, and his heart started to drag through his chest painfully. Ventricles came to life and stiffened, while Enzo shook his head and sighed.

'Khaleesi,' a gentle, kind voice echoed though his mind, and Enzo scoffed out a breath before looking up at the sky.

"What's going on?" he asked the moon, his arms flapping at his sides, frustration stabbing through his veins like long, heated needles. "Look, okay, I get it. I'm the freakin soulmate janitor but why is everything going so quick? And why am I being set up with people who are in love with other people, or who *just* end up being my friend? Am I meant to fall in love with all these people? Why am I different? And what am I supposed to do? Am I just…?" His eyes fell to the floor, his hair flopping into his eyes. "Am I just gonna be alone forever? Or am I supposed to keep doing this forever? Coz I don't know how much longer I can do my job or live in my crappy flat. I don't know how much longer I can hide the fact that I'm bi from my dad. Is my life *ever* just…"

A sharp sigh escaped him as his eyes lasered the floor, a serious, painfully hot squish pressed through his heart and caused his back to straighten. "Is my life ever just going to be mine?"

'Khaleesi,' the voice insisted once more, and Enzo sighed sharply then turned on his engine.

"I guess not. On my way, Khaleesi."

Chapter 18
KHALEESI

Kal had never put much stock into soulmates. It's not that he didn't believe in love or in romance or any other things. It was hard not to believe in romance when you studied in the most romantic city in the world. Seriously, he could walk outside and see six couples making out outside bakeries, cafes, schools and varying other things. People in Paris didn't really have a good sense of what was appropriate PDA and what wasn't. They just kissed and touched each other and, well, it was gross, and Kal didn't want to be a part of that.

He'd had a voice since he was eighteen, like everybody. It was just this guy named 'Noah,' who had a slight American twang. They'd never met, and Kal doubted that they would ever meet, given that he was twenty-two, and there was just no sign. It wasn't that he didn't care, or that he wouldn't be excited to meet the person who the universe had picked for him. It was just that life was fine without him.

He lived in a beautiful city. He had lived there for a year now, and he still had another year to go on his master's course. His painting had gotten much better since he'd moved from Dublin, and he spent basically every day on his crappy fire escape, just painting the clouds and the moon and the sky. He'd spot people across the road and paint them too. He loved it. He got lost in worlds and found new colours. It was awesome.

She'd woken up one day, uncomfortable in her thick, masculine pyjama trousers and sports bra. She took a shower, then put on her long, red, floral dress with her black, lace-up boots and thin tights. She'd taken her short, wavy, blonde hair down, shoved on a bit of red lipstick, as well as some pale-pink eyeshadow, some light-brown mascara and a tiny bit of concealer on some frustrating spots. She had looked in the mirror and grinned, feeling that today was a 'Leesa' day. Her lightly bronzed skin glittered perfectly in the low lights from her pale blue bathroom. Her shoulder-length, dirty-blonde hair fell in perfect waves down the sides of her small, rounded face. Her tight, red, button dress clung to her slim, tall form, falling to the middle of her calves. She double-checked her make-up, gently rubbing off a bit off mascara from the corner of her right eye, before chucking on her denim jacket and her little backpack and walking out of her tiny, pink apartment.

It was about eight a.m. on a Sunday morning. She was pretty sure it was January, but she wasn't a hundred percent sure. It was cold, but it didn't feel like Christmas. There were people out and about, but not many. Valentine's merch had started to appear in stores, along with Easter eggs and Mother's Day things. January always felt like one of those 'nothing' months and Leesa didn't really care for it. Last year she had spent January wandering around the city and taking pictures with her new, vintage camera, then printing them off in her school's dark room.

This year she was doing the same, then she was heading to the Louvre, because she wanted to make the most of her last weekend before classes properly started again.

She'd appeared over the Seine River in no time, the sun just starting to rise, bathing the world in deep pinks, reds, oranges, and yellows. The light was bright, white and beautiful, shimmering over the water and causing little glittery patches to appear on Leesa's copper skin.

She pulled out her camera and took some simple, basically composed shots, aiming specifically at capturing the light effects on the water. A few people were up and wandering about, smiling through the sunlight and eating pastries. The air was cool, but the breeze was warm. Her muscles chilled and froze, then warmed as the heated breeze ghosted over her skin.

She grinned through the light, looking out over the breeze and catching lights slowly appearing through the buildings in little, orange squares. It was beautiful and warm. It already looked like something out of a painting, and Leesa just closed her eyes and breathed through the silence with a wide grin.

Wait, silence? Her eyes blinked open quickly, her eyebrows lowering as a sharp, warm breeze slapped at her cheeks and a stabbing pain jabbed through her ears.

She cringed and bit her lip as a tall, dark figure started to appear from the other end of the bridge.

She squinted in a desperate attempt to make out the man across the way. He was clearly a guy, with his boots, jeans and navy jumper. His hair was long and flowing, but she couldn't make out any other details until he took another six steps forward, and Leesa's eyes went wide in shock. The guy had pale, glimmering skin with little freckles over his nose. His eyes were a beaming gold, and everything about him felt familiar and warm. Had she seen him before? It felt like she'd seen him before, when a voice quaked through her head and every muscle in her body felt numb.

'Enzo,' it stated, and Leesa grinned then pointed to the man.

"Enzo?" she asked.

"Khaleesi?" he asked, and she nodded.

"Well, Leesa, right now, but yeah," she corrected, and Enzo nodded in understanding. "Wanna get a pastry?"

Enzo blinked in surprise. "Sure, but you don't, like... you're not..." he began, then gestured between the pair of them. "You're not, like, freaked out by..." He gestured again, and Leesa shrugged.

"Nah, soulmate or not, I haven't had breakfast today," she stated then began to wander off the bridge.

Enzo blinked in confusion then followed her to the little, green pastry shop.

They grabbed a table in the far corner. Enzo ordered a croissant and a cup of tea, while Khaleesi ordered a cup of coffee and a *Pain au chocolat*. Each nursed their mugs while staring around at the flowers crowding and covering the walls of this place. There were multi-colour, rectangle plant pots dangling from the ceiling and overgrowing with roses and daisies. The whole place smelt like chocolate and coffee. It had wall-to-wall and ceiling-to-floor windows that showed a glittering view of the Seine.

A few silent moments passed as the pair nibbled on their pastries and sipped at their warm drinks before Leesa dramatically slammed her mug onto the table with a smug grin. Enzo jumped, then stared at her with a cocked eyebrow and a half-smirk.

"So, how old are you? Where are you from? How did you get here?" she queried.

"Twenty-three, Wickhampton, and I took an early morning plane from Norwich," he explained, "You?"

"Twenty-two, Dublin, and I walked," she replied. "How'd you know where I was?"

Enzo grinned wickedly, causing a flicker of fire to dart through Leesa's chest.

"I just did," he explained vaguely, shrugged, then drank his tea.

"You realise that that's more creepy than intriguing, right? Did you stalk me or something?" Leesa asked, and Enzo's eyes went wide.

"What? No. I... I just know," Enzo said. He nibbled on his croissant, and Leesa's eyes widened.

"Okay, now that's intriguing. How did you know?" she asked, and Enzo grinned.

"Seriously, I just know," he replied, then shrugged. "I'm a little different – soulmate-wise – than most people."

"Different how?" Leesa asked with squinted eyes.

"Different in that I get a new one every couple of months," he explained with a short sigh, before staring down at the table.

"A new... you what?" Leesa asked and Enzo shrugged.

"My soulmate changes. I've never heard the same voice in my head for longer than about four months," he explained, and Leesa's eyes went wide once more.

"Right, that explains this," she stated, then gestured between the two of them. "Am I just gonna not have a soulmate when you leave, or do I, like, get a million soulmates like you?"

"You're not gonna end up like me. This soulmate thing isn't infectious." Enzo sighed and gave a small, subtle eyeroll.

"Sounds like you've been asked that a lot," Leesa stated, then cocked a brow. "I mean, I don't really care either way. Soulmates are just kinda... they exist." She shrugged.

"That's it?" he asked, and Leesa shrugged once more while looking into his eyes.

"Yeah. I mean, I get it. It feels like I already know you, and it's nice and kinda cool, but it's not like the be it and end all," she said.

"Huh," Enzo said slowly, while cocking an eyebrow.

"What?"

"Nothing, that's just… uh… you're different," Enzo stated.

"Different… bad?"

"Different, interesting," Enzo stated, with a little cheeky smirk. "You really don't care about soulmates? You ever met yours?"

"You mean aside you?" she grinned. "No, I haven't. I think he's in California or something, and I'm not about to hop on a plane to try and hunt him down. Not all of us have soulmate GPS."

Enzo chuckled. "But you really don't care?"

Leesa shrugged. "Yeah. I mean, soulmates are great if you have 'em, but I don't need one to be happy," she said, and Enzo blinked in slow shock with a little, wistful smile.

"Well, that's refreshing," he admitted, his smile growing slightly.

"Refreshing?" Leesa asked.

"Lot of people have very stilted attitudes on soulmates," Enzo explained. "How we all only get one and they're supposed to be together forever, even if they don't talk, or fight all the time, or cheat, or end up hating

338

each other. Soulmates are forever, and we don't have to try– it's all very false."

Leesa scoffed then stood, grabbing their mugs and plates and placing them on the counter.

"You up for a trip to the Louvre? Was planning on going there before…" she began, then pointed between the pair of them.

"Sure," he said.

The pair wandered down the Seine, sunlight beaming over them and getting brighter and brighter as the sky turned from pink, red to a pale, glimmering blue like the water beneath. A few candyfloss clouds appeared in the sky, as the sun glowed over and through the pair. Leesa led the way, her eyes continually staring at Enzo as they walked.

He was about the same height as her. He had dark hair, light-brown eyes, little freckles on his nose, sharp features and tall posture. He was one of those guys that you'd look at across the street and think 'Hey, he's cute', then move on. His smile was kind and understanding, but there was something grey and drifting through his glittering gold-brown eyes. His freckles seemed to beam out refracted rainbow light, glowing through his eyes and making them brighter. Leesa got a weird sense from him – beyond the 'he stalked her across the country' feeling, that turned out to be technically untrue.

"Why are you like this?" she asked suddenly, and Enzo sighed sharply, coming to a stop just before a display case full of sarcophaguses.

"I don't know," he admitted, and a weird silence flew over them as Leesa cocked an eyebrow. "I just am. It's a long story."

"Well, our souls are bound for eternity; I think we got a little time," Leesa said with a little smirk, and Enzo rolled his eyes.

"Not exactly how it works, Leesa," he replied.

"I know, but you can still talk to me. I think you might need to, buddy. You're all broody and silent," she explained then gestured to him widely.

"I am not broody," he stated and Leesa rolled her eyes.

"And defensive," she added and Enzo scoffed.

"Fine. I don't know why I'm like this," he sighed. "Well, okay. I had a soulmate when I was eighteen; this guy named Tim who was like my best friend. He was sweet and we had fun. We knew each other before we knew we were soulmates, and we were two weeks in and planning our future together; talking about going to Uni together, where we wanted to travel to in the future, and whether we wanted kids. Looking back on it now, it was *insane* to plan that far ahead, at eighteen." He realised aloud.

"Yeah, no shit."

"But we were soulmates, and that's how these things worked, right?" He asked, disbelief clear in his tone. "You're bound to each other and meant to be, and everybody believes it. You get one person – one person who you spend the rest of your life with, regardless of whether you grow apart, whether the other person cheats, or whether one person works out they're a lesbian and they're dating a guy. Like, what are the limits? People can be bound to anyone, and we're just supposed to stick together, regardless of how much we grow and change, how different we are, or whether your partner is disloyal or cruel. Soulmates add this stupid contract or addendum to relationships. They add this pressure that *no one* can handle or live up to, because people aren't perfect. No one is great at confrontation or perfect with communication. We all have issues telling people things that they don't want to hear, and it's not okay. It's never been okay, and people act like losing their soulmate is this awful, shameful thing. Being single in this world is freakin impossible because everybody looks at you with pity in their eyes, and it just hurts. And everybody thinks that being single is just terrible, when being single is good for people. It's good because you get the chance to figure yourself out and just relax. Relationships are a lot of pressure, and you're always around that other person. There's just no time, so you just start putting what you want and who you are to the side, and you start losing the things that make you special, until you're just a part of that other person. Then that relationship doesn't work out, and then they leave, or they cheat, and you're lost," Enzo rambled off, pacing back and forth with wild, frustrated hand gestures. His voice had gradually gotten louder and louder, until the small crowd of people around them were either staring or walking away with wide eyes that read, 'Yep, that dude's mental.'

"My parents hate each other, yet they're not splitting. My dad drinks and my mum hides away, but they're soulmates, so they're stuck together. *So* many people I've met have met their soulmates and just assumed they'd be fine, until communications slip and they just start changing and falling apart. But they stick it out – not because they love each other but because they're obligated to stay, and it's easier to stay. They don't know who they'd be if they weren't with their soulmates. They also just hate the idea of telling their family or friends that they screwed up and lost the person that the universe decided was their perfect, freakin match. It's just impossible; having a soulmate is an impossible, ridiculous fantasy."

"Wow, okay," she said eventually.

Enzo sighed. "But," he continued, then turned back to look at the sarcophaguses, "sometimes it all feels great, and you fall head over heels. You laugh, and you joke, and you have fun. You forget about this stupid soulmate pressure for a minute because you just want that other person. You just want to see them smile and hear them laugh, and you just want to get to know them. But then the universe decides, 'Nope, onto the next guy', and the next guy is great. All the people I've met

– except for one, but she might even be alright; she just screwed up and needs to fix it – needs to stop being so self-involved, but yeah, it doesn't matter. They're all great, and it all feels the same. Like we already know each other, and things are fun and cute and sweet. Talking to my soulmates is like talking to an old friend, but I've been doing this for five years, and all I do is appear and tell people to put themselves first and figure things out; take a break and just relax about relationships. But what if that was wrong?"

"What do you mean?" Leesa asked.

"I wanted my soulmates to be secure in themselves, whether they had another person or not. But recently, I don't know. My soulmates have been weird, and I've just been helping them connect to people – soulmate or not – because they were in love and just, urgh," He sighed sharply, running a frustrated hand through his hair and tugging a few scruffy strands into his eyes. "I don't know how I feel about this anymore. Relationships are complicated. It's about wanting, not needing someone. Soulmates are just people and people screw up. Sometimes relationships don't work out and that's fine. It's all communication and taking time for yourself and just trying not to get lost. It's all ... I don't know. I haven't been in a relationship in *so* fucking long. Hell, before the end of last year, I hadn't kissed anyone since I was eighteen. I don't know anything, and I go about the country telling people to think of themselves and not date and just be secure in being

343

alone. Should I have been telling them to put themselves out there and fall in love with someone else? What's the right answer? Coz being alone freakin sucks. It does. It's good sometimes, but sometimes things are just so quiet, and you just start thinking about how much you missed out on and how much you hate your job. You just want someone to be there so you can rant and rave and let things out. You just want a sounding board; someone who'll listen and make you smile when you feel like shit. Someone who'll hold your hand and let you know that you're not alone. Someone who helps you believe in you when you don't know where to start. It's not wrong to want that, and I get it, but just..." Another sigh.

"It's okay to be alone, and it's okay to not want to be alone. It's not okay to stay in a relationship where you're unhappy because you feel pressured to stay, and it's not okay to ask too much of your partner. Everyone is entitled to their own opinion, and nobody *has to* do something for the sake of someone else. Relationships are about choices, honesty, loyalty and figuring things out together while working on yourself. Is that right? Coz I don't freakin know! It just feels... it feels like you're either alone and can figure yourself out, or you're in a relationship and you're stuck. I don't want that to be true because none of us know who we are at all times. We're always changing and growing. Nobody's perfect and life is crazy, and it's a lot. Relationships are a lot."

Leesa just blinked at him, as the small crowd slowly dissipated. Enzo began collapsing in on himself, his arms wrapping around his chest as the words in the air began pressing down on his shoulders and darting through Leesa's ears. She just stared at him and tried not to feel the new weight pressing through and squeezing juice out of her heart. Her hand reached out and pressed into his shoulder.

He jumped and turned to her with wide eyes.

"You've been holding that in for a long time, haven't you?" she asked with a raised eyebrow, and Enzo scoffed.

"You have *no* idea," he answered, and turned to her, his posture falling back to normal as he unfolded himself. "Sorry."

"Hey, it's all right," she said. She retracted her hand and shrugged. "You're not wrong to be fair. I mean, I've never been in a relationship, so I don't really uh… well, okay, I've dated and I've kissed people and hooked up, but I've never fully dated anyone. I don't really care about soulmates. My parents split up when I was a kid. They were soulmates but they just weren't working out, so my dad left. They're still friends now, and they're both remarried and happy. Like, it happens. They're still technically soulmates, but I think they've both sort of agreed to be 'friend soulmates'. Just accepted that they were meant to be a part of each other's lives forever, just not in the way that they thought," she explained, and Enzo blinked in surprise.

"So, friend soulmates are a thing?"

"I mean, I don't know if it worked out for other people, but it works for my parents, so…" She shrugged. "I think the key to anything is just doing whatever you're comfortable with and trying to be true to you. No one gets everything right all the time, Enzo."

Enzo rubbed his upper arm and gave a little gulp, his eyes falling to his feet as Leesa looked at him curiously.

"So, who are they?" she asked, and Enzo jumped.

"What?"

"I mean, I don't know if you're straight or not. I'm assuming not, since I'm fluid, and we're soulmates, so…" She shrugged. "But something's obviously triggered this, and you were talking about being alone and about not feeling like you can be yourself in relationships but wanting to. So you *want* to date someone, but you feel like you can't."

"You considered joining the FBI? You'd be a pretty good detective," Enzo stated.

"I mean, you were just laying it all out there," Leesa returned easily, then folded her arms and cocked her eyebrow knowingly. "So? Who?"

"He was named Danny," Enzo began, "and is basically the reason that my brain has been fucked on relationships for the past four or five months. Well, okay, he was the spark that ignited that stupid flame, and it doesn't matter, coz I'm messed up for some reason. I can't have a soulmate for longer than eight hours now, so…" He shrugged. "What you gonna do?"

"What do you mean?"

"I mean, I'm messed up and I don't know why. I know that most people don't get just one soulmate, but they usually get soulmates that last longer than a day or a week or a month, and it's usually after they've met and lost their original soulmate, that I appear. Then I leave, then they get another, and they're just together forever – it's easy for them. It's supposed to be easy and happy. I don't know. I like doing this, or I liked it. I liked travelling around the country, meeting people and helping them, and I think I *have* helped them. I don't know. I can't stop thinking about how cynical I've been, and how much I've encouraged people to focus on them and not think on relationships. Was that the right thing? It feels like I was forcing my ideals on them, and now they're all cynics, like me, who are gonna end up alone."

"Do you know that they are? Do you really think you had *that* much of an effect on these people? No offense." Leesa added, and Enzo smirked.

"I mean, I'm pretty charismatic," he stated, and Leesa rolled her eyes. "I don't know. I don't think I went in and saved them or did everything correctly. I like to think that I started them on a good path. That's all. I came in and pointed something out, but they pushed themselves to be better, and now they're happy, but that's not the point."

"The point is – why are you like this and how can you stop being like it?" Leesa asked, then raised her eyebrows up her head slowly.

"I, yeah… I don't know."

"You don't know if you want to stop, or you don't know why this started in the first place?"

"Both," he scoffed.

"How do you feel about relationships, and how did you feel about them when you got your second soulmate?" Leesa asked curiously.

"I uh… I was heartbroken and depressed. I thought I had no chance in finding someone new. Then I did, and they were great. Well, they'd just lost their soulmate, too, so we kinda bonded. I helped them, and we helped each other. I don't know. It was nice. Then I got another and another and, yeah, they were all great, and I've been doing this for so long that I just can't imagine not doing it."

"But you want to?" Leesa asked, and Enzo gulped. "You know it's your choice, right? Soulmates are ultimately just a name in your head. They don't control you, and life goes on without them."

"That's easy for you to say when you don't know where they are," he stated.

"Yeah, I guess, but you said you've been going around and trying to tell people that life goes on without soulmates, but it just kinda sounds like your life *is* soulmates."

"Yeah, you're telling me," Enzo replied, and the pair started to slowly trudge through the museum.

"No, seriously, Enzo. Okay," Leesa said, then grabbed his shoulders and forced him to turn to her. "Seriously, you're not getting this. I get that you know where your soulmates are, and you're right that *knowing* that would change things, but it's still just a name in your head, okay? That's all it is. *We're* what gives them reason, and we are what puts pressure on soulmates and relationships. Everything is a choice, and every person you date doesn't have to be a soulmate. It's about *you*. That's it. You have to do what's right for you. People can figure things out and move on. It's not your responsibility to make sure that they do, though I'm sure you have helped people and given them a reason to. How long have you been doing this?"

"Five years," Enzo sighed, and Leesa's eyes went wide.

"Dude, I think it's time that you started thinking about what you want. Stop letting the names dictate you," Leesa stated with a little smile, pulling her hands back and staring through his eyes. "I think you should go home."

Enzo blinked in shock. "But your name isn't... your voice isn't..."

"I know, I know. Yours isn't either, and I don't really want you to go. You're the most interesting thing that's happened up here in a long while, but I think you need to go. I think you need to start taking your own advice," she suggested, while looking into his glistening, golden eyes.

He opened his mouth a couple of times while trying to think of something to say, but Leesa had him locked down, and she knew it.

She smirked and folded her arms, before reaching forward with her hands and shaking his shoulders. "Get a flight and just start thinking about things, okay? I'll be fine, and your other soulmates are fine, I'm sure. Just take a break and do something for you, otherwise you will go mad – trust me."

Enzo cocked a brow, and Leesa handed him a small bit of paper.

"Okay, here's my number. Now freakin go, okay? And call me, just to, like, let me know that you're okay."

Enzo cocked a brow in surprise at that last statement before she reached forward and shoved him towards the exit.

"Fine, fine. I'm going, I'm going," he muttered, then trudged off, rolling his eyes slightly and smiling.

He reached the exit to the Louvre, turned back and waved, as Leesa rolled her eyes and gestured for him to move. He smiled then disappeared.

"Right, well, that was an interesting morning."

Chapter 19
ENZO

The flight home was quiet and slow. Finding his bike in the airport car parking was slow and painful. It took him three hours and six circles of multiple car parks. He was frustrated, tired and confused, and he didn't have a clue what to do or where to start. Khaleesi's voice was still spinning around his head. He should've stayed. Coming back felt wrong.

Khaleesi's number was still in his pocket, so he pulled out his phone and typed in the digits, sending a quick 'Got home safely' message, before jumping on his bike and taking the long trek home.

Khaleesi's name faded a day later, and silence hit Enzo like a shot. His head was empty and foggy as he showered, worked, tried to tidy his flat and just get through the days. He didn't know what to do or where to begin. He was just waiting on another name. Another name would appear, and he'd be out of his flat and on his bike in no time, because that was his life.

Three days went by in silence.

Four days.

Eight.

Fifteen.

And Enzo was starting to freak out. He'd had silence before. He'd had gaps in soulmates, but they didn't feel like this. This felt heavy and final, and it was slowly driving him mad. What was he supposed to do if he didn't get another voice?

He worked every day, did overtime and talked to people about their service. His mum showed up twice and slept on his couch after having pizza. She left the next morning without a word, and Enzo was lost. He was miserable and the world was grey, lifeless and confusing. He was stuck and stumbling in the dark. What was he supposed to do? Where were the names? Marlow had messaged a few times; Khaleesi, too, and Danny. A few people from the past five years had popped up but Enzo hadn't replied. He hadn't read them. He just sat and worked.

His mind was falling numb and his eyes were falling tired. People were being idiots but he was barely processing it. More days passed in silence and it started to feel like Enzo was drifting – like nothing made any sense – and he hated it. He hated himself. What was wrong with him? He'd been doing this for five years, not his whole life. He could handle life without another name. Heck, he wanted life without another voice. He wanted his life to be his own and now, maybe it was.

And what was he doing? He was working a crappy customer service job that he hated and never leaving his flat. He hadn't talked to anyone in days. He barely had motivation to leave his bed. It was like he was eighteen again.

"What the heck am I doing?" he muttered, then shook his head. He forced himself out of bed, stumbled into the living room and pulled out his laptop, deciding that maybe he should look at other jobs. Jobs that involved interacting with more people and leaving this flat. Maybe he should go back to school? What would he study?

When he was eighteen, he was going to study history and become an archivist, which now sounded like the most boring thing in the world. He liked people. He liked helping people and travelling the country. Maybe he should go and study travel or tourism or something. Wait. Travel...

Enzo's eyes drifted across his flat, landing on a little plane ornament that sat under his TV. It'd sat there for years, just collecting dust behind his DVDs. He'd never touched it or moved it. His mum had bought it for him when he was fourteen. He'd wanted to be a pilot. How had he forgotten that? He had been obsessed with looking up courses and figuring out how to get his license but had stopped when he'd gone to college. The thought of becoming a pilot now made him feel a little nauseous. He thought he could do it, but there was a lot of training involved and not a lot of talking to people, and...

Maybe he could be an air host? His heart jumped at that idea, a shocked smile appearing on his face as he blinked. Yeah, he loved the idea of doing that. Travelling and talking to people and the suits and the training. He loved airports – was that weird? It was probably weird. He didn't think on it for more than half a minute before he was typing in air host training programmes on google and looking up available positions. He found several positions at Norwich airport and applied, taking full-body pictures and sorting out his passport, grinning through all of it. His heart was beating in anticipation that he hadn't felt in a long time.

It felt weird. It all felt weird. He was used to having another name and having to disappear – he wasn't used to being in his flat. He wasn't used to having time to think. He was used to disappearing and only working when he could find a spare day. He was used to living in crappy hotels and on people's couches. He'd forgotten so many things. He'd forgotten what it was like to be home.

Damn, Khaleesi was right. His life was soulmates. That's all it was. He didn't have time for it to be anything else. Holy crap. He was a hypocrite. There was no way around it. He spent his life going around the country, telling people to have a life beyond soulmates and put themselves first but he'd never had time to do that. He didn't know what he wanted to do with his life until ten minutes ago.

Okay, it didn't matter. The world seemed a little brighter and clearer now. Things seemed a little more hopeful. He should start to go for things he wanted. He should've years ago, but everything had been so crazy, and he just hadn't had time.

The silence quaked through his mind as he smiled and stared down at his phone, looking up his messages and replying to everyone he could within ten minutes. Marlow and Khaleesi asked if he was okay. Danny had sent a quick 'Hi' at three a.m., but nothing else for days. Enzo didn't know what to do with that, so he just sent a 'Hello' back.

He then spent hours looking up more air host courses and figuring out what he needed to do to do this. He squealed excitedly when he got an email about a video interview. He knew that it wasn't guaranteed and that he still needed to work his current job until he got a placement, but it gave him this weird, warm feeling. It felt like his heart was beaming, and he just couldn't stop smiling and picturing himself in training, just talking to people and learning new things and doing those stupid safety announcements. He'd never been excited about work before. Was this what being excited about work felt like? His job was just a job. It was a convenient, little thing that he could revolve around his soulmates.

Crap. What if he got another name, and another name, and another? What would he do then? He felt his heart plummet when that thought occurred to him. He couldn't disappear from this job. What if he was mid-air? No. No. It didn't matter. It was just a name. Just a name. It didn't mean Enzo had to run off to help them. They'd be fine. That's the point. He wasn't just the soulmate guy. His whole life couldn't revolve around this stupid curse. He needed to let go and figure out his own crap.

And if he didn't? He just didn't want to wake up in another five years and realise that he'd only worked a job that he hated and that he'd wasted more time. He didn't want to be thirty and stuck. He needed to let go and start again. He needed to do what he should've done at eighteen.

A heavy sigh suddenly fell through his living room. Enzo's gaze jolted up to spot his mother in the doorway, weary, watery eyes, and a pained, fake smile that snapped Enzo's heart into a million sandy granules. Her hair was a mess, her irises were dark and grey and her loose, green jumper dress was falling off her slim, bony shoulder.

"Can I stay here tonight?" she asked quietly and Enzo sighed, his heart falling through him as a little gulp jolted through his throat.

He nodded after a second, and she sat herself down on the couch, resting her arms on her lap and her head in her hands.

The silence in Enzo's head got heavier as he looked over her. She always looked so small when she came here. She always looked so thin and vulnerable, but she never talked. Why wouldn't she talk?

"What happened?" Enzo asked and she jolted, her wide, watery eyes turning to Enzo in slow shock.

"What did he do, Mum?"

She bit her lip, tears falling down her cheeks, as her slim form shook and her short, blonde hair got scruffier. She looked awful. Black circles deeply engorged her eyes and made her look like a panda. She couldn't stop shaking – Enzo could see the couch cushion moving beneath her.

"Mum, I'm sorry. I know you don't like talking about this stuff, but you need to, okay?"

"Enzo, you don't get it. I can't."

"Coz it's about me?" he asked.

She jolted, her gaze falling to the floor as her teeth chattered.

"Yeah, it's about me."

"No, no. It's not that."

"Mum, have you told Dad that I'm bi?" Enzo asked, with a slightly raised eyebrow. "Does he know why I travel around the country? Does he know about my soulmates?"

"He um… he knows that you're special, Ennie," she whispered, wrapping her arms around herself.

"And that means?"

"He doesn't know that you're bi, and he doesn't know about your soulmate situation, but he does know… He knows that something isn't…"

"He knows that I'm not normal." Enzo sighed. "And he takes it out on you."

"No, no. That's not what this is! That's not why I'm here. We're just not… he's just not…" She sighed, crumpling further into herself as tears fell. "We're not talking about this."

"Mum," Enzo grunted, then glared through her eyes. "It's been years of this crap. You can't keep going like this."

"Why? You not gonna let me stay anymore?"

"No, you're always welcome," he stated with an eyeroll, before closing his laptop and shoving it onto the couch. "You *shouldn't* keep going like this. It's not fair on you. You're miserable and tired. Your back's gotta be killing you from sleeping on my lumpy, old bed."

"I'm fine, Enzo. It's not your job to take care of me."

"Then why do you keep coming here?" he asked sharply.

She jolted up, her eyes glaring into Enzo's as her heart fell.

"Why do you keep doing this to yourself? Why don't you just leave?"

"You know why," she replied.

"Coz he's your soulmate?" Enzo asked, eyes rolling as she nodded. "So? He's a drunken idiot."

"Don't talk about your father like that," she snapped.

"He's barely my dad," Enzo argued. "I haven't talked to him properly in years, and I don't want to coz he does this crap to you."

"Enzo."

"No. Just, no." Enzo sighed. "Mum, you don't *have* to stay with anyone just coz you're soulmates. If you're not happy then leave. Just freakin leave."

"It's not that easy."

"It is! Come on, you can't still love him. He's a drunk and an ass, and he never deserved you."

"He needs me."

"For what?" Enzo asked in deep confusion.

"Enzo, he's got a problem. It's not his fault."

"What?" Enzo scoffed. "Mum, he's an alcoholic. It's not up to you to fix that."

"But I can't just leave him. What if he hurts himself? Or hurts someone else? What if he spends all our money and we lose the house? He can't survive on his own. I'm his soulmate – it's my responsibility to support him."

"You're his soulmate, not his carer," Enzo spat out sharply.

"What's gotten into you?" she asked and Enzo rolled his eyes.

"I'm just tired of seeing you like this." He sighed.

"I can go?" she offered.

"Mum, are you happy? Okay, if you and dad weren't soulmates, would you be together right now? Would you have left?" he asked, and she opened her mouth silently before staring at her shoes. "Taking that as a yes, you would've."

"But it's not that simple."

"It is, though," Enzo stated. "Mum, soulmates aren't permanent, uncontrolled things. Just coz you're linked to someone, doesn't mean you *have* to stay with them. It's not a contract. You're unhappy, be logical and leave. It's simple if you make it simple. The world isn't, or shouldn't, be full of people staying together, just coz the universe freakin dictated it. You have to do what's right for you. It's *that* simple."

A heavy silence settled onto their shoulders, as Enzo stared into his mum's eyes, feeling years and years of pent-up frustration fade away in the air between them.

His mum sighed gently, then slumped into the couch beside him, each getting lost in their own worlds as the TV turned on and the silence between them flittered away.

Weeks went by like days after that. Silence still quaked through Enzo's brain. His parents talked and talked and talked, ultimately deciding that they just weren't meant to be. His dad moved out.

Enzo left his job and rented a new, little house down the road, before signing up to an air host training course and sorting out all his documents.

It was like a snowstorm of change. One flurry led to a blizzard, and everything was different within two weeks. Enzo didn't feel like the same person, and he was a little lost on how to feel about it. He felt normal, and that was weirding the heck out of him. Seriously, what do normal people do with themselves?

He'd moved all his crap from his flat to his new house within twelve hours. His mum had helped but had to leave to go to work, but even then, eighty percent of the job was done. His house was basically set up.

It was just a small, cottage-style house with a built-in bathtub. The carpet was brand new, fluffy and cream, and Enzo had wasted no time in placing his new, black, faux-leather corner couch on it, in the left corner against the wall. His large, flat-screen TV was in the centre with his Xbox and DVDs beneath. His bedroom had a new double bed with a memory foam mattress, as well as all the new flatpack furniture that had taken him and his mum four hours to build. The bedside tables seemed a little rickety, so there was maybe a screw or two missing. The blackout curtains were grey and pulled closed to hide the slowly fading daylight outside. The heating had been on for a couple of hours, so the place was cosy; it was like the air was a fluffy blanket. The kitchen, living room and dining room were all separate. There was a bathroom downstairs and a bathroom upstairs, and one master bedroom. It was a home. It looked like a home, and it felt like a home, and it was all his.

He'd been sitting alone in his house, sipping at a bottle of beer while leaning back into his squishy couch. His mind and eyes glazed over as he watched some pointless gameshow on his new TV. It took an hour of this before he started to get restless and decided that he needed to get out. He needed to know that there were other humans on the planet besides him and his mum, so he chucked the empty beer bottle in the bin, grabbed his keys and headed to the little bar around the corner.

It was a small, old building with a giant, winking frog stuck out the front. The bar was called 'The Winking Frog' and was a classic, British pub. It was about eight p.m. in late February, so the sky was already pitch-black and drenched in twinkling stars. A full moon lit Enzo's path to the red, wooden door. He stepped through and trounced across the dusty, burgundy, beer-stained carpet, slumping onto a bar stool with a little, calm smile.

"Hey, you're new. What can I get ya?" a gentle, sweet voice stated, and Enzo jolted.

His eyes looked up to find a small, middle-aged, blonde lady standing behind the bar with a half-empty bottle of whisky in her hands. She wore an apron over a floral shirt and jeans. Her frizzy, platinum blonde hair was tied back in a tangled, little ponytail. She had a smile like his mum's; it was relaxed and calm with awkward elements behind it.

"Uh... just a uh... cider," he replied awkwardly, then pointed to the kiwi cider in the fridge behind the bar.

The lady smiled, placed down the whisky before opening the fridge and grabbing the cider bottle, popping the top off with her bare hands. She placed it in front of Enzo, and he gently started sipping it with a little, wistful smile.

"Thanks."

"First one's on the house for newbies," she stated, and Enzo blinked in surprise, the bartender shuffling off as Enzo debated getting out his wallet and paying her anyway.

She reminded him of his mum and that hurt his heart a little They'd spoken a lot over the past few weeks, bonding in their lack of soulmates. His mum had taken a different path to what Enzo did when his soulmate broke his heart. She'd gone from sad to angry and back again, not quite landing on anything more productive. She helped Enzo a lot but she spent a lot of her time picking up extra shifts and not really thinking about things, about what she wanted in the wake of her life blowing up.

She'd told Enzo that she was proud, that she didn't understand him sometimes but was proud of how he'd handled his 'curse' and was happy that it was over.

Enzo didn't know how to feel about that. He didn't know how to feel about anything, really. His life was loud and manic last week. He was in Paris a few months ago, he'd slept on the couch of multiple strangers. He'd had adventures, collected stories and lived a crazy-ass life that still made no sense.

He felt like Frodo when he'd come back to the shire. Like his story had ended and he didn't know what came next, maybe nothing did. Maybe life was normal, life was his. He got a job and made new friends, had a house. Maybe he'd live and soulmates would fade to obscurity, his stories falling to legend... not that they meant anything to anyone but him and his soulmates, anyway.

A part of him still felt itchy, though. The silence in his head making him jittery on some days. He wanted to wake up tomorrow and hear a new voice but it felt like that side of his tale was over, like the silence was unending. The universe had dictated that he ended up alone.

Years of having a new voice every few months and flitting about the country. Years of being too busy to notice how quiet his home was, years of life being crazy had amounted to this.

To sitting alone in a strange bar with a Kiwi cider in his fingers and a winking frog on the door.

Enzo thought it was oddly poetic. Some stories ended in a blazing glory, others ended in a winking frog. Enzo was happy to be in the latter part of that phrase.

He sighed, leaning into the bar and sipping at his cider with a wistful smile and a breath of relief. Silence floating around him as he processed his new state of life, trying to let go of this 'what now?' feeling.

Because, what now? What did he do now? His story was finished, the curse was over. It felt like he'd conquered a great evil and come out alive, gasping in ashy air and glaring up at a bloodred sky. He'd finished, gotten a job and a house. In the blink of an eye, he'd become an adult after years of existing in limbo. It felt like he'd given into social norms, like he'd become domesticated and could no longer do anything crazy.

Maybe he wanted that though, a little time to figure things out and move forward... silence enveloping him as he learned to listen to his own, stupid voice for once.

But again, it was too quiet. It'd been too quiet for months and Enzo didn't have a clue how to feel. It felt like his skin was crawling on some days. His ears were buzzing, his heart was waiting and he wasn't sure what for?

Did he want a soulmate? Did he want another voice? He didn't know what it'd mean now. Soulmates had become his whole world and he wasn't going to let that happen again.

Five years. It'd taken Enzo five years to realise that soulmates weren't this inexplicable, unfightable power. They were just voices. They were just one sound bite in the back of people's minds. The world was full of people who weren't soulmates, it was full of friends and enemies, people we were destined to meet for varied reasons but we were allowed to react and be who we wanted with them in whatever moment we chose.

Enzo chose to be a person who'd helped and as stupid as he felt about some of the things he'd advised, he couldn't regret that. It was a good story and a good life, he'd loved the people he'd met and the things they'd taught him. He hoped they were happy, that they were okay in whatever decision they'd made. He just needed to be happy in his decision too.

A bell chimed and a breeze gushed in, footsteps echoing behind Enzo as he stared at the bottles behind the bar. The silence in his head started to get a little deafening as it surrounded his eardrums in a strange, balloon-like layer. Moments passed, and it felt like the balloons had started to inflate through to his brain. The bottle in his hand started to blur, the coolness of the glass against his palm started to get a little warmer and a little more unclear, as a sharp ringing began darting through his ears, blurring his vision further as he placed the bottle on the bar.

A strange warmth settled over his heart, and his back collapsed calmly, though the stool didn't exactly hold him up.

"Well, this is a classic scene," a voice stated.

Enzo's entire body froze, his heart twanging through his chest like someone had snapped a piece of elastic through it.

"Whoa, you okay?" the voice asked, and Enzo blinked in slow shock as a man appeared beside him.

He wore a blue, tartan shirt wrapped around his hips, light blue jeans, a navy-blue T shirt and lace-up black boots.

The silence in Enzo's head began wrapping around his brain as light-blue eyes stared through him.

A ringing sound quaked through Enzo, and a little gulp rang through his throat. 'Danny,' the familiar voice whispered through his mind.

"Yeah." He gasped out and Danny slid onto the seat next to him. "What are you doing here?"

Danny just shrugged and grinned, not taking his eye off Enzo. "I suppose that's a long story."

Chapter 20
DANNY

It'd been a weird day at school. It'd been a weird few weeks. Life was going by quickly. He was planning lessons and working out, adjusting to his new routine. He went out with Bexxie a couple of times, falling asleep on his sofa with boxes of pizza on his lap when he did. She took the bed then brought him painkillers in the morning, before shoving him into his own bed.

He did start talking to some new guys and girls; just talking, nothing more than that. He'd befriended a few of the parents at school and had been in contact with some friends of friends, to get his friends off his back. He still hadn't rejoined those sites or re-downloaded those apps but he was marginally less lonely, and he spent less nights staring at Enzo's contact on his phone, thinking about whether to message him or not.

One night, he was drunk and almost called him. *Almost*. He ended up sending a quick 'Hi' at three a.m., then collapsing in bed. He woke up and immediately regretted it when he saw that Enzo had read it and not replied. He wanted to text back and explain that he had been drunk and that it was just a mistake, but he couldn't make himself do that.

Anyway, it didn't matter now. He was moving on, and life was good. He'd gained a bit of muscle. He was laughing with his old friends and properly befriending the other teachers at school. He hadn't thought about soulmates or Allison or Enzo in weeks because life was just too busy. His days were full, and he was smiling and laughing, loving it.

He did appreciate the solitude he had when he came home from work. Well, he hated it and appreciated it. It was one of those things. He didn't feel lonely anymore, and he didn't really feel like he needed someone around to feel good or happy in what he was doing, but he'd be remiss to admit that his flat could be a little too quiet some days.

Anyway, it had been a weird day at school. It was Parents' Day, so Danny stayed behind for a couple of hours to talk to parents about their kids. He tried to be as honest as he could, without explicitly telling some parents that he hated their kids. Well, hate was a strong word. There were a couple of kids in class who didn't have a clue what they were doing and were unwilling to try and learn. It was infuriating, and Danny didn't know what to do with them, so to those parents he said, 'Your kid is great. Has a little issue concentrating in class', then he moved on to other topics before the parent got defensive.

It hit about six p.m., and Danny had talked to a lot of parents. It was the last Friday before February half-term, so Danny would have a week of just chilling on his couch – which he'd earned. He had been working non-stop the past couple of months –lesson planning, marking and various other things, as well as trying to have a social life and work out. He needed a breather, so when he got home he collapsed onto his couch with a yawn, his eyes closing slowly as some random gameshow played on his TV.

The gameshow faded to silence, the emptiness of his flat making him dizzy. He remembered Allison singing and hmm-ing as she cooked. He remembered her making him tea in the evenings, kettle whistling through the thin walls. He remembered how warm this place had felt with another person here. He thought of Bexxie staying over, his parents appearing and his friends. He thought of their laughter and their stupid games before his eyes blinked open again, gameshow rattling through his ears and making his temples twinge.

A pair of gold eyes appeared and he sighed, small smile appearing when something sharp tugged on his heart and Danny collapsed into the carpet.

His brain fell epically silent –painfully silent – before a ringing shook through his eardrums. His entire, lit-up vision began to horrifically blur and blend, the corners darkening and reddening until a deep, familiar voice whispered through his mind. A shocked grin appeared on Danny's face, his heart still tugging and his head still spinning, as the word 'Enzo' flooded his head, and a warble of kind, wonderful warmth shook through his muscles.

His heart tugged forward, and Danny shook his head, his eyebrows lowering as his gaze tilted to his door. "Enzo," he whispered, then stood and grabbed his keys, walking out the door and out to his car.

He had *no* idea where he was going, or why. His heart was pulling him in the right direction, and Danny was just following it. He drove for maybe twenty or thirty minutes before appearing outside a little, crappy bar that was barely lit up. He parked quickly and ran up to the door, his eyebrows drawing together in confusion.

He wandered in and headed to the bar, the blonde girl grinning at him then handing him a cider.

Danny's gaze locked onto the back of his head – long, dark hair glimmering through the low bar lights – Danny walked over and stood at his side, taking in the sight before him in disbelief.

The man wore a long, navy jumper, light-grey jeans and light-grey slip-on shoes. His dark hair was wavy and scruffy, tied up in a little, awkward ponytail that seemed to be falling out. His eyes were glowing a blinding gold in the light, while his freckles glittered like stars.

Danny was having a lot of trouble believing this was reality right now. He caught sight of Enzo scraping the label off his cider bottle, and a stupid, cheeky idea appeared in his head.

"Well, this is a classic scene." He echoed Enzo's words and actively watched as the man froze in shock. "Whoa, you okay?" he asked without thinking.

"Yeah," Enzo stated, and Danny just jumped onto the stool opposite him, as the man grinned. "What are you doing here?"

"I suppose that's a long story," Danny admitted, then vaguely explained the heart-pull and the name.

He hoped he didn't sound insane, but then he remembered who he was talking to. Enzo's grin only got wider, and his bright eyes only got brighter. The air around the pair was warm, wonderful, familiar, magical and ridiculous, and when Danny stopped talking, their faces were a lot closer than he'd remembered. His face was on fire as he looked over Enzo's cherry-red cheeks and wide grin. He could feel water filling the corners of his eyes, while his brain flooded in happy warmth, Enzo's voice and name quaking through him loudly like a gong.

"So, what now, blue-eyes?" Enzo asked, and Danny smiled.

"I don't know, freckles. How long do we got?" he asked, and Enzo rolled his eyes, his face leaning closer to Danny's.

The warmth of his skin began tracing his cheeks as they looked deeply into each other's eyes, each gasping for breath as their grins fell to shocked, shaky smiles.

"Oh, you're not getting away this time," Enzo stated, and Danny blinked in surprise.

"Even if…" he began, then pointed to his head awkwardly.

"Even if," Enzo confirmed, and gently pressed their lips together, as the warmth around them got blindingly hot.

It settled through their bones and their muscles as they slid into each other, their arms wrapping around each other's backs, as they got closer and closer. Enzo's dark hair started tickling Danny's cheeks. Danny's mousy hair started tickling Enzo's nose. They both had to hold back smiles until they pulled away, arms still wrapped around each other. The warmth cradled them in shaky, body-numbing waves that made them feel calm. It was like they were floating out in space, stars twinkling through their bright eyes and Enzo's freckles. Neither stopped smiling as Enzo leaned his forehead into Danny's, their eyes linking properly once more.

"So," Danny began, causing both men to jump slightly. "I think we've got some catching up to do since the last time you appeared in my head."

"Yeah, no kidding, Dann-O," Enzo stated.

"Since when don't you care about the names in your head?" Danny asked, and Enzo scoffed with a little, fond smile.

"Since I kinda fell for this cute, blue-eyed guy about six months ago. Haven't been able to shake him." Enzo shrugged and Danny felt his face burn.

"Then why didn't you come back?"

"Coz I still had some things to figure out," Enzo admitted. "Sorry for making you wait."

Danny just rolled his eyes and shuffled to stand, retracting his hands and leaning his head back to look at Enzo's shocked face.

"Well, if you made me wait, you'd better make this worth it, huh?" Danny stated sassily, then pressed a hand out towards Enzo.

The gold-eyed man blinked at it in slow shock before looking back into Danny's eyes curiously.

"Let me take you out on an actual date," Danny offered.

Enzo grinned, taking Danny's warm, shaking hand slowly before standing up.

"We're not going bowling this time."

Enzo scoffed, and the pair started heading towards the door. "Only coz you know I'd thrash you."

"In your dreams, freckles."